I0643346

George Farquhar Jones

Family Record of the Jones Family of Milford, Massachusetts

George Farquhar Jones

Family Record of the Jones Family of Milford, Massachusetts

ISBN/EAN: 9783337379872

Printed in Europe, USA, Canada, Australia, Japan

Cover: Foto ©Andreas Hilbeck / pixelio.de

More available books at **www.hansebooks.com**

"THE OLD JONES HOUSE."

Built 1703. Enlarged 1733. Demolished 1874.

FAMILY RECORD

OF THE

JONES FAMILY

OF

MILFORD, MASSACHUSETTS,

AND

PROVIDENCE, RHODE ISLAND,

WITH ITS

CONNECTIONS AND DESCENDANTS,

Together with the Ancestry and Family

OF

LORANIA CARRINGTON JONES,

Wife of George F. Jones.

Collected, compiled and edited

BY

GEORGE FARQUHAR JONES.

Philadelphia, 1884.

IN LOVING MEMORY

OF MY

Father and Mother,

ALEXANDER AND MARY FARQUHAR JONES,

I DEDICATE THIS BOOK.

TO THEIR UNCEASING AFFECTION, THEIR WISE COUNSELS, THEIR GOOD
EXAMPLE, AND THEIR CHRISTIAN PROFESSION AND PRACTICE,
THEIR CHILDREN AND GRANDCHILDREN

ARE EVER INDEBTED.

THEY SOWED THE GOOD SEED,
THEY WATERED IT WITH THEIR PRAYERS,
AND A HARVEST HAS BEEN GATHERED; A LARGE MA-
JORITY OF THEIR CHILDREN, AND THEIR CHILDREN'S CHILDREN
HAVING EMBRACED THE TRUTHS OF THE BLESSED
GOSPEL, HAVE "PROFESSED THE FAITH
OF CHRIST CRUCIFIED."

"Blessed are the dead, who die in the Lord,
For their works do follow them."

INTRODUCTION.

MANY years ago I began a family record book, which contained such information as I could gather from my father, mother, and elder sisters. Many of the dates of births, marriages and deaths, were imperfect, or entirely unknown, with regard to our ancestors, and some of the collateral branches. As the years went on, I added from time to time, such items of interest as I could secure, with such obituary notices and newspaper paragraphs as came into my possession. The record was fragmentary, imperfect and unsatisfactory to me, because there seemed to be many "missing links," which I supposed could never be discovered or supplied. Although the prospect showed much that was discouraging, I decided to make a strong effort to obtain all the information that was possible, and to spare myself no trouble or exertion of which I was capable. I therefore resolved to make the record as full and as perfect as it could be made under the circumstances. This involved a correspondence which I foresaw would be tedious, laborious, and probably vexatious; but I started it, and with the determination to have a successful result. One great difficulty to overcome, was the indifference of many with regard to the matter in view, but I wrote letters to numbers of our relations and connections, and after many difficulties, gradually secured information of the collateral branches of the family, and such as I had long desired. One result of the numerous letters that were written, was to awaken an interest in the record, and this, I am happy to state, has largely increased. It is perhaps useless to relate the many difficulties and disappointments experienced, but at times they seemed to be almost insurmountable. By perseverance, however, and contending with them at all points, I have met with such success as the following pages will show. I have endeavored to have each and all the branches of the family represented, so that all the descendants may find much that will be of interest to them.

Consulting Savage's work, the Genealogical Register, and more particularly Ballou's History of Milford, Massachusetts, I have been enabled to secure much valuable information with regard to five generations of "The Jones Family." From the last named book I have made copious extracts. I am also much indebted to Mr. Lloyd B. Hoppin (my wife's brother), for the fruits of his patient research, in that he has enabled me to add a complete record of my wife's ancestors and family.   G. F. J.

PATERNAL ANCESTORS

OF

GEORGE FARQUHAR JONES.

FIRST GENERATION.

Thomas Jones, born probably in 1598 to 1600, in Wales or England.

Ann Jones, his wife, maiden name and date of birth and marriage unknown, but supposed about 1600.

According to my father's account, his ancestors came from Wales, but in the History of Milford, Mass., it is recorded that Thomas Jones came to America in the ship Confidence, and landed at Hingham, Massachusetts, with his wife Ann, and their oldest children, in 1638. Later in life, he settled in Hull. The history also states, that Thomas Jones was "a native of Caversham, Oxfordshire, England."

The dates of their deaths have not been found.

Their Children were:

2. Joseph Jones, born probably in 1634.
    Benjamin Jones, "   "   " 1636.
    Abraham Jones, born "   " 1638.
    Robert Jones,   "   "   " 1640.

    And some others not on record.

If it were not for the great amount of trouble, and the heavy expenses involved, a search in and among the records in England, might show still further back, some generations there.

SECOND GENERATION.

Abraham Jones, son of Thomas, born probably in 1638, in England.

Sarah Jones, his wife, born probably in 1640. Her maiden name and the date of their marriage unknown, but probably during the year 1660.

2

CHILDREN:

3.   Benjamin Jones, born about 1661.
  Thomas Jones, " " 1663.
  Abraham Jones, " " 1665.
  Joseph Jones, " " 1667.
  John Jones, " " 1670.
  Ephraim Jones, " " 1672.
And a daughter not named " 1675.

Abraham Jones must have been a man of ability, prominence and respectability. It is on record that he enjoyed the good opinion and confidence of his fellow-citizens, for "he was made a freeman in Hull in the year 1673, and elected Representative of the General Court of His Majesty's Colony of Massachusetts in 1689."

The dates of his, and his wife's death are not recorded, but his will was dated January 8th, 1717, which would make his age to be at least about 80 years.

THIRD GENERATION.

John Jones, or Elder John Jones, (as he was called by every one, and is thus designated in the annals of the town,) was born in the year 1670.

Sarah Jones, his wife, born in 1668, exact date unknown, and maiden name also unknown. Date of marriage not on record, but supposed to have been 1693.

CHILDREN OF ELDER JOHN AND SARAH JONES:

Sarah Jones, born in Hull, 1694.
Bridget Jones, " " " 1696.
Mercy Jones, " " " 1697.
John Jones, Jr., " " " 1699.
Nathaniel Jones, born in Hull, March 31, 1702.
Lydia Jones, born at the Dale Farm, September 17, 1705.
Abraham Jones, born at the Dale Farm, July 2, 1708.

4.   **Joseph Jones,** born at the Dale Farm, December 27, 1709.

Elder John Jones died March 28th, 1753, aged 83 years.
Sarah, his wife, died March 3d, 1750, aged 82 years.

Grandchildren of Elder John and Sarah Jones.

Sarah Jones married **Daniel Corbett,** December 4th, 1717.

CHILDREN:

Mercy Corbett, born September 2, 1718.
Daniel Corbett, " July 8, 1720.
Sarah Corbett, " May 4, 1722.
Nathaniel Corbett, " March 21, 1724.
Bridget Corbett, " February 25, 1726, married Aaron Morse, February 9, 1744.
Lois Corbett, born December 24, 1727.
Eunice Corbett, " May 4, 1729, married Samuel Warren, May 20, 1754.
Priscilla Corbett, born May 9, 1732.
Alice Corbett, " February 23, 1733, married Dudley Chase, August, 23, 1753.

Elder Daniel Corbett and his brother-in-law, John Jones, Jr., in about 1742, exchanged farms, and he afterwards held some 400 acres in the North Purchase. He was elected Elder in 1749, and was an influential member of both civil and religious society. He died in 1753, and among the personal property, in the inventory of his estate, was one item: "A negro boy and his bed and hoe, £40 4s. and 5d," showing that there was once a little pious slaveholding among our ancestors. His widow married again in 1755.

Bridget Jones married **James Wood**, May 17th, 1716.

CHILDREN:

Sarah Wood, born January 14, 1718.
Mary Wood, " April 8, 1720.
Martha Wood, " February 18, 1723.

Mercy Jones married **John Thwing**, probably in 1718.

CHILDREN:

John Thwing, Jr., born probably in 1719, married Thankful Edwards.
Mercy Thwing, " February 9, 1720.
Sarah Thwing, " February 28, 1722, married Samuel Torrey, second, Andrew Adams, and third, Rev. Amariah Frost.
James Thwing, born March 3, 1725.
Nathaniel Thwing, born July 27, 1728.
Benjamin Thwing, " May 25, 1732.
Martha Thwing, " March 10, 1735, married Josiah Kilburn, October 31, 1760.
Thomas Thwing, born July 15, 1737.

John Jones, Jr., married **Abigail Holbrook**, born August 19th, 1697, July 1st, 1723.

CHILDREN:

Cornelius Jones, born April 20, 1727, became a clergyman.

Abigail Jones,   "   March 28, 1731, untraced.

David Jones,   "   February 19, 1734, married Hannah Pratt, April 25, 1754.

Hannah Jones, born August 20, 1736, married Joseph Pratt, January 30, 1755.

John Jones, Jr., after the death of his wife, married again, and in some five years after that, losing his second wife, married a third time, but the names and dates are not on record.

Nathaniel Jones married (date not found) **Priscilla Corbett.**

CHILDREN:

Nathaniel Jones, Jr., born July 19, 1723.

Sarah Jones, born (date not found), married Azariah Newton.

Priscilla Jones, born July 21, 1738, married Daniel Gage.

Samuel Jones,   "   October 3, 1744.

Seth Jones, baptized April 17, 1748.

Deacon Nathaniel Jones acquired considerable landed estate from his father, his wife's father and by purchase. He maintained his high position in the church and an influential standing in the community, and left to his descendants, not only a fair heritage, but a good name. His son Samuel became one of the most distinguished and influential citizens of the town, and was always called "Squire Jones."

Something more than the above notice of Samuel Jones, Esq., should be recorded here, for he occupied a number of high positions accorded to him by his fellow-citizens. He married Mercy Parkhurst, March 27th, 1766. They had no children, except by adoption. At various times his fellow-townsmen conferred on him nearly every office of distinction within their gift, by choosing him for the most responsible positions. He proved himself to be fully worthy of their confidence, every duty incumbent on him being faithfully performed. He was commissioned as Justice by Governor Samuel Adams, March 2d, 1797, when that office was held in much higher esteem than in our day, and held it reputably for twenty-one years. He died December 2d, 1819, aged 75, leaving the memory of a man highly intelligent, capable, upright and estimable in all his relations. His widow, Mary Jones, survived him sixteen years, dying January 25th, 1835, aged 89 years.

Lydia Jones married **Jonathan Whitney,** January 26th, 1726.

CHILDREN:

Susanna Whitney, born February 12, 1728, married Isaac Tenney and Noah Wiswall.

Jonathan Whitney, Jr., born October 18, 1729, lived only one day.

Jesse Whitney, born November 24, 1730.

Lydia Whitney, " November 18, 1732, married Samuel Bowker.

Jonathan Whitney, born July 26, 1734, married Esther Parkhurst.

Sarah Whitney, " (not recorded), married Wales Cheney.

Ruth Whitney, baptized April 11, 1742.

David Whitney, " September 21, 1746.

Jonathan Whitney seems to have become a prominent and trusted citizen, an influential member of the church, and a staunch coadjutor of his father-in-law, Elder John Jones, in establishing the new precinct. He was nominated in his will and that of his own father as co-executor, and as things turned had almost the entire responsibility of settling their estates. He died in 1756, and his wife, Lydia, some years later, but dates not found.

Elder Abraham Jones married **Keziah Whitney** (who was born July 31st, 1706), probably in 1730 or 1731, date not on record.

CHILDREN:

Susanna Jones, born February 8, 1732, died November 1, 1736.

Jonathan Jones, " November 13, 1733, died November 6, 1736.

Keziah Jones, " November 23, 1737. ⎫
Sarah Jones, " December 16, 1739. ⎬ Died between the 6th and
Hannah Jones, " November 8, 1741. ⎭ 21st September, 1744.

John Jones, " March 23, 1744, married Abigail Cheney, December 9, 1762.

Abraham Jones, Jr., born May 3, 1746, married Oliver Bates, October 30, 1765.

Solomon Jones, born April 3, 1748, died young.

It is somewhat remarkable, that of the eight children, six died young: two within five days, and three within fifteen days. In the record of all the descendants, from that date to the present, only one similar case has occurred, but that (as will be seen in another place) was far more terrible and distressing, and might almost be termed unprecedented. Elder Abraham Jones was a solid and highly influential man among his Christian brethren and fellow-citizens. He was chosen Deacon in 1743, and Elder in 1754. He died February 25th, 1792, and his wife, Keziah, June 29th, 1791.

Joseph Jones, the youngest son, married **Mary Whitney**, and the births, names, marriages, etc., will appear under the head of the Fourth Generation.

RECAPITULATION.

Sarah and Daniel Corbett	had	9	children.
Bridget and James Wood	"	3	"
Mercy and John Thwing	"	8	"
John, Jr., and Abigail Jones	"	7	" (3 by another wife.)
Nathaniel and Priscilla Jones	"	5	"
Lydia and Jonathan Whitney	"	8	"
Abraham and Keziah Jones	"	8	"
Joseph and Mary Jones	"	8	"

Grandchildren of Elder John Jones, 56 children.

There were many other families of the Jones' race, springing from our first ancestor, Thomas Jones, and his son and his grandson, but to record each one with their children and their children's children, would swell this record to such large proportions, I must omit them, only giving names, marriages, etc.

Dearing Jones,	married	Rebecca Benson, January 7, 1729.
Sarah Jones,	"	Azariah Newton, February 20, 1746.
Nathaniel Jones 3d,	"	Rachel Chapin, May 20, 1747.
Priscilla Jones,	"	Daniel Gage, January 1, 1756.
John Jones 3d,	"	Abigail Cheney, December 9, 1762.
Abraham Jones 3d,	"	Olive Bates, October 30, 1765.
Jonathan Jones,	"	Mary Ball, May 7, 1767.
Timothy Jones,	"	Ann Scammell, December 3, 1771.
Mary Jones,	"	John Robinson, March 1, 1773.
Mary Jones (another),	"	Oliver Chapin, April 29, 1784.
Mary Jones (another),	"	James Sumner, July 7, 1784.
Clarinda Jones,	"	Benjamin Gibbs, April 13, 1786.

From the above marriages there were 73 children.

The family of Elder John Jones, with those of his sons and daughters, were connected by marriage with many others of that and the two succeeding generations that settled and flourished in the Mill River precinct and town of Milford. I frequently heard my father mention the names of Chapin, Corbett, Scammell, Nelson, Sumner, Parkhurst, etc., when I was a boy. He told me that he was named Alexander, after Alexander Scammell, who entered the Revolutionary war, was an officer, became major while the American army was encamped around Boston, and afterwards general. He was a brave and notable officer, and served his country faithfully for six years, ending his life at the early age of 34 years, being mortally wounded (after capture) by a cowardly, brutal Hessian mercenary at Williamsburg, Virginia. He was a tall, well-built, handsome man, full 6 feet 2 inches in height, and of graceful deportment, a bright scholar, a genial companion and of attractive manners.

Immediately after the battle of Lexington, as soon as the news came to Milford, it stirred the feelings of the people to the highest pitch. Their acts of patriotism showed the depth of their bitterness against King George and his ministers. "Two Mill River companies" of soldiers were formed, and among the names enrolled were —— Jones, sergeant, John Jones, Jr., Joseph Jones, Abraham Jones and Samuel Jones. From the facts of Elder John and his sons starting the project of Milford becoming a town, and aiding it with their names and influence, to bring it to a successful result; their forming a new and flourishing church, and that his sons, grandsons and nephews had the fires of patriotism burning in their breasts, we can infer that our progenitors were worthy citizens, and truly religious as well as patriotic people. They felt their responsibilities as men, as citizens and as Christians. They strove earnestly to fulfil the duties incumbent on them as such. And from the old records we learn that they faithfully performed those duties and in the fear of God. In this testimony there is cause for pride and rejoicing among their now numerous descendants, that their ancestors were men of noble stamp. In the simple pioneer, and afterwards long and prosperous lives of Elder John Jones and his sons, what a field there is in which the imagination can work!

I was told by my father (Alexander Jones) when I was quite a young lad that Elder John Jones, his great grandfather, was *the first settler in Mill River precinct*, now the town of Milford, Massachusetts. That he first boarded in Mendon, the next settlement, and daily went to the land he had located, taking with him his axe, gun and dogs and his "Johnny cake" for his midday meal. He always kept his gun near him while at work making a clearing, to protect himself against an attack by some wild animal or stray Indian. Here he worked with great energy and perseverance to clear a place in the forest for a dwelling and barn. After he had succeeded in his efforts, he built a primitive log house, and went to Hull to bring his wife and children to their new home. Lydia, his sixth child and fourth daughter, was the first girl born in Mill River precinct, as it was then called.

Elder John Jones was an honest, pious and God-fearing man. As he was prospered, he added other lands to his possessions until he held a large number of acres, and "The Dale Farm" became large, productive and beautiful. That farm or homestead in itself (not counting other tracts near by) contained about 150 acres, and through it, near to the afterwards venerable house, ran the clear and beautiful little stream called Mill River. Between the years 1818 and 1825 my father frequently took me with him when he drove "up to Milford" from Providence to see the farm, the tenant and his family, and always to visit "Uncle Rawson," who lived on the next farm, and who had married (some 50 years before) his mother's sister, Elizabeth Nelson. Well do I remember this venerable pair, their remarkably dignified appearance and their deep religious feeling, which somewhat awed my youthful mind and heart. Vividly do I remember all my visits to the farm, the beauty of the place and all the persons comprising the family of Mr. Daniels, the tenant. One visit (that I was permitted to make alone, and which lasted three weeks, with a number of little incidents that occurred) is fresh in my recollections, and was greatly enjoyed. The place was lovely, and the association with the boys and girls of the family (with whom I worked daily, out of bed at daylight in the morning and again in bed early in the evening) was pleasant and healthful. It was a visit full of boyish delight, and I often recur to it with great satisfaction. Three generations of our family were born there, and after being in the family for one hundred and thirty-nine years, my father sold it to Hastings Daniels, the eldest son of Elisha Daniels (the tenant), who was the seventh in lineal descent from Robert Daniels.

In the history of Milford, Elder John Jones occupies quite a prominent position, and, as his first appearance there took place *almost* 200 *years ago*, all that relates to him, his family, etc., must be of interest, even to his most remote descendants, and is worthy of record here. The Rev. Mr. Ballou, in the history named (the indefatigable and industrious author), writes as follows: "The name of Jones has been conspicuous in our records from the first settlements on our territory downward. Elder John was previously of Mendontown, but became possessed of some 10 or 12 acres located where what was afterward "The Dale Farm." There his own pious and stalwart hands felled the sturdy forest and hewed him out a clearing, which gradually broadened into one of the noblest farms east of Neck Hill. Captain Seth Chapin was one of the original plantationists who came to Mendon from Braintree in 1680 to 1682, and became a distinguished proprietor and citizen. He was the father of fourteen children and a contemporary and near neighbor of Elder John. The oldest recorded laying-out of land to him (Chapin) bears date May 26th, 1700, and in the deed it says, 'westerly to 10 acres of land laid out to, and in possession of, John Jones.' This indicates plainly that Elder John Jones was in possession prior to the year 1700."

It is further recorded that he seems to have been attracted to Mendon when about 21 or 22 years old, and to have acquired taxable estate *there*, as he was assessed for the support of the *Rev. Grindal Rawson* (one of my wife's ancestors by the Rawson and Hoppin side) in the rate bills for the year ending October 25th, 1691. The Elder ripened with his years into a substantial inhabitant, and was evidently an enterprising and executive man, as well as an eminently pious and devoted church-member. Report says "that in clearing up his first acres he came down from Mendon Hill (where he had his domicile or lodgings) through the woods, and generally single-handed, with only a dog for companionship, and plied his axe vigorously all day in felling the lusty, primitive trees that studded the soil. He brought with him for his dinner plenty of Indian bannock and a bottle of milk. At noon he spread out before him his wholesome but frugal repast, either on a suitable rock or on one of his newly-cut broad stumps, yet never tasted it 'till first he had knelt and solemnly invoked the divine blessing. Breakfast and supper he took at home, prudently quitting work in time to return by daylight to avoid the wolves and other beasts of prey that then made the night hideous. When his clearing was sufficiently advanced, he built a strong log barrack and began to stay over night on the premises. The late venerable Jared Rawson said that when he worked for Elder John's great-grandsons during the years 1805, 1806 and 1807, he and his fellow-workmen dug up the ancient hearthstones and embers of that barrack. It is rather likely that this log barrack was already up in the Spring of 1700."

"The Elder increased and prospered. He soon afterwards *built the first framed dwelling-house in these parts*, east of Neck Hill. Meantime he had possessed himself of the valuable house-lot at the town seat, and began to have various-sized tracts of land laid out to him on Mill

River. Having located his family in "The Dale," and provided himself with a small stock of cattle (fed at first chiefly with hay cut on
'Beaver Meadow'), his wealth began to increase rapidly and especially
in lands. The proprietary records show that year after year through
his long life he was having parcels, here and there, laid out to him.
Most of these were near his homestead, but some were miles distant
and in different directions."

He brought to his new home, in 1701, from Hull, his wife, three
daughters and two sons, and they afterwards had one daughter and two
sons born in "The Dale."

In the year 1741 a petition was sent to William Shirley, Esq., Cap-
tain-General and Governor of His Majesty's Province of Massachusetts, to create a separate town (from Mendon), and it was first signed
by Elder John Jones, and was called, "The petition of John Jones and
others." Among the signers were the names of John Jones, Jr., and
Abraham, Nathaniel, Joseph and Dearing Jones. The petition was
granted.

In the same year (1741) some members of the First Church, who
"considered themselves aggrieved," met and formed a new church, and
among them were John, Joseph and Abraham Jones. John was elected
first Elder, and it was called the Second Church. In that same year
the new church "appointed a day of solemn fasting and prayer, and it
was duly observed at 'The Dale,' the home of Elder John Jones."
"Two acceptable sermons were preached." Also "in forming the new
and so-called *Second Church of Mendon*, other days of fasting and
prayer were observed, and the meetings, the ordaining council and the
ordination of the Rev. Amariah Frost, all took place at the Jones
house in 'The Dale.'"

When I was a boy of 10 to 12 years old, in my frequent visits to
Milford, I went to this same church (a meeting-house, as it was then
called) with my father, and heard "Parson Long" preach sermons that
lasted an hour and a quarter.

THE WILL OF ELDER JOHN JONES.

In the name of God, Amen! The twenty-sixth day of June, Anno
Domini 1735.

I, John Jones, of Mendon, in the County of Worcester, in His Majesty's Province of the Massachusetts Bay, in New England, Husband-
man, being very sick and weak in Body, but of perfect mind and
memory, Thanks be given unto God therefor; calling unto mind the

mortality of my body, and knowing that it is appointed for all men once to Die; do make and ordain this my last Will and Testament: that is to say, principally and first of all, I give and recommend my Soul into the hands of God that gave it; and my Body I recommend to the Earth, to be buried in Decent, Christian Burial, at the Discretion of my Executors; nothing doubting, but at the General Resurrection, I shall receive the same again, by the Mighty Power of God. And as touching such Worldly Estate, wherewith it hath pleased God to bless me in this life; I give and Demise, and Dispose of the same, in the following manner and form:

Imprimis. To Sarah, my Beloved Wife, I Give the east end of my now Dwelling-house, with the Cellar thereto appertaining, with one-half of my barn, with one-third part of the Issues and Profits of my Homestead (viz.): that part which I shall here Decypher, and Set over unto my son, Joseph Jones, to be by her, my said Wife, quietly and peaceably possessed and enjoyed, for and during the time of natural Life; and after her Decease, the said third part, with the Dwelling-house and barn as aforesaid, to be and remain my said son Joseph's, as hereby this my Will shall be expressed. And further, my will and meaning is, that my said Wife shall and may hereby enjoy the whole of my Household implements and Utensils, with two good milch cows, to be taken out of my stock of cattle, with one horse, for and during her natural Life, as aforesaid: and after my said Wife's Decease, that the remaining part of my said Household Utensils, and the cows, and horse aforementioned, if any there shall be left, To be Divided equally to, and amongst my four Daughters (viz.): Sarah Corbett, Bridget Wood, Mercy Thwing, and Lydia Whitney, or those that shall legally represent them.

Item. To my beloved son, John Jones, over and above what I have already given him, I give him all my wearing apparel.

Item. To my beloved son, Nathaniel Jones, over and above what I have already given him, I give him the sum of five pounds, which I lent some time past, unto him my said son, Nathaniel.

Item. To my beloved son, Abraham Jones, to him, his heirs, and assigns forever, I give the whole of my land situate, lying and being in Mendon aforesaid, on the north side of a durable spring, commonly called and known by the name of The Living Spring: in such manner and form as that a due nor-east and sou-east line shall be run, acrost my farm, acrost the spring aforesaid, to render the matter convenient, as well for my son Joseph's cattle coming to water, as for him the said Abraham's cattle coming to the same; which said nor-east and sou-west line shall be the dividing (or divisional) line, betwixt my sons Abraham and Joseph Jones: with a five-acre right, in all after divisions of land that are to be made in Mendon aforesaid, from and after the ninth division; always excepting fifty acres of land, on the North corner of my farm, that I intend for to give unto Robert Sanders, to be measured off. And further, it is my will that my said son, Abraham, pay unto my granddaughter, Mary Thwing, the sum of fifteen pounds, when she shall come to the age of eighteen years.

Item. To my youngest son, Joseph Jones, to him, his heirs and assigns forever, I give the whole of my homestead, whereon I now dwell (excepting the Issues and Profits reserved for the use of my wife aforesaid, during her natural life), with the Edifices and Buildings thereon erected, excepting the east end of the Dwelling-house, and part of the barn, reserved for the use of his Mother, as aforesaid, and after her decease, for him, my said son, Joseph, to take the possession thereof. A due nor-east and sou-west line, acrost my land as aforesaid, by aforesaid spring, that my son Abraham's land, heretofore in this instrument given him comes to, which said nor-east and sou-west line, is a division line, and shall remain so to be, betwixt my said sons Abraham and Joseph. More to be given to my said son, Joseph Jones, a five-acre right, in all future divisions of land in said Mendon, from and after the ninth division, with all and singular, my husbandry implements. And further it is my wish, that my said son, Joseph, pay unto my granddaughter, Mary Thwing, the sum of fifteen pounds, when she shall come to the age of eighteen years.

Item. To my beloved daughters, Sarah Corbett, Bridget Wood, Mercy Thwing, and Lydia Whitney, their heirs and assigns forever, over and above what I have already given them, I give unto my said daughters, Sarah, Bridget, Mercy and Lydia, equal in co-partnership, all my personal or moveable estate: except what I have in this Will given to my sons: to be equally divided amongst them, my said daughters, after my just debts and funeral charges are paid, and the charges of settling of the Estate in the Probate office: but my said daughters not to have that part of my personal estate that I have left for my said wife's improvement, until her decease.

Item. I give unto my granddaughter, Mary Thwing, the sum of thirty pounds, and to be paid unto her by my sons, Abraham and Joseph Jones (viz.), to pay fifteen pounds apiece, as soon as the said Mary comes to the age of eighteen years, as aforesaid.

Item. I give unto Robert Sanders, my servant, if he shall remain in my service, or with my assigns, until he come to the age of twenty-one years old, Fifty acres of land, to be set off to him, at the north corner of my farm; and that it be set off to the said Robert by my executors, and if he tarry with my assigns the term of time aforesaid.

And further, my Will and Meaning is, and I do hereby appoint my beloved sons, John and Nathaniel Jones, to be my Executors of this my last Will and Testament; hereby authorizing and empowering them, my said Executors, to make Sale and Disposal of so much of my stock of cattle or sheep, as may be needful, in order to pay the just debts and funeral expenses, and other charges, for settling the estate in the Judge of Probate's office; before the division of that part of my personal estate, that I, in this instrument, give to my four daughters, be made.

And lastly. I do herereby revoke, renounce, disallow, and make null and void, all other Wills by me formerly made; allowing this, and no other, to be my last Will and testament.

In testimony whereof, I, the said John Jones, have set to my hand and seal, the day and year above written.

Signed, sealed, published, pronounced and declared by the said John Jones, as his last Will and testament.

JOHN JONES.   [SEAL.]

In the presence of us, the subscribers:

> NATHANIEL NELSON,
> HABIJAH FRENCH,
> SETH CHAPIN, JR.

This Will (original and written by himself), is now in the possession of Mrs. Ellen M. Dabney,

Ballou, in his history of Milford, states that Elder John Jones made another and later will, and writes thus: "Elder John Jones, owning many tracts of land, prospered greatly both in temporal and spiritual affairs. All his children, sooner or later, became church members. He was a large landowner, and otherwise rich; married off his daughters and sons influentially, and endowed them liberally, with either lands or goods. He made gift deeds of lands, years before he died, to John, Jr., Nathaniel, Abraham and Joseph, retaining the latter as his partner on the homestead. His last will bears date December 11th, 1749 (about four years before his death), and specifies, with proper references, his wife, Sarah, his sons, John, Jr., Nathaniel, Abraham and Joseph; his daughters, Sarah Corbett, Mercy Thwing and Lydia

Whitney, and eight grandchildren, the children of his deceased daughter, Bridget Wood. He gave his large bible to John, Jr., which, if I could have seen, would have saved me days of anxious research. It (the will) ordained his two sons-in-law, Corbett and Whitney, as executors." The Elder lived a long, useful and successful life. He lived to see incipient Milford become a thriving precinct. He came to it when all was crude, wild and sparsely populated, and after becoming an aged patriarch among his family, neighbors and friends, he was called to his reward in the life eternal.

REFLECTIONS.

The Rev. Mr. Ballou indulges in these so happily and forcibly, I adopt his thoughts and words, without attempting to write my own. In his History of Milford, he writes as follows: " It may be well not to forget the crude state of things and the peculiar circumstances amid which our pioneer settlers labored and succeeded. They breasted a howling wilderness. Their clearings were few and small. Their dwellings little other than log huts, and their barns, rude hovels, their fodder (when they had any in store), was in stacks. Their roads were rough cart-paths and uncouth drift-ways. They had no grocery-store, much less post-office or school-house. Blacksmiths, carpenters, shoemakers and other mechanics were few and distant. 'Mendontown' was their material dependence for such necessaries, as they could not produce on their own raw clearings. But Mendon depended on other places, some fifteen or eighteen miles distant, and these again on Boston. Food, raiment, and all the necessaries and comforts of domestic life were mostly coarse, simple, home-wrought, and often scanty, though happily, healthful. They were religious, Puritanical people, the adults (with rare exceptions), church members, and their children baptized. They were punctillious and devout attendants on public worship, no one staying at home on the Sabbath without good excuse. Away to the town seat they posted on the Lord's day, barefoot or shod, on horseback (single and double), or on their own sturdy legs, to sit under the ministrations of Parson Rawson, on uncushioned seats and in the coldest weather, in a plain, unwarmed, old-fashioned meeting-house, through services, generally two hours long, and both forenoon and afternoon. Were they downhearted? Were they cheerless, discontented people? Not at all. Anything but that. They were healthy, active, robust and hopeful. They were bound to subdue the wilderness, to master the wild beasts, and achieve a victory over all difficulties. Gigantic trees fell before them, and well-burned fields grew green with grass and grain from year to year as they advanced. Fresh immigrants came prospecting their closely adjacent wild lands, assuring them of new neighbors soon to arrive. Thus they were expectant, resolute and cheerful. If we imagine that their hardships, privations and toils made them miserable, we probably mistake their mental condition. We may safely guess that they uttered fewer groans under their *real* wants, than we now do under our artificial and unreal ones. Doubtless they extracted health, content, and even merriment from their scanty resources, quite as successfully as we do from the plethora of our luxuries. They had their frailties, faults and woes, but pity would be wasted on their lot. It was one rather to be envied and admired. We can but honor them as heroic pioneers and bless their memories for the heritage they transmitted to us. Successive generations have reaped, and will continue to reap, the harvest they sowed, with mingled tears and gladness. They thinned off direful beasts and venomous reptiles. The rugged earth became fruitful under their labors, and civilized habitations, though humble, superseded the transient wigwams of savageism. Domestic flocks and herds grazed peaceably on hill-tops and plains, but recently wrested from the occupancy of ferocious bears, wolves and panthers. Meadows, orchards and gardens yielded fragrance and fruitage, where a little while before an unbroken wilderness bred only dreariness and terror. 'The wilderness blossomed like the rose.'

"Thus commenced the settlement of our now populous, enterprising and prosperous domain. We will not forget 'the rock whence we were hewn, and the hole of the pit whence we were digged,' neither will we 'despise the day of small things.'

"Our ancesters, our fathers, *came to stay*, and they possessed a goodly land for themselves and their posterity. Let us all appreciate their achievements, improve our inheritance, and deserve well the benedictions they distil upon us from the mansions of immortality."

THE PURITANS,

There has been much said and written about the Puritans during the last 250 years, and there still remains a wide difference of opinion with regard to them throughout our country. While many look upon them as religious fanatics who strove to subvert and destroy all proper forms of order in the church and in the worship of Almighty God, others seem disposed to consider them as almost perfect in their belief, their laws, their customs and their simplicity of worship. But without acknowledging either side as competent or impartial judges, it must be conceded that there is much to approve and admire (when the peculiar circumstances of their position is in review), in their self-denial, their uprightness, their adherence to bible truths, and their determination to worship God according to the promptings of conscience. This latter privilege is one that the inhabitants of our favored land have always held as sacred and inalienable.

In the mother country, the Puritans suffered from the imposition of heavy taxation; their liberties were circumscribed, their complaints disregarded, and under the reigns of James I and Charles I, they had to endure persecution. These two kings, impressed with the belief that they held the position they occupied "by divine right," insisted that their assumed prerogatives should be believed in and respected. This caused the flame of liberty to become brighter, and liberty of the person and of the conscience was preached and maintained. And that desire for liberty, that struggle for it, has resulted in our present liberty in this our glorious country, which is everywhere proclaimed as "a home for the oppressed" and "the land of the free." It is recorded in history that the methods of taxation were unequal, arbitrary and oppressive at that time in England. Opposition to these methods was considered as uncalled for, regarded as most flagrant sedition, and as unlawful resistance to tyrannical authority. Again, not only political but religious questions assumed great importance, and were discussed with all the bitterness that human nature was capable of. The established church, under the influence and guidance of Archbishop Land, introduced new customs, ceremonies and observances in its ritual, many of these showing doctrines more in accordance with Papistical than Protestant belief. Many were shamed and exasperated by these proceedings and bitterly denounced them. Both civil and religious obligations became antagonistic, strong partisanship was evolved, and both sides became embittered, violent and implacable. These two kings set forth doctrines that were utterly subversive of civil and religious liberty, and the people rebelled against them. Parliament, which represented the people, opposed the King, and in return the King fought Parliament. Human nature is always pugnacious, and it is not surprising that a bitter state of feeling was engendered and increased. The Puritans went as far one way as their opponents did the other, but the former had the principle of civil and religious liberty to contend for. The lover of liberty must approve the principle, if they cannot applaud all the methods used to secure it. Many

JOSEPH JONES, JR.
Born 1737.   Died 1799.

who felt their liberty restrained, who could not approve the new ritual in the church, who considered that they were contemned and oppressed, felt themselves forced to give up home and country, and to seek a new home and a refuge in a new land, where they could be governed by equal laws and enjoy *"freedom to worship God."* They came to America, suffered hardships of all kinds, but with commendable and heroic spirit they persevered and founded a home and a country whose name is now famous throughout the world. With all their rigid laws, their stern and unpoetic lives, there is much to admire in their heroic self-denial, their wonderful fortitude under great and depressing difficulties, their strict adherence to the truths of the gospel, and their entire and absorbing religious devotion.

FOURTH GENERATION.

Joseph Jones, youngest child and son of Elder John Jones, married **Mary Whitney** (born May 28th, 1710) in the year 1732, probably.

CHILDREN:

5.	Susanna Jones,	born Nov. 10, 1733, untraced.
	Hannah Jones,	" Jan. 3, 1736, died young.
	Joseph Jones, Jr.,	" Sept. 29, 1737, married Ruth Nelson.
	Mary Jones,	" Oct. 16, 1740, " James Sumner.
	Lydia Jones,	" April 2, 1744, untraced.
	Jonathan Jones,	" Aug. 11, 1746, married Mary Ball.
	David Jones,	" July 10, 1749, died young.
	Timothy Jones,	" April 25, 1751, married Ann Scammell.

Joseph Jones died April 3d, 1796. Mary Jones died July 9th, 1788.

This son of Elder John Jones always lived with his father on the original homestead. The records show that he was given a part of the land of the farm, and that the father and son were, to a considerable extent, partners in the management of business, from about the year 1730 downward. As such they reconstructed and greatly enlarged the mansion, known in its latter days as "The Old House." They put up a crude dam across the river, and set up a saw-mill. This was between 1730 and 1735, the last date being that at which their mansion was enlarged.

Joseph Jones must have been a large landholder in his time, and a man of prominent influence in the community. He was one of the original members of the church organized in 1741, but was not inclined to hold church offices. He lived a long, honored and useful life, extending to more than 86 years.

FIFTH GENERATION.

Joseph Jones, Jr. (my grandfather, and born September 29th, 1737), married **Ruth Nelson** (born November 10th, 1743), December 28th, 1763.

CHILDREN:

Alexander Jones,	born	Aug. 8, 1764,	died	March	19, 1840.
David Jones,	"	Mar. 24, 1767,	"	Sept.	29, 1841.
Nathaniel Jones,	"	Mar. 22, 1769,	"	May	22, 1808.
Lucinda Sophronia Jones,	"	June 4, 1771,	"	Sept.	15, 1776.
Joseph Jones 3d,	"	May 17, 1773,	"	July	16, 1791.
Hannah Jones,	"	June 28, 1775,	"	Aug.	16, 1836.
Lucinda Jones,	"	Aug. 26, 1778,	"	Jan.	12, 1852.
Betsey Jones,	"	Nov. 1, 1781,	"	Nov.	13, 1800.
Nancy Jones,	"	Mar. 9, 1783,	"	July	25, 1845.
Noah Jones,	"	Nov. 21, 1785,	"	Dec.	14, 1813.
Wiswall Jones,	"	Oct. 22, 1788,	"	Aug.	8, 1842.
Leonard Jones,	"	Mar. 10, 1791,	"	same day.	

Ruth Nelson was the daughter of Nehemiah Nelson (born October 4th, 1716), of one of the best families in Milford. His wife was Hannah Sheffield (born February 28th, 1723), daughter of Lieut. William and Mary Sheffield. Nehemiah Nelson's father died when he was about 12 years old, and he was placed under the guardianship of Elder John Jones. This is somewhat singular, as Ruth Nelson's father was in the care of Joseph Jones' grandfather. Her great-great-grandfather, Thomas Nelson, was born in England, date not known, and his was one of the twenty families that emigrated to America with the Rev. Ezekiel Rogers, from Rowley, in Yorkshire, in December, 1638. Another singular circumstance is, that, without doubt, Thomas Jones, our first ancestor known, came, with his family, at the same time. The maiden name of Thomas Nelson's wife was Joan Dummer, date of birth not known, and they had five children, two born in England and three here. He was made freeman in May, 1639, chosen Deputy to General Court in 1640 or 1641, and "appointed to join persons in marriage in the town of Rowley." Thus promoted to positions that were responsible and honorable, he seems to have gone steadily forward to prominent wealth and responsiblity. Called to England on important business, he made his will and sailed, and while there was taken ill and died in

RUTH NELSON, WIFE OF JOSEPH JONES, JR.
Born 1743.   Died 1825.

1648. His son Thomas married Ann Lambert, date not known, and they had seven children, the sixth being Gershom Nelson, born July 11th, 1672. He married Abigail Ellithorpe, July 16th, 1700, and they had seven children, the same number his father and mother had. And (another still more singular coincidence) his sixth child was Nehemiah Nelson. He was married to Hannah Sheffield, October 29th, 1742, and they, too (also very strange), were blessed with the same number of children, so that the son, the father, and the grandfather each had seven children. My grandmother was the oldest child of Nehemiah and Hannah Nelson, and was born November 10th, 1743. And here it may also be mentioned, as somewhat singular, her sister Elizabeth Nelson, born March 30th, 1746, married Deacon Nathaniel Rawson March 24th, 1768, and he (born in Mendon, July 9th, 1745) was a brother of my wife's grandmother (Anne Rawson, born May 8th, 1749), who married Col. Benjamin Hoppin, of Providence, R. I. Thus a grandnephew of Mrs. Elizabeth (Nelson) Rawson married a granddaughter of Anne (Rawson) Hoppin. Thus were two of the third generation, from Ruth Nelson and Anne Rawson, married, and by that marriage the two families of Jones and Rawson again connected after a long interval of time.

The Nelson family, its progenitors and descendants, occupied prominent positions in Mendon, Mill River and Milford for six generations, and in both secular and religious matters. Those positions they filled with ability and honor, deserving and receiving the praise of their fellow-men.

Of my grandmother, Ruth Nelson Jones, the Rev. Adin Ballou, in his "History of Milford," writes as follows: "In a conversation with the late venerable Jared Rawson (son of Deacon Nathaniel and Elizabeth Rawson), then over 90 years old, he extolled his Aunt Ruth Jones as one of the noblest women ever raised in this vicinity. Joseph Jones, Jr., and his wife raised a large, talented and enterprising family."

Joseph Jones, Jr., died at the house of his oldest son, Alexander Jones, in Charleston, South Carolina, of fever, August 22d, 1799, aged 62, and was buried in St. Philip's churchyard. Many years after, his granddaughter and her husband, Mr. and Mrs. Dabney, caused his grave and the stone, which had fallen into decay, to be fully repaired. After Alexander Jones had left Charleston and established himself and family in Providence, he tenderly cared for and supported his mother, who suffered and was almost helpless from paralysis for 20 years, until she entered into rest, August 16th, 1825, at the age of 82.

"Blessed are the dead who die in the Lord."

Additional items of interest, accidentally omitted, should be here recorded, though limited space renders it necessary to be brief.

When quite a small boy, I frequently heard my father speak of "Aunt Sumner," and cousins by the name of Parkhurst, but not making any particular inquiries at the time, I never understood the relationship until within a few months. In reading Ballou's "History of Milford," with its really remarkable biographical register (which I saw for the first time the latter part of March last) it became perfectly plain. James Sumner married a daughter of Joseph and Mary (Whitney) Jones, and was a man of note in his day, exercising a leading influence in the community. He held the various offices of clerk, chief committee man of the precinct, assessor, coroner of his vicinage, etc. He was born December 10th, 1718, and lived to the age of 77 years, dying August 29th, 1795. His wife Mary was born October 16th, 1740, and died April 29th, 1791, in the 52d year of her age.

James Sumner, Jr., his son, born May 31st, 1747, married Melatiah, daughter of Jonathan and Mary Jones, born June 1st, 1746. He died September 22d, 1775, and in March, 1778, she married again. The Parkhursts married into the Jones and Rawson families, and some of the Jones families married Parkhursts, but as a record of them would run into an almost interminable length, it is perhaps best to omit it. The "History of Milford" contains many interesting matters relating to old houses, farms, homesteads, etc., and in a record of some of the latter, it says: "The Old Jones House" (as it has been called for many long years), "situated on 'The Dale Farm,' was built in 1703, enlarged and improved about 1734 or 1735, and was demolished in October, 1874, many parts of it being 171 years old." I well remember my first impressions of it, and that it was then 115 years old, when I passed my first night under its roof.

At the centennial celebration in Milford, in 1880, many old and curious articles were exhibited, and among them there were a few of special interest to us who are descendants of the Jones' families. First: "a pair of snowshoes, worn by the ancestors of Sarah Jones" (it does not state which Sarah) "about 200 years ago." Also, hand-made spikes from the timbers of the old house in the Dale; also, a horn drinking cup, carried through the Revolutionary war by Col. Samuel Jones, used in the war of 1812 by Captain Henry Nelson, and the same was afterwards carried through the late civil war by Henry Nelson Parkhurst; also, the sword worn by Capt. Ezekiel Jones at the battle of White Plains; also, the clothes worn by the children of Capt. Ezekiel and Mary Jones at their baptism in 1782, 98 years before. In addition to these, the coat of arms of the Jones family, and portraits of Col. Sumner and his wife, together with the coat of arms of the Parkhursts', both these families being connected with the Jones family. These were shown at the town hall of Milford, at the celebration of the Municipal Centenary, the 10th of June, 1880. Many other items of great interest *to me* are recorded, but the want of both time and space forbids my continuing them farther.

SIXTH GENERATION.

Alexander Jones, the oldest child and son of Joseph, Jr., and Ruth Jones, was married January 28th, 1790, in St. Philip's Church, in Charleston, South Carolina, by the Rev. Thomas Frost to **Mary Farquhar,** daughter of George and Elizabeth Farquhar.

CHILDREN:

7. Harriet Farquhar Jones, born in Charleston, Jan. 3, 1791.
    Eliza Ruth Jones,   "   "   June 16, 1793.
    Mary Margaret Jones,   "   "   Jan. 30, 1795.
    Alexander Jones, Jr.,   "   "   Nov. 8, 1796.
    Joseph Jones,   "   "   Sept. 15, 1799.
    Caroline Flagg Jones,   "   "   Jan. 31, 1802.
    Jane Sherwood Jones,   "   "   Nov. 26, 1803.
    Frances Nelson Jones,   "   Providence, Jan. 7, 1806.
    George Farquhar Jones,   "   "   Feb. 11, 1811.
    Ellen Maria Jones,   "   "   June 30, 1812.
    Emily Matilda Jones,   "   "   Aug. 16, 1814.

Eleven children, all of whom lived to maturity, and ten of the number were married.

Alexander Jones graduated at Brown University, Providence, R. I., in 1782. In the Spring of 1783 he went to New York as a clerk. In 1784 he went to England as clerk. In 1786 returned home, and kept a school through the Winter of 1786 and 1787. In the latter year he went to Charleston, S. C., and was clerk and bookkeeper until December, when he went into business. Continued it with success, married in 1790, and lived in Charleston until 1805, when he removed with his family to Providence. There he became a cotton merchant, and sold the first bale of cotton to the first manufacturer in this country, Samuel Slater. In 1813 he bought the mansion on Angell Street, about a half mile from the centre of the town, which he named "Bellevue." In 1827 he retired from business, which he had carried on successfully for 22 years in Providence, being (what was called in those days) a rich man. Eight years afterwards my mother died at the age of 62, and four years and six months from the time of her death he followed her, entering into "the rest that remaineth to the people of God," March 19th, 1840, aged 75 years, 7 months and 11 days. The husband and wife lived together 45 years, and they both left a record and a memory ever to be valued by their children and grandchildren.

REMARKS.

In closing this part of the record of "the Jones Family of Milford," I feel a strong desire to impress upon the minds of their descendants who are now living, the important fact that their ancestors were men and women of excellent character and abilities. They occupied a prominent position in the community in which they lived. Their deportment and conduct were such as to elicit the esteem and the commendation of their fellow-men. That they well deserved this, no one can doubt who reads what has been recorded of them. Their whole lives, as citizens, as heads of families, and, above all, as professing Christian men and women, were such as to show that they were actuated by a desire "for the glory of God and the good of their fellow-men." They aimed high, they put up a high standard, and they did not fall short of the mark.

In consequence they have left behind them, as they have been "gathered to their fathers," a record and a legacy of which we have just cause for pride. And this pride of ancestry is not only pardonable, but it is an incentive to us who follow after (and we, too, must soon, like them, all be gathered to our fathers) to emulate their virtues, to pray that their mantle may fall on us, so that we, too, may leave the same excellent record to our posterity. If we, like them, faithfully perform all the duties of life, and with the same desire that was theirs, to glorify God and to benefit our fellow-men, our record will be "known and read of all men," our inheritance will be an eternal habitation in Heaven and our reward: "Well done! thou good and faithful servant!"

What a noble heritage is ours! what a strong incentive to us, to "go and do thou likewise!" If we, too, aim high and live up to an exalted standard, our record, like theirs, will be handed down to our children and our children's children with a sweet fragrance that will cling to it as long as time shall last. No higher motive can be ours than to advance the cause and add to the glory of our Creator and our God, and to promote the welfare and happiness of our fellow-men. Such a record will be imperishable.

ELIZABETH (SHERWOOD-FARQUHAR) CHRISTIAN.
Born 1746.   Died 1813.

MATERNAL ANCESTORS

OF

GEORGE FARQUHAR JONES.

FIRST GENERATION.

John Sherwood was born in England in the year 1713.

Elizabeth Sherwood, his wife, maiden name unknown, born December 26th, 1714.

The date of their marriage unknown, but supposed in 1745.

SECOND GENERATION.

Elizabeth Sherwood, daughter and only child of John and Elizabeth Sherwood, was born in Charleston, October 15th, 1746.

George Farquhar, her husband, was born in Scotland, April 13th, 1745.

They were married October 5th, 1770.

John Sherwood, died Dec. 11, 1755.
Elizabeth Sherwood, " June 7, 1775.

THIRD GENERATION.

CHILDREN OF GEORGE AND ELIZABETH (SHERWOOD) FARQUHAR:

Margaret Manson Farquhar, born July 29, 1771, died Dec. 2, 1806.
Mary Farquhar, " Dec. 24, 1773, in Milledgeville, Ga.
Lalier Elizabeth Farquhar, " Jan. 19, 1776, died Oct. 6, 1776.
Elizabeth Farquhar, " Oct. 2, 1777, " May 24, 1778.
Jane Farquhar, " May 31, 1779, " Feb. 19, 1780.

My grandfather, George Farquhar, died September 20th, 1779, aged 34 years.

Elizabeth Farquhar, about two years after her husband's death, married **Robert Christian** on his birthday, October 28th, 1781. He was born in England, October 28th, 1753.

THEY HAD BUT ONE CHILD, A SON:

Charles Christian, born July 20, 1785, who was lost at sea in 1815.

Mrs. Elizabeth Christian, my grandmother, died April 10th, 1813, aged 67.

During the Revolution George Farquhar remained "loyal to the king," and, being a soldier in the British forces, was no doubt a strong and active partisan, for he was very obnoxious to the patriots. While away from his home, they ransacked it, destroying his furniture, bedding, etc., and it is with good reason supposed that all his papers were burned or lost. Among them, without doubt, were family records, so that nothing can be traced with regard to his family or ancestors in Scotland. This became a matter of great regret, as we heard some years after that a large property was held, belonging to the heirs of the Farquhar family, in England and Scotland and awaiting claimants.

In St. Philip's Churchyard, Charleston, S. C., there is the following:

The mortal part of

ELIZABETH CHRISTIAN

Lies buried under this stone, waiting for the resurrection of the just.
She had for a number of years been a member of St. Philip's
Church, and died in the blessed hope of Salvation
through faith in Jesus Christ, on the 10th
of April, 1813, aged 66.

Contiguous lie the remains of James C. Green,
who died May 29th, 1803, aged 30,
and
Margaret M., his wife,
who died December 2d, 1806, aged 35,
also of Nathaniel Jones,
who died May 22d, 1808, aged 39.

The following is also to be seen in St. Philip's Churchyard:

Died the 22d of August, 1799,

JOSEPH JONES,

of Milford, State of Massachusetts,

in the 62d year of his age, after three days' sickness of an

epidemic fever. He left a wife and four children in

Milford and five children in this city to

lament his sudden death.

This stone is erected to the memory of an affectionate parent

by his oldest son.

There were but two of the children of George and Elizabeth (Sherwood) Farquhar that lived to maturity, my mother, **Mary Farquhar,** and her older sister, **Margaret Manson Farquhar.** The other three children died quite young.

I now give the record of her marriage and the list of her descendants.

Margaret Manson Farquhar married **James Carey Green** (who was born in Providence, R. I., June 4th, 1772), on the 16th of March, 1797.

They were married by the Rev. Thomas Frost, rector of St. Philip's Church, who had also previously married her sister Mary to Alexander Jones.

THEIR CHILDREN WERE:

James Farquhar Green, born Feb. 13, 1798, died Apr. 6, 1882.
William Hayward Green, " Aug. 6, 1799, " Oct. 29, 1800.
Edward Geo. Farquhar Green, " Jan. 19, 1801, " Aug. 16, 1801.
Charles Leverett Green, " Nov. 29, 1802, " date unknown.

James Farquhar Green married **Margaret Reid** (born in Charleston), September 25th, 1824.

CHILDREN :

Elizabeth Green, born Sept. 15, 1825, died date unknown.
Robert Maxwell Green, " May 28, 1827, " Aug. 20, 1883.
James Farquhar Green, Jr. " Apr. 3, 1829, " Feb. 19, 1859.
Jane Hall Green, " Sept. 23, 1830, " Apr. 17, 1876.
William Stuart Green, " Aug. 30, 1833.
Mary Belcher Green, " July 21, 1835.

Margaret (Reid) Green died in 1846. Exact date not given.

Robert Maxwell Green married Mary Farquhar Jones, December 21st, 1859.

List of Children under Head of George F. Jones' Family:

James Farquhar Green, Jr., died unmarried at the age of 30 years.

Jane Hall Green married Joseph Middleton Wilkinson, December 15th, 1853.

CHILDREN:

Margaret Green Wilkinson,	born Dec.	4, 1854.
Aramintha Jenkins Wilkinson,	" July	4, 1856.
James Farquhar Wilkinson,	" Apr. 14, 1858, died June, 1859.	
William Clement Wilkinson,	" Feb. 26, 1860, " Feb., 1864.	
Mary Elizabeth Wilkinson,	" Dec. 12, 1864.	
Maxwell Green Wilkinson,	" May 23, 1866.	
James Farquhar Wilkinson,	" May 31, 1869, died May 13, 1873.	

Mrs. Jane Hall Wilkinson, died Apr. 17, 1876.

Margaret Green Wilkinson married John Joseph Lewis, December 21st, 1881.

CHILDREN:

Robert Earle Lewis, born Dec. 17, 1882.

Aramintha Jenkins Wilkinson married Henry Philip Sitton, of Pendleton, S. C., February 27th, 1877.

CHILDREN:

James Middleton Sitton, born March 17, 1878.
Charles Vedder Sitton, " Sept. 22, 1881.

Mary Elizabeth Wilkinson married William Harper Hughes, April 30th, 1884.

Mary Belcher Green married John Arnold Hubbard Brinsdon, of Devonshire, England, November 30th, 1870.

CHILDREN:

John Joseph Brinsdon,	born Nov. 29, 1871, died May 6, 1873.	
Charles Edward Brinsdon,	" July 1, 1873.	
Mary Pickens Brinsdon,	" Feb. 28, 1875.	

James Farquhar Green, Sr., married second, Rachel Keith Dickinson, June 6th, 1848. They had one child, Lawrence Lee Green, born March 12th, 1849.

Lawrence Lee Green married Mary King Clement, February 28th, 1877.

CHILDREN:

Charles Farquhar Green,   born Jan. 6, 1878.
Mary King Clement Green,   "   Feb. 28, 1881.

The remains of James Farquhar Green and his wife, Margaret (Reid) Green, and his son, James Farquhar Green, Jr., lie buried in St. Peters' Churchyard, Charleston, S. C.

James Farquhar Green was a man of very pleasant social qualities, a good friend, an honest man and a gentleman. It was often said by my mother, that he was the only blood relative that she had living. He was always a favorite with her, and continued so to the day of her death. He was a man of good business abilities, but retired from business many years before his death, removing to the upper part of the state, to Pendleton, where he passed the last years of his life. He lived to the good old age of 84 years, and died in his chair, April 6th, 1882. He was a man of fine personal appearance, and his genialty was remarkable, making him a very pleasant and agreeable companion.

DEATH OF ROBERT MAXWELL GREEN.

Died in Summerville, Georgia, on Monday, August 20th, 1883, R. Maxwell Green. He had gone there from Charleston to pass the Summer months, for rest and recuperation, but the dread disease (consumption) had progressed too far, and he was called upon suddenly to lay down the burden of life, which he did almost literally, in the arms of a young friend who had gone there to see him. But we have the assurance that he, who was a sincere Christian in life, was ready for the summons that called him hence in death.

The writer of this knew him to be a strictly honorable man, and one whose integrity was unquestionable, whether in business transactions or those of life generally. His abilities and qualifications for business were excellent, and he carried on with considerable success the exportation of the finest grades of cotton to Europe, until compelled, by the state of his health, to abstain entirely.

The death of his son, George Farquhar Green, at Sewanee College, Tennessee, at the interesting and promising age of 18, was a heavy blow to fall upon him, for he was not only very fond of him, but proud of his conduct and abilities, which presented to his father's and to the eyes of all, a prospect for great usefulness and capability in manhood. But God took him in the flower of his youth, and many wept his early death. Faith aids us in looking beyond this vale of

tears, and leads us to hope that the loving father and the affectionate
son are inheriting the reward of the blessed.

THE LIFE OF ALEXANDER JONES.

As written by himself on his 70th birthday; Providence, R. I., August 8th, 1834.

It having pleased Almighty God to prolong the life of Alexander
Jones to the great age of "threescore years and ten," he would, on
this anniversary of his birth, pour out his heart in gratitude and
thanksgiving to Him for His long forbearance and tender mercies to one
so unworthy of His favors, and express his determination to devote
himself anew to the service of his Lord and Saviour Jesus Christ
during the short remnant of his days.

I write this biographical sketch of my unprofitable life for my
own gratification and for the information of my dear children and
grandchildren, having been father of eleven of the former, of whom,
blessed be God, nine are now living, and fifty of the latter, of whom
thirty-eight are now alive.

I was born in the town of Mendon, in that portion called Mill River
Precinct, now the town of Milford, county of Worcester, Massachusetts, on the 8th of August, 1764. When a boy, my father being a
farmer, I did light work on the farm until about 12 years old, when,
as I was more fond of books than labor, not robust and being very
small, and the oldest and favorite son of a too indulgent father, he
placed me under the tuition of the Rev. Amariah Frost, the minister
of the parish, who prepared me for college.

I stop here to relate a wonderful preservation of my life when
about six years of age. I went into the barn (about ten rods from
the house) on Sunday to look for eggs and to play. I fell from the
great beams, about twenty feet, to the threshing floor, striking against
the plank of a scaffold, cutting a large hole in the upper part of my
forehead. My brother David ran to the house saying that I was dead.
My mother ran and found me, as she supposed, dead, carried me into
the house, and laying me on her lap, she perceived that I breathed,
and then made a little moaning noise. Dr. Scammell was sent for
and I recovered. "Oh! how good and gracious the Lord is! Let
this casualty be a solemn warning to my children and grandchildren
not to desecrate God's holy Sabbath day."

I will relate a second preservation. In the year 1775, in Summer,
when Washington and the American army were encamped in Cam-

ALEXANDER JONES.
Taken at the age of 32 years.

bridge and Roxbury, the British holding Boston, my father and mother drove to the camp to visit Major Alexander Scammell, who named me. I sat in a little chair (being very small, indeed), before them in the chaise. In going over a small ditch in Cambridge, I was pitched out and fell under the wheel, which stopped against my neck and soiled my collar. Two inches further and I must have died. This was a *second* remarkable preservation. I return to the narrative:

In September, 1778, I entered Cambridge College as Freshman. It being during the Revolutionary war that I was admitted, and my father, finding the expense there very heavy, he concluded to place me to board and under the tuition of Rev. Mr. Ustick, of Grafton, one of the professors of the Rhode Island College, at about half the expense, to pursue the studies of the first year, with the understanding that I should enter the Sophomore class the next year, which was accordingly done. In Providence I boarded at Mr. Wm. Holroyd's, down town, for a long time, and then at Capt. Paine's, and lastly at Ralph Earle's in Weybosset Street. Our little class consisted of Joseph Jencks, Obadiah Brown, William McClellan and self, under the direction of and at Dr. Manning's house, the first president, and now occupied by Dr. Francis Wayland. In the year 1781, Brown, McClellan and self studied mathematics with Mr. Ustick, in Grafton (as Dr. Manning did not teach that branch), and Jencks studied with Dr. West. The first Wednesday in September, 1782, we passed a private examination in the chapel, and took private degrees. We went "through college" without residing in the building, as it was occupied a part of the time as a hospital for the French army. John Greene, Samuel Snow and Dr. Levi Wheaton (who had regular standings in college before the war), received their degrees at the same time.

I went home to my father's, a young and dwarfish stripling of 18 years. My father having sold his farm for paper money, which became almost worthless, and becoming embarrassed in trade, found it difficult to pay for my education. I had nothing but a little learning, and did not know what course to pursue. My father procured me the place of captain's clerk on board a privateer, but while my fond mother was preparing my clothes, wetting them with her tears, news came that a preliminary treaty of peace was signed. A kind Providence smiled upon me in this respect.

The Winter following, I kept school in Hopkinton, and had male and female scholars older and stronger than myself. I boarded at Mr. John Hayden's, and while in this kind family, was taken very sick with bilious colic—was taken home in a sleigh, covered with a blanket—

and after ten days' of extreme suffering, in which I lost twenty pounds of flesh, I recovered from this dangerous disease. In this *third* preservation, I *now* see the kind forbearance of my Heavenly Father to his erring, sinful child in his 19th year.

In the Spring of 1783, I went to New York and resided in the family of Captain Goldsbury, corner of Beekman and Water Streets. A part of the time I was clerk to Mr. Livesey, in his grocery in Beekman Street, and a part was clerk to Levi Thayer and Mr. Lyman. Every afternoon I went to a slaughter-house in Whitehall, to take receipts from the midshipmen of the British fleet, for quarters of fresh beef. Prince William Henry, now King William the Fourth, was then a midshipman on board Amiral Grave's fleet.

I boarded part of this time at the Bullshead and Plough and Harrow Inns, in the Bowery. While in Captain Goldsbury's family (he was a Loyalist, and had fought against his country), I was dangerously ill of bilious or yellow fever, and at one time my life was despaired of, so much so that Captain G. spoke to a friend of his for a place for me in a vault in St. Paul's churchyard. To the goodness and mercy of God, and His blessing on a skillful physician's prescriptions, and the kind, affectionate and untiring attention and good nursing of Mrs. Goldsbury (who placed me in her own bed), and that of her three excellent daughters, Betsey, Priscilla and Sally, who watched with me alternately (and if I had been a son or brother, more kindness could not have been shown me), I recovered. I was deranged and not conscious of my danger, neither did I, when convalescent, feel the least gratitude to God for this *fourth* preservation from the grave. Oh! the hardness and impenitency of the sinner's heart! How vile! and yet how unfeeling!

In 1783, a little before the evacuation of New York by the British, I returned home, and in December I sailed with Captain Connell in a schooner for Shelburne, Nova Scotia, and had charge of about $1,000 in fresh beef, furnished by Captain Bullen, of Medway. I arrived safely after a cold winter passage, boarded again in Captain G.'s fine family in a log house. At the breaking up of winter I took passage in a sloop for Marblehead with the proceeds in guineas, and walked from thence to Boston, Medway (where I paid over the money) and to Milford.

In the Spring of 1784, I took passage again in the sloop —— , Captain Cornell, as *supercargo* of a cargo of unslacked lime in the hold, and twelve heavy live oxen on deck. In a dreadful gale of wind (in which we could carry no sail), the oxen falling on deck, made it leak, and the seas breaking continually over us, being on or near a shoal of George's Bank, we could not scud before the wind, and the lime beginning to smoke, the Captain ordered the decks cleared, which was done with great difficulty. The oxen perished and the gale soon abated. We all survived and arrived in safety. We were in imminent danger. I prayed for mercy, from a sense of fear, probably, for the first time in my life, but soon forgot all and kept on sinning. In this *fifth* preservation from death I see the finger of God, and would "call upon my soul and all that is within me to bless and praise His great and glorious name."

Early in August, 1784, I sailed in a brig, Captain Collins, from Shelburne for England, as a clerk for Levi Thayer and Philip Jarvis. Arrived at Dover and went by land to London, where I remained in furnished lodgings in Salisbury Court, Fleet Street, until November, when we all sailed in the ship Good Hope (same captain), and after a boisterous passage arrived in Shelburne and opened a ship chandlery store for Thayer & Jarvis. I was a clerk for some time in Robertson & Rigby's dry goods store and boarded with Mr. Rigby. Thayer & Jarvis failed in 1785, and *ran away* in 1786. I got a passage to the United States in a fishing schooner, and again went to my own home in Milford, poor and destitute.

My father and the family then resided in Noah Wiswall's house at twelve dollars a year rent, for he had lost money and become poor. In the Winter of 1786 and '87, the time of Shay's insurrection, I again kept school at Chestnut Hill, Mendon, at six dollars per month and boarded at Colonel Reed's and Major Taft's.

In the Summer of 1787, Moses Smith, who owed my father money, proposed going to Charleston, South Carolina, and said he would pay for my passage. I had nothing but character, clothing not very good, and a little money; and well knowing how sickly the Southern climate was, there seemed to be no other course for me to take but this desperate one. I proceeded to New York and there, on the 4th of July, falling into respectable company with some dissipated acquaintances, I spent nearly all the money I had—about four dollars. Oh! let my children who read this, caution their children to beware of dissipated companions, however respectable their standing. I was ashamed and confounded, and made solemn resolutions, which I kept firmly afterwards.

, I proceeded on in the sloop ——, Captain Elliott, to Charleston, Commodore Chauncey, then the cabin boy, where I arrived on the 19th. I ought here to relate a *sixth* preservation. Our vessel got aground on a shoal in the bar and in the breakers, and we were in such danger as to prepare to *swim ashore* if it was possible. We, however, at last thumped over the shoals into deep water and all was well.

When I landed in Charleston *I had only eighteen coppers in my pocket*, but a number of letters of introduction to Mr. Russell, Mr. Crafts, and several to Thayer, Bartlett & Co. These I had procured from my friends in Providence and Boston, and by them I hoped to procure a situation as clerk in a store, or as teacher in an academy or private family. On my passage (afterwards a remarkable coincidence), I became acquainted with Mr. Samuel Brenton (uncle to my son-in-law Rev. Samuel Brenton Shaw), who had a little property with him. He formed a friendship for me, and said he would divide with me while what he had lasted. We went to board at Mr. Hall's in the Bay at four dollars per week.

A very important era of my life was now about to take place. I lost no time in delivering my letters, but after being received with much politeness by all, none gave me encouragement as to employment. I had seen Mr. Williams Thayer several times (his partners being in Providence), and fortunately for me all his clerks except William Dabney (who afterwards married my sister Hannah), and he was in want of some one to bring up the books and accounts and make out bills and collect the amounts. And besides it appeared that he was pleased with me, "for," said he, "I suppose you have not a great deal of money and you had better come and stay with me and I will see what can be done for you. In the meantime, if you have a mind to do some writing, it is very well." I accepted his offer with avidity, entered into his business with spirit, made out bills, collected money and brought up the books. Soon after this he said: "Well, Jones, you shall not work for nothing. I will allow you ten dollars a month." About this time he gave me a suit of clothes (of brown cassimere), which I very much wanted, as I had a poor wardrobe. Business increased, I worked hard, my heart as light as a feather and I was happy, but not worth a dollar. In the Autumn both partners returned with three or four clerks and I was not wanted. My best friend said: "We will not turn you adrift." I was still a favorite.

Now comes one of the most important occurrences of my whole life —commencement of business. An old gentleman named Henry Caldwell, Sr., wished for an active young partner to commence the retail grocery business and to board with him, a bachelor. This business was much overdone, and the currency was paper money at

17½ per cent. discount and a flood of copper coin. We tried the experiment, and opened a small grocery store in a small building of one story in Church, a little south of Tradd Street, under the firm of Caldwell & Jones; Thayer, Bartlett & Co. turning out and loaning me West India goods to the amount of £100 sterling for my part of the capital, Caldwell putting in the same amount in cash. This was in December, 1787. I commenced sales at retail by myself *at cheap prices, early and late,* and principally to blacks. Business increased and I extended it by running into debt. This so alarmed my partner that in two months we dissolved, and Thayer, Bartlett & Co. paid him off and took his place. The firm was then Alexander Jones, in the books Alexander Jones & Co.

My business increased rapidly, and my credit was undoubted in this year, 1788. I was active and delighted to have property at command to assist my father's family, who were quite poor. I went upon the plan of *selling cheap* and therefore had a great run of business. My store was too small, and my friends Thayer, Bartlett & Co. hired a lot next door at the corner of Longitude lane and employed some Northern carpenters to put a large cheap store, a small kitchen and a stable for their horse. A small shed room was put up for me, large enough for a cot bed, a pine table, two chairs, a trunk and an iron chest. In this small room I kept "bachelor's hall" and lived happily and contentedly. My brother Joseph was a very good and active clerk, and afterwards my brother Nathaniel. James C. Green and Robert Maxwell were also in my employ.

About this time my Aunt Sumner died, but being without heirs-at-law, the half of my grandfather Joseph Jones' farm, which he had previously given to her, reverted back to him, and he gave it to my father, and he deeded the same to me. Here was now a pleasant home for my father's family.

In the course of this year I became acquainted with *Mary Farquhar, daughter of Mrs. Elizabeth (Farquhar) Christian,* and was pleased with her. In 1789, I paid her more particular attention, and became attached to her, and at length was engaged. After a short courtship I was made happy by being married to her by the Rev. Thomas Frost on the 28th of January, 1790. Mrs. Christian then resided in Elliott Street and we boarded with her until July. This I consider the most important epoch of my life. At twenty-five (nearly) I married the lady of my choice, aged sixteen. Neither of us had property (or myself but very little), but I had health, activity and a good run of

4

business. I took this important step after obtaining the approbation of *my best friend*, Williams Thayer.

I ought here to mention another important subject. For about two years I had a seat in Mr. Thayer's pew, in the Baptist Church, and sat under the close and excellent preaching of Rev. Mr. Furman. I, however, frequently attended St. Philip's Church, and being of a light and thoughtless disposition, I preferred Mr. Frost's preaching, as it did not alarm my conscience. I was pleased, too, with the Episcopal service, and especially with the music, and chanting of the choir of singing boys. I became an Episcopalian, and hired a pew in the south gallery, in Mrs. Christian's name. I afterwards purchased a pew in the centre of the Church, and paid for it £150 sterling.

In July of the above year, we commenced housekeeping, having purchased a little furniture, and hired a chamber and garret room, for £18, in Capt. Brown's house, near my store. About this time, my friends (T. B. & Co.), after clearing away my shed-room, and their stable, built on the store lot, in Longitude lane, a small brick house, 36 feet in length, of two stories, and only four rooms. In this house we lived happily and contentedly, about eight years. God prospered and blessed us with four fine children: Harriet F., Eliza R., Mary M. and Alexander.

I might have before stated, that in 1792 we visited our friends in Milford, with our only daughter, Harriet, and "Minty," nurse. I purchased my father's half of the farm. We returned by way of New York and Philadelphia. In the following year I dissolved with Thayer, B. & Co., and paid them £1,000 sterling for their part of the profits. I had used up my part, and had but little active capital left. My credit being good, however, I went on in my business successfully.

About 1795 or '96 I began to discount notes and bills of exchange, which was a very lucrative business, and about this time sold my stock of groceries to Mr. Lauderdale, and gave up that business. I set up my brother Nathaniel in the grocery business, who was successful, and paid me in two years about $2,000 profit. I also set up James C. Green, and was a dormant partner, by which I sustained a loss of about $15,000.

In May, 1798, I purchased a large three-story house of Mr. Wright, at the corner of Tradd and Orange Streets, and removed there. I laid out about $4,000 in repairs and additions. We were blessed with health and lived happily in this pleasant situation seven years, and had three more children: Joseph, Caroline F. and Jane S. My father died in my house, of yellow fever, on the 22d of August, 1799. In

1800 I went to the North, to assist my mother in settling my father's insolvent estates, and to see my poor, sick sister, Betsey, before she died, which was in November. I purchased while there the other half of "The Dale Farm."

In 1802 there was a great change in my constitution, or habit, as to perspiration. Before this time, I had sweat profusely, and could bear the heat of the climate very well. In an unaccountable manner, the pores of my skin became closed, so that I could not perspire at all (perceptibly), except on the right hip (a place about as large as a silver dollar), and on the right side of my neck. This habit has continued until this time. My sufferings from the heat in South Carolina were extreme, and have been equally great in very hot weather at the North. On this account I passed the Summers of 1803 and 1804 in my native air at the North, and for the same reason I removed my family to Providence, R. I., in June, 1805, after selling my mansion-house, garden, etc., in Charleston.

Now commences another important epoch of my life. I became an inhabitant of Providence, R. I. We first resided in T. Foster's house, in Westminster Street, now owned by S. Tillinghast. Our daughter, Frances N., was born in this house, in January, 1806. In this year we removed to Billings' house, now Wm. J King's, Union Street. I also began to sell a little cotton. In 1807 we removed to Capt. Packard's house, in Westminster Street, and afterwards to "the Power House," corner of South Main and Transit Streets, in December, 1809. George F. was born here in February, 1811, and Ellen M. in June, 1812. In 1813 I purchased (by exchange of Dr. Moser) the mansion house in Angell Street, which I called "Bellevue." Our youngest daughter, Emily M., was born here in August, 1814, and here we continue to reside. I carried on a heavy and successful business in cotton, from 1809 to 1819, by commission and importation, notwithstanding that I made heavy losses by bad debts and otherwise. I continued, after 1819, to do a small business in the same line until 1827.

I must now go back a number of years, and refer to the most important subject, and the most important era of my whole protracted life, as it has reference to "the life that now is, and to that which is to come." I mean *religion*, and the conversion of myself, my wife, and several of my children. Laus Deo!

I hired a pew in old St. John's Church, in 1806, and purchased one in the new church, in 1810. About this time I began to be anxious as to my state, and to feel compunctions of conscience as to investing property in a church where the gospel *was not preached in its spiritu-*

ality. It pleased Almighty God, however, about the year 1814, to *convert* my minister, Dr. N. B. Crocker, and my son, Alexander (now a clergyman), and in that year my eldest daughter, Harriet, became pious, and joined the communion. (On the 14th of October, 1823, she departed and joined the church above.) Eliza R. and Alexander (three children) became communicants at this time.

In 1815 prayer meetings were established in St. John's Church, and were held at my son-in-law's, J. B. Wood's house, conducted by students of the college, *Benjamin B. Smith* (now bishop), *Alexander J. Marshall, Cutler*, etc. In the year 1815, I was convinced and convicted of sin, and shed floods of tears of contrition. I had imbibed the notion of natural inability and passivity—was of the opinion that salvation was all of grace—that the work of conversion was all of God, by the special operation of His Holy Spirit (which I now believe), and that, therefore, the sinner *could do nothing* but wait for the special operation of the Holy Ghost to compel the acceptance of proffered mercy. I became convinced that this was a great mistake, and found that religion was not to be obtained without effort, and in January and February, 1816, I began to pray, and to "work out my salvation with fear and trembling." God graciously heard my cry for mercy, pardoned my sins, and gave me "the witness of the Spirit" and the consolation of His promises, and the Saviour of sinners became precious to my soul. I believed on His name at the age of 51 years, and with my wife and my dear daughter Caroline (at the age of 14) joined the communion of St. John's, in March, 1816. In this year about 70 became members of our church. My wife had obtained hope in Christ before me, and waited to join the Holy Communion with me. I was baptized before a large congregation, and felt no reluctance to confess my blessed Lord before men. Oh! what a precious rest to weary and heavy laden souls!

My dear daughters Mary M. and Frances Nelson joined the church a few years later, and since then two of my grandchildren, M. J. Alden and H. R. Wood, have become communicants in the Episcopal Church. "Oh! how shall words express the gratitude I owe."

On the 16th of August, 1825, my honored mother departed this life in the 82d year of her age, having been a pious professor of religion nearly 50 years. "Blessed are the dead who die in the Lord."

My son Joseph died in Tampico, Mexico, November 12th, 1831.

There are now six of us, brothers and sisters, Alexander, David, Hannah, Lucinda, Nancy and Wiswall, and all professors of religion.

On looking over the foregoing pages, and reviewing my long, protracted and checkered life, I can say, in the language of the holy Psalmist, "surely the goodness and mercy of God have followed me all the days of my life." To *Him* be honor and glory forever and ever.

I can discover a protecting, superintending Providence, from my infancy to the age of 70 years, and especially in *six* remarkable preservations from death. My Heavenly Benefactor has prospered me in my temporal concerns, and enabled me to bring up and educate, and assist a family of eleven children. I have been highly favored, as to my health, *not having been confined to a sick bed, probably, more than thirty days in seventy years.* My health is as good now as at any former period. Above all, I glorify God's holy name for "Heavenly blessings in Christ Jesus," and for "a name and place among His people," and the evidence that my unworthy name is "written in heaven." Glory to God in the highest. Amen.

> "My life's brief remnant all be Thine,
> And when Thy fixed decree
> Bids me this fleeting breath resign,
> Oh! speed my soul to Thee."

Signed,

ALEXANDER JONES.

The following was added afterwards:

A great calamity and distressing Providence came upon me suddenly! My beloved wife departed this life on the 5th of September, 1835, in the 62d year of her age. We had lived happily together more than 45 years.

"The will of the Lord be done."

On the 16th of August, 1836, my beloved sister Hannah was called to the church in heaven.

On May 1st, 1837, I sold my estate at Bellevue to Mr. John Stimpson for about six thousand four hundred dollars, and on the 3d removed to Mr. Franklin's brick house on Westminster Street, opposite Grace Church. My daughter Ellen has kept my house since the departure of her mother to this time, January 30th, 1838.

On the 3d of April, 1838, I sold my farm in Milford, Massachusetts, to Hastings Daniels for four thousand eight hundred dollars. This farm had been in the Jones family since 1696.

On the 13th of July, 1838, I removed my family to Capt. Wilbur Kelley's house, No. 37 Benefit Street.

Signed,

ALEXANDER JONES.

To the foregoing plainly and tersely told life history, it is but proper to add (what he would naturally have declined to do) something as to his characteristics, habits, etc. My father was a man of pure spirit and perfect, unquestioned integrity. One who always endeavored to carry out the Saviour's injunction, "Do unto others as you would they should do unto you."

His reputation as a merchant was excellent. He was the first to sell cotton, and sold it to the first manufacturer (Samuel Slater) in New England. Among his fellow-men as a man, a gentleman, a citizen and a Christian professor, his record was unblemished, and he held the respect and esteem of all who knew him. Though offered public positions, he assumed none, disliking to attract public attention to himself. In all the relations of life, and especially as a husband and father, he was gentle and affectionate, cheerful and pleasant. But it was as a Christian that his character and disposition shone most brightly, for he was a consistent and faithful follower of his Lord and Saviour. Though a devoted member of the Episcopal Church, his spirit and religious feeling was so truly catholic, he loved intercourse with Christians of other denominations, and there are those yet living in Providence who have heard his voice in prayer or exhortation in the conference or the prayer-meeting in the various churches. He was elected regularly a delegate to the General Convention of the Episcopal Church for 24 years and felt an absorbing interest in its proceedings and deliberations. His hospitality was almost unbounded, and he was never better pleased than when his pleasant home was filled with relations and friends.

When nearly 76 years of age God called him to "come up higher," and he died beloved and mourned by his numerous children and grandchildren. With a modest estimate of himself and with an humble but sure faith, he ordered that only his name, birth and date of death should be placed on his tombstone, and

"A sinner saved by grace."

MRS. MARY (FARQUHAR) JONES,
Wife of Alexander Jones.

"Died at Bellevue, the residence of her husband, in Providence, R. I., Mary Farquhar, the beloved wife of Alexander Jones, Esq., in the 62d year of her age. Born in Milledgeville, Georgia, December 24th, 1773, married in Charleston, South Carolina, January 28th, 1790, and entered into rest September 5th, 1835. She was the mother of three sons and eight daughters, seven of the children being

MARY FARQUHAR, WIFE OF ALEXANDER JONES.
Taken at the age of 23 years.

born in Charleston and four in Providence. All her daughters and two of her sons married, and all her children are professed followers of that Saviour whom she loved."

> "Still let me dream my mother's kiss
> Is warm upon my brow,
> Still let me dream familiar tones
> Come to me, sweet and low."

> "Rest remaineth, rest from tears,
> Rest from parting, rest from fears."

"She was ever an affectionate and very loving mother, a good wife, a sincere friend, really a lady in its full sense, and a sincere, unobtrusive Christian. No monument is needed to record her virtues, for they are enshrined in the hearts and the memories of her children and grandchildren. Many others, friends, acquaintances and even strangers, remember her many excellent qualities and her cheerful and warmhearted hospitality. Her sympathy for and her benevolence to the poor and needy has embalmed her memory with them and in many hearts."

OBITUARY OF ALEXANDER JONES,

which first appeared in the *Christian Witness*, and afterwards in the New York *Evangelist:*

At his residence, in Providence, R. I., on the 19th of March, 1840, Alexander Jones, Esq., in the 76th year of his age. It is our privilege and our duty to record the virtues of those who, having finished their course in the faith of the gospel and in the bosom of the church of Christ, now "rest from their labors." This subject was emphatically an example of every Christian grace, and his death has cast a gloom over the hearts of kindred and friends beloved, which the hopes and consolations of the gospel can alone dispel. It is not our object to portray the character of our departed friend, for to those who knew him this were a needless task, and for those who knew him not, it is not necessary. Few have passed through the changes of three score years and ten more free from reproach or possessed "a conscience more void of offence towards God and man." *He was truly an honest man, and in all his relations to society, and in all the business transactions of a busy life was governed by principles of the strictest integrity.* To the poor and needy he gave freely of his abundance, and no object worthy of his support applied in vain to his liberality.

In his domestic arrangements, provision was made for the most enlarged hospitality, and thousands are living who have partaken of his bounty. Above all, he was a sincere Christian and a devoted churchman. The evidences of his piety were not of a fitful, periodical character, requiring the stimulus of periodical efforts to bring them out, but they were seen in an humble daily walk with God, and a well-ordered life and conversation. True, he was ever zealously affected in a good cause, but his zeal did not evaporate with the occasion which specially excited it. Although his Christian feelings were of the most expansive kind, inducing him to acknowledge as fellow-Christians *all* who honored the Christian name, yet of the strength of his attachment to the church of his choice he gave the most abundant proof.

Until after leaving college and his settlement in Charleston, S. C., he was connected with another communion, as had been all his ancestors, but attracted to the Episcopal Church by its moderation, its dignity, and the devotional purity of its worship, his love for her peculiar features increased with increasing years, and her prosperity was an object of his greatest solicitude. For 30 years he represented her in the diocesan and general conventions, and he ever spoke with unaffected emotions of her increasing piety and numbers. He *loved* the church as the spouse of his Redeemer, and as the channel of His grace, and never will the writer forget the fervor with which he asserted his interest in her welfare in the touching language of one of our most beautiful hymns:

> " For her my tears shall fall,
> For her my prayers ascend,
> To her my cares and toils be given,
> Till toils and cares shall end."

It was, therefore, a source of unspeakable satisfaction to him that so many of his children (*all*) and grandchildren were the professed followers of the Lamb, and partakers with him of like hopes and privileges. To them, his loss is truly great, as his efforts for their good were untiring, and although death came in an unexpected hour, they are nevertheless consoled by the assurance of his having entered a holier, happier state, where there is no decay, and where Christian friends shall " meet to part no more."

" I heard a voice from heaven saying, write, Blessed are the dead who die in the Lord, for they rest from their labors, and their works do follow them."

Servant of God, well done!

ALEXANDER JONES.
Taken at the age of 63 years.

"Christian! I praise thee not,
   Thy virtues were not thine,
But His—who made thee
   Splendidly to shine,
With much humility,
   With heart sincere,
And fear of God,
   Which knows no other fear."

"Oh! that thy prayers, departed saint!
Even now the answer,
Of thy pitying love might find;
That I, that all, in spirit e'en as thou,
Were humbled, changed, renewed
In heart and mind.
Oh! that, like thee,
'Twere ours, to live by faith
And see as thou,
Heaven's portals op'd by death."

"The spirit, whom 'twas Thine
   To counsel, soothe and guide on life's dark way,
Who read in Thee the power of grace divine,
   Who shared Thy prayers and precepts many a day,
Back to the world's vain scenes no more must turn,
But still, with holiest hopes and wishes burn."

PREAMBLE AND RESOLUTIONS ADOPTED AT THE DIOCESAN CONVENTION OF RHODE ISLAND.

At the Fiftieth Annual Convention of the Protestant Episcopal Church of Rhode Island, which met in Providence on the 9th and 10th of June, 1840, the following preamble and resolutions were adopted:

WHEREAS, It has pleased Almighty God in His wisdom to take from this world *the venerable Alexander Jones*, for a long series of years the treasurer of this convention, and a lay delegate from St. John's Church, Providence, Therefore:

Resolved, That we lament the loss we have sustained by the death of this sincere follower of Christ, and this valued associate in the councils of the Church.

Resolved, That while we cordially express our sense of his excellence as a Christian, and of his singular devotion to the interests of the Church, we desire to thank God for the good example of his servant, who, having now finished his course in faith, rests from his labors.

Resolved, As a further expression of our respect for the character of the deceased, that these resolutions be entered on the journals of this convention.

SEVENTH GENERATION.

Harriet Farquhar Jones married **John Barnet Chace**, November 3d, 1811.

CHILDREN:

John Alexander Chace,   born Aug. 17, 1812, died the same day.
Alexander Blodget Chace,   "   Apr. 24, 1814, " Nov. 9, 1873.
John Barnet Chace, Jr.,   "   Oct. 11, 1815, "   "   1849.
Harriet Jones Chace,   "   May 21, 1817, " Aug. 6, 1817.
Samuel Chace,   "   "   25, 1818, " Mar. 7, 1820.
George Jenkins Chace,   "   June 22, 1819, " Sept. 25, 1819.
Caroline Frances Chace,   "   Jan. 22, 1821.

8. **Alexander Blodget Chace** married **Laura Esther Bates**, June 23d, 1842.

CHILDREN:

Albert Arnold Chace,   born April 13, 1843, died April 10, 1860.
John Barnet Chace 3d,   "   Jan. 29, 1850.

8. **John Barnet Chace, Jr.**, married **Susan Pauline Fuller**, April 20th, 1842; no children.

8. **Caroline Frances Chace** married
      First, **Aaron Mount**, in 18—
      Second, **Joseph Sanford**, Dec. 30, 1868. } No children.
      Third, **Henry Fuller**, in 18—

Major John B. Chace was a man who won the good will and regard of his relatives, friends and acquaintances. Though somewhat eccentric and peculiar in speech and in manner, he was a man of most perfect integrity and honesty. No one coming in contact with him could fail to see his simplicity of character, his great cheerfulness of disposition, and above all, his deep religious feeling. A writer in one of

MARY FARQUHAR, WIFE OF ALEXANDER JONES.
Taken at the age of 54 years.

the papers said of him, "there is no blot on his record, there is no stain on his integrity, there is no impeachment of his truth."

For more than fifty years he was an active, energetic and influential member of St. John's Church, and under all circumstances, lived a most consistent Christian life. Among the poor, the unfortunate, the criminal, he went regularly to speak to them of God and of eternal life, and endeavored to cheer them and bring them to a knowledge of "the truth as it is in Jesus."

He was born April 13th, 1782, and died August 23d, 1863, in the 82d year of his age. As the funeral procession was passing along the streets, every head was uncovered, for he was held in universal esteem by all classes of the city of Providence.

Mrs. Harriet F. Chace died in early womanhood, October 14th, 1823, at the age of 32. She was a great favorite among all who knew her in society, in the Church, and especially among the poor. Her voice in singing was one of uncommon sweetness and richness, and her musical talent quite noted. Her calmness, when death came to her, was exhibited in the heroic manner in which she bore great suffering, for her reliance was on Him, who, to her, was all in all.

Her pastor, the Rev. Dr. Crocker, wrote of her as follows:

"Active benevolence to the poor and ignorant shed a lustre on her character, and has embalmed her memory in the hearts of the unfortunate. Exemplifying the loveliness of religion, she was cheerful, yet watchful, shrinking from applause, and afraid to trifle with temptation. Her time, her talents, her influence, were devoted to the service of God, and her conversation constantly showed that her affections were in Heaven. Her piety flourished even on the borders of the grave, and the sudden termination of her life can be viewed in no other light than as a translation to glory."

SEVENTH GENERATION.

Eliza Ruth Jones married **Joshua Brackett Wood**, of Rutland, Mass., October 4th, 1810.

CHILDREN:

Mary Elizabeth Wood,	born July 14, 1811, died Aug 3, 1843.
Harriet Ruth Wood,	" Jan. 15, 1813.
John Matthias Ehrick Wood "	Feb. 25, 1815, " Oct. 26, 1815.
Joshua Crocker Wood,	" Dec. 24, 1816, " Mar. 2, 1820.
Normand Knox Wood,	" Mar. 3, 1819, " Sept. 5, 1840.

Edward Whiting Wood, born July 1, 1821, died Dec. 19, 1823.
Eliza Ann Jones Wood,   "   Aug. 27, 1823.
Frances Placidia Wood,   "   Dec. 22, 1825.
Samuel James Wood,   "   Feb. 26, 1828, " Mar. 14, 1828.
Josephine Howard Wood,   "   Mar. 18, 1829.
Alexander George Wood,   "   Nov. 12, 1831.

8. **Mary Elizabeth Wood** married **James H. Cutler**, May 20th, 1840; no children.

8. **Harriet Ruth Wood** married **Rev. Samuel B. Bostwick, S.T.D.**, October 12th, 1841.

CHILDREN:

Theodora Harriet Bostwick, born Sept. 2, 1842.
*Edward Breck Bostwick,   "   Jan. 15, 1848.
Arthur Wood Bostwick,   "   Feb. 10, 1849.
Mary Elizabeth Bostwick,   "   Oct. 2, 1850.

9. **Theodora Harriet Bostwick** married **Frank Edgar De-Graw**, May 13th, 1869.

CHILDREN:

Lilian Conover DeGraw, born May 7, 1871.
Annie Howard DeGraw,   "   Dec. 16, 1873.
Ruth Farquhar DeGraw,   "   Mar. 15, 1876.
Arthur Bostwick DeGraw, "   Oct. 14, 1878.
Theodora DeGraw,   "   Apr. 6, 1883.

9. **Mary Elizabeth Bostwick** married **Arthur Breese Davis**, August 11th, 1874.

CHILDREN:

Edward Livingston Davis, born June 19, 1875.
Marian Bostwick Davis,   "   Jan. 29, 1877.
Ruth Chandler Davis,   "   Apr. 23, 1879.
Margaret Wood Davis,   "   Nov. 17, 1882.

8. **Eliza Ann Jones Wood** married **Rev. Edwin A. Nichols**, July 26th, 1843.

---

* Edward B. Bostwick graduated at Hobart College, delivering the valedictory of his class.

CHILDREN:

Eliza Augusta Nichols, born June 3, 1844.
George Gideon Nichols, " Jan. 10, 1846.
Charles Edwin Nichols, " Feb. 17, 1848.
Mary Josephine Nichols, " Dec. 28, 1849.
Caroline Dodge Nichols, " Mar. 4, 1851.
Walter Wood Nichols, " Feb. 26, 1854.
Edith Adelia Nichols, " " 4, 1861.

Rev. E. A. Nichols is a clergyman in the Episcopal Church, and formerly lived in Saugerties, N. Y., but for many years past in the City of Brooklyn, having no charge on account of poor health.

9. **Edith Adelia Nichols** married **Francis Jackson Palmer,** of Brooklyn, N. Y., September 17th, 1884.

8. **Frances Placidia Wood** married **Rev. J. Breckenridge Gibson,** May 13th, 1847.

CHILDREN:

Breckenridge Stuyvesant Gibson, born Mar. 25, 1848.
Alexander Jones Gibson, born July 7, 1851, died July 25, 1880.
Fanny Grace Gibson, " Jan. 20, 1854, " Aug. 28, 1855.
Annie Wainright Gibson, " Feb. —, 1857, " aged one week.
Lily Margaret Gibson, " Dec. 25, 1860.

9. **Breckenridge Stuyvesant Gibson** married **Mary Eleanor Sheldon,** July 2d, 1872.

CHILDREN:

Breckenridge Stuyvesant Gibson, Jr., born Aug. 8, 1873.
Margaret Eleanor Gibson, " June 27, 1879.
Edith Gibson, " July 19, 1881.
Mary Frances Gibson, " May 24, 1883.

9. **Lily Margaret Gibson** married **Ralph Brandreth,** June 20th, 1883.

CHILDREN:

Ralph Brandreth, Jr., born March 21, 1884.

Rev. J. Breckenridge Gibson, D.D., was at one time Rector of the Episcopal Church in Haverstraw, also in Saratoga, N. Y. He also had charge of the large school at Burlington, N. J. He afterwards took the control of the school at Sing Sing, for many years managed by Marlborough Churchill, now St. John's School. It is a large and flourishing institution of high order, and under the care of Dr. Gibson, with the assistance of his oldest son, will no doubt continue successful.

8. **Josephine Howard Wood** married **Rev. E. Gay, Jr.**, October 6th, 1863.

CHILDREN:

Alexander Wood Gay, born Oct. 17, 1869.

And here should be recorded the remarkable fact or facts, that in the marriages of four daughters of Col. J. B. and Mrs. E. R. Wood, in each case the husband was a clergyman in the Protestant Episcopal Church, and at one time (before the division of the diocese), all in the diocese of New York. It is doubted if another similar case could be found throughout the length and breadth of our country.

The House of the Good Shepherd, under the rectorship and care of the Rev. E. Gay, Jr., deserves more mention than that of a mere passing notice. As stated elsewhere, it is the outgrowth of the wishes and prayers of that now sainted woman, Mrs. Eliza R. Wood. Under the care of Mr. Gay, and his ready and helpful wife, it has grown to be a large, industrious and noted institution. It has the aid of many who love Him who loved little children, as well as the poor, the sick, the distressed. It was formed in faith, carried on in faith, and will be continued in faith, that God will provide the means to do for the bodies and the souls committed to its care.

It is situated on the west bank of the Hudson, the main building some 150 feet above the river, and at Tompkins' Cove, Rockland County, New York. The property includes about ninety acres of land, with a number of buildings, all in use; among them a hospital building, solidly built of stone, erected and furnished by Mrs. Ellen M. Dabney, as a memorial thank-offering for godly parents. It possesses all the means and appliances to bring quiet, rest and comfort to those who may happen to become its inmates. Want of space prevents a more detailed account of this lovely little hospital.

The same want also denies the pleasure of describing this lovely place, this noble institution, and its great advantages. It has been a real blessing to many a poor and slighted child, it has taken in, sheltered and cared for—many a sick and weary body—many a sick and weary soul. It has pointed out to the ignorant and sinful, "the way of salvation," and has brought peace and joy to the dying. It is a work where sympathy is ready to flow, where mercy is alive and active, and where help is ever ready for the poor child, or the sick and weary man or woman. The body and the soul are both cared for.

The natural advantages of the place are very marked. Pure air, a lovely prospect, and delightful and constantly changing views of the noble river and the surrounding country, all unite in making the location a highly attractive one. The finances of the institution are under the control of a Board of Trustees, and great assistance is given by "The Ladies' Association in aid of the House of the Good Shepherd." To this last named, the institution is largely indebted for its prosperity. Many a Christian churchman's heart has been warmed into becoming a giver and a helper to this noble charity. It appeals strongly to our humanity, to our pity, to our Christian love.

A description of the buildings, the inmates, the discipline, and the numerous things with regard to this institution, tempt us to enter on it fully, but time and limited space forbid. To any one who will visit and examine the House of the Good Shepherd, its usages, its government, its every-day life, we can say: your sympathies *will go out to it and for it*, your feelings will be touched, your pity excited, your admiration evoked, and if you have the means, your money will be cheerfully given to help its progress. "Inasmuch as ye did it to one of the least of these, ye did it also unto Me."

8. **Alexander Geo. Wood**, married **Emily Victoria Wilmot**, October 11th, 1864.

CHILDREN.

Alexandra Victoria Wood,	born September 25, 1865.
Wilmot Farquhar Wood,	" January 3, 1869.
Warden George Leveret Wood,	" February 2, 1876.

Alexander George Wood has for many years been in business as a stock broker in Wall Street.

OBITUARY NOTICE OF MRS. ELIZA RUTH WOOD.

Died, at her residence in Haverstraw, Rockland County, New York, Eliza R. Wood, wife of the late Col. Joshua B. Wood, and second daughter of Alexander Jones, of Providence, R. I., May 23d, 1867, aged nearly 74 years.

Many loving hearts will receive this announcement with keen regret, tempered by the recollection that our loss is her great gain. A clear and quick mind, added to a warm and genial temperament and unbounded hospitality, and a deep, though unobtrusive Christian character, made this venerable lady precious to a large and widely extended circle of relations and friends.

Naturally fond of children, she always delighted in their society, and in her early life (in connection with the now senior Bishop of the Protestant Episcopal Church, Bishop Smith of Kentucky), established the first Sunday School in Providence, R. I.

Even while an invalid, and a great sufferer, she gave her best interests and efforts towards the establishment of the Orphan House, at Haverstraw, *now* the House of the Good Shepherd, at Tompkins' Cove (same county), and of which her youngest daughter is the housemother, and her husband, the Rev. E. Gay, Jr., is the rector and housefather.

Most prized where best known, her relatives and friends will ever mourn her loss most deeply, even while thanking God, that her long years of weary and almost incessant sufferings, are exchanged for the happy rest of the people of God. Unmurmuring in pain, patient even to the last, and rejoicing at the near approach of her loved Saviour's presence, she has

"Fallen asleep in Jesus."

My sister was a woman of great vivacity and ability. Her conversational powers were also remarkable, and charmed the young, the middle aged and the old. With quick perceptions, a bright intellect and a somewhat satirical vein of thought, her conversation and her letters were marked by a flowing and easy expression, that gave great pleasure and delight to those who received them. At one time, when blessed with plenty, her house was called *the home of hospitality*, and in after years, when reverses had dimmed the prospect, she still had a warm and cheering welcome for her relations and her friends. The fond mother, the devoted wife, the loving friend and the true Christian, she carried with her, into her declining years, the love and admiration of all who knew her in the bright days of prosperity and the dark ones of adversity. She experienced many trials and troubles, but passed through them with unabating faith, and came out as "pure and fine gold," "meet for the Master's use." She fought a good fight, and finished her course, and now rests in the presence of her Lord and her Redeemer.

Colonel Joshua B. Wood was a gentleman with a warm and generous heart, and of a sociable and genial disposition. He was remarkable for his great hospitality (in which he was warmly seconded by his wife), and it was a great pleasure to him to have visits from relatives and friends. He literally kept an open house. His business, located in Providence, R. I., grew to large proportions, as exchange broker, and extended to Boston and throughout the New England States. It necessitated frequent visits to New York and Boston, and in those days, when the rates of postage were very high and express companies unknown, passengers to and from these cities took not only a large number of letters, but packages of money. On one occasion, as Col. Wood was about leaving New York for Providence in the Sound steamer, a friend asked him to take for him a package containing several thousand dollars. He did so, giving it, as was his regular custom, to the barkeeper of the steamer with his own package of money. Just before the steamer left, while he had gone on deck to speak to some friends, it was discovered that some one had stolen the packages. The alarm was at once given, the police called, and orders were issued that no one was to leave or come on board the steamer. A rigid search was instituted, all the passengers submitting to an examination, but without success, and the money was gone.

Afterwards, the friend (?) who asked Mr. Wood to take the package to oblige him, brought a suit to recover the amount lost. Mr. Wood endeavored to secure the services of the celebrated Daniel Webster, but his opponent had been before him, and he was obliged to get such as was available. The case was tried at court, and the verdict was against Mr. Wood, who was obliged to pay the amount, with interest and costs.

At this time the lottery business was not only reputable, but a very large business in this country, and Mr. Wood had the sole agency for the sale of tickets in New England. It was the custom to report by mail, on the days of drawing, the number of tickets unsold, and the numbers of the tickets on hand, to the principal house in New York City, and on one occasion the clerk reported to Mr. Wood, at the appointed hour for mailing, that there were but two whole tickets unsold. Mr. Wood said: "Charge them to me, report all sold and remit." One of these two tickets drew the highest prize. Crowds of friends and acquaintances, on hearing of his good fortune, poured into his office with their congratulations that he should thus fortunately receive the amount he had been forced to pay.

Mr. Wood afterwards (about 1828) removed to New York, where he carried on the exchange business for a number of years. He was a member of the vestry of St. Luke's Church, Hudson Street, and living a consistent and faithful Christian life, was called to his reward in the life to come.

He was born in Rutland, November 18th, 1779, and died in the city of New York, March 2d, 1852, in the 73d year of his age.

OBITUARY NOTICE OF MARY ELIZABETH CUTLER.

Died in New York, on Thursday, August 3d, 1843, in the 33d year of her age, Mary Elizabeth, wife of James H. Cutler, eldest daughter of Col. J. B. Wood, and oldest grandchild of Alexander Jones, after a long and painful illness, which was borne with true patience and Christian resignation, sustained throughout by a lively faith in her Redeemer. She committed her spirit into His hands, and died (to use her own words) in peace with God, and perfect charity with the world. Admired by all who knew her, a wide circle of relatives and friends will lament her early death, yet let them find consolation in this promise: "Blessed are the dead who die in the Lord: yea, saith the Spirit, for they rest from their labors."—E. A. N., in *New York Churchman.*

It was the lot of the writer of the few lines that follow, to know most intimately, and from early childhood, the subject of the foregoing notice, and he cannot refrain from adding his tribute to her memory. Brought up to womanhood by the most kind and indulgent parents, her life was, until a few years past, "gay and happy." Surrounded with many friends and acquaintances, whose sole object seemed to be the enjoyment of life, she seemed to care but little for "the life to come." Blessed with an ardent temperament, and a bright and lively disposition, she was "the gayest of the gay," and her presence gave pleasure and animation to all around her. Her amiability of character was so sweetly blended with her mirth and gayety, that she won the love and admiration of all.

A few years since her mind and thoughts became deeply awakened to a sense of sinfulness, and she saw and felt the necessity of making "her calling and election sure." She gave heed to the call of the Holy

Spirit, and made her peace with God. Joining the Communion of the Church, she became a faithful "follower of the meek and lowly Jesus." Her character, before so much admired, under the influence of the Gospel, shone now with far greater brightness, and was clothed with Christian graces.

Though suffering greatly in her last, long illness, her mind continued calm and clear to the last. If it pleased God to restore her to health, or to take her hence, she was resigned to His will, but her wish was "to depart and be with Christ." Shortly before the day of her death, she partook of the Sacrament of the Lord's Supper, and while those present were singing the well-known and beautiful hymn, "Rock of Ages," although very weak, her voice (noted for its purity and sweetness when in health) was distinctly heard throughout, and afterwards she repeated, with energy:

> "In my hand no price I bring,
> Simply to Thy cross I cling."

Her whole dependence was on her Saviour. "I can do nothing—all my hope is in Him." Calmly and quietly, and with the words: "Lord Jesus, receive my spirit!" she passed away from life here to life everlasting.   G.

August, 1843.

THE REV. SAMUEL B. BOSTWICK, S.T.D. and D.D.

While visiting at the house of his brother-in-law, the Rev. Dr. Gibson, in Sing Sing, that pure-minded and holy man of God, the Rev. Dr. Bostwick, was called by the Master he had so faithfully served: "*Come up higher*," March 16th, 1881.

Samuel B. Bostwick was born in Jericho, Vermont, March 15th, 1815. He graduated from Vermont University, in 1835, and was admitted to orders in 1842, and was Rector of St. Thomas's Church, Brandon, Vt., in 1844. Two years later he accepted an election to the Church of the Messiah, Glens Falls, and St. James' Church, Fort Edward, New York. In this connection he taught school to supplement his salary, and founded Zion Church, Sandy Hill, which, with its stone edifice, was the crowning work of his life. After the parishes at Glens Falls and Fort Edward were detached from his field, he continued his rectorship at Sandy Hill (laboring there for thirty years), until Easter Day, 1877. During two years, he taught a select school there, and in the Spring of 1880, accepted an election to Trinity Church, Gouverneur, New York.

He was still in charge of this parish when he died at Sing Sing. He was also a member of the Standing Committee of the Diocese, and discharged, for twelve years, the duties of his office with singular fidelity and ability.

Such is a brief sketch of the life of Dr. Bostwick, but it would take a volume to tell what that life was. To record in just and appropriate terms his abilities, his disposition, his deep piety, his character and his work, would require an abler pen than that of the writer. His whole life, his demeanor, his conversation, all showed the great depth of his religious feeling, his entire devotion to God and His Blessed Gospel. His purity of mind and heart was seen, and known, and felt, by all who came in contact with him, and shone brightly in his daily life and conversation. I never have seen a man so thoroughly imbued with the spirit of Christ—so confident in the faith, yet so humble—so rooted and grounded in the faith, yet so guileless and childlike in his conduct. In speaking of this faithful minister of God's truth, I feel myself at a loss to do so in proper language, for words fail me. I revere his memory. I have ever admired his character, but I cannot do them justice by my faint endeavors. I therefore quote from the resolutions passed by the vestries of Zion and Trinity Churches, as follows:

" *Resolved*, That we express our sense of the deep loss we have sus-
" tained in the death of one who was at all times the friend in the pas-
" tor, and the pastor in the friend. That we will, by God's grace, ever
" keep before us the example which we were privileged to have, of a
" life holy and acceptable to God, by reason of its humility, purity
" and faith."

" *Resolved*, That while we are filled with sorrow, and mourn that his
" face will be seen no more among us, we are yet grateful that the bless-
" ing of his presence was allowed to us for a few short months, during
" which he endeared himself to every member of his parish, and won
" the respectful esteem of the entire community.

" *Resolved*, That by his death this parish is deprived of a devoted
" pastor, in whom the word of Christ dwelt richly in all wisdom, the
" society of a courteous, dignified, Christian gentleman, venerable, not
" so much by his years, as in the fulfilled perfectness of a holy life,
" from which ever emanated the influence of personal religion, pure
" and undefiled, whose memory, cherished in our hearts, may help to
" bring the blessing his continued life would have given."

As Enoch of old " walked with God," so did this pure and holy man
—this faithful pastor—this wise counselor; and now he will receive

God's reward: " Well done, good and faithful servant, enter thou into the joy of thy Lord."

IN MEMORIAM OF ALEXANDER JONES GIBSON.

Fell asleep July 25th, 1880, on Sunday, God's day of rest, Alexander J. Gibson, in the flower of his youth and promise. This sad announcement will carry sorrow to the friends of this noble young man and Christian gentleman. He had no enemies, he made and retained friends everywhere. "None knew him but to love him, none named him but to praise."

Alexander Jones Gibson was born July 7th, 1851. He was educated at St. Stephens' College, Annandale, N. Y., where he graduated in 1872 with honor. Admitted to the bar in 1875, he commenced the practice of law in this village. New York offering a better and larger field for his talents, he entered the office of Messrs. Chase & Bestow, where his quick perception and devotion to business was of great service to them as managing clerk. A little more than a year ago he began practice for himself. His assiduity, ability and genial disposition brought him considerable business, and a brilliant and successful career as a lawyer appeared certain.

Last August he was seized with a fatal disease, and was soon after compelled to retire from practice. He lingered for many months on a bed of sickness and suffering, which he bore without complaint and with the faith of a Christian martyr. His gentle disposition, unfailing cheerfulness and resignation manifested themselves amid his greatest sufferings. His devoted mother for nine months hardly left his side, and his affianced bride was only happy when ministering to him. But the greatest medical skill and most devoted care could not stay the approach of the great destroyer, and he passed peacefully away, leaving behind him a memory fragrant with the perfume of his goodness, amiability, talent and integrity.

An affectionate son, a tender and considerate brother, the bereaved parents and family have the heartfelt sympathy of the community in their affliction. A gracious and warm-hearted friend, his companions mourn the loss of an associate, the remembrance of whom recalls nought but pleasant things. The sorrow is only for us. He is free from suffering. Life's dark ending is eternity's bright beginning.

Sing Sing, N. Y.   B.

ALEXANDER JONES GIBSON.

Entered into rest at Sing Sing, N. Y., Sunday, July 25th, 1880, Alexander Jones Gibson, the second son of the Rev. J. B. and Frances P. Gibson, after a long illness, which he bore with Christian fortitude and resignation.

Born and reared a true child of the Church, gentle and loving to all, humble, docile to parents and teachers, a beloved and esteemed graduate of St. Stephen's College, studious and talented, though not ostentatious, he was quietly pursuing the study and practice of law, with assured hopes and every human prospect of an honorable and successful career.

Amid the refining influences and lovely scenery of a Christian home, of excellent social position, combining the tenacity and wisdom of his ancestor, *Governor Stuyvesant*, with the warm religious character of his maternal ancestor, *Alexander Jones, of Providence*, whose name he bore, pure in mind, sunlike in a bright and happy temperament, how favored seemed his lot a year ago! But the time of trial came like a dark thunder cloud at noon. Stricken down with a dread disease, he bowed in quiet submission. For nearly a year, hoping against hope, his anxious parents watched and strove for his recovery, only to see their fair flower droop and die, he all the while cheerful, uncomplaining and loving as ever to all. How precious his memory! How manifest his victory over death and the world and its attractions!

"Blessed are the pure in heart, for they shall see God." And surely our loss is their gain, when thus taken from all earthly possibilities of ill to the bright world

> "Where saints in light, our coming wait,
> To share their holy, happy state."

Brooklyn, N. Y.   E. A. N.

SEVENTH GENERATION.

Mary Margaret Jones married **Cyrus Alden, Esq.**, May 24th, 1813.

CHILDREN:

Mary Jones Alden,	born Mar. 18, 1814.	
Charles James Alden,	" " " 1816, died Sept.,	1856.
Caroline Perkins Alden,	" Oct. 21, 1817, " May 6, 1855.	
Jane Frances Alden,	" " 4, 1821.	
William Baylies Alden,	" July 31, 1823, " June 29, 1829.	
Eliza Wood Alden,	" May 21, 1826.	
Harriet Farquhar Alden,	" Apr. 14, 1829.	
Alexander Joseph Alden,	" Feb. 25, 1834, " June, 1835.	

8.   **Mary Jones Alden** married **George Washington Little,**
July 20th, 1840. He was born July 30th, 1806, and his first wife was
Clara Churchill, sister of Ann, wife of Rev. Alexander Jones. He
died October 21st, 1882.

CHILDREN:

Caroline Frances Little,	born Sept. 13, 1841.
Emily Alden Little,	" " 19, 1843, died July 10, 1869.
Mary Alexander Little,	" July 1, 1845, " Oct. 1, 1847.
Louise Berry Little,	" June 27, 1847, " Mar. 20, 1849.
William Cyrus Little,	" Feb. 23, 1849.
Jennie Elizabeth Little,	" Apr. 15, 1851.
Harry J. C. A. Little,	" July 20, 1853.
Marion Chase Little,	" Sept. 2, 1860, " Jan. 24, 1864.

9.   **Caroline   Frances   Little** married **Joseph   Doddridge
Russell,** October 22d, 1862.

CHILDREN:

Frank Alden Russell, born Nov. 16, 1863.
William Hill Russell, "   Mar. 24, 1865, died Mar., 1879.
George Little Russell, "   May 14, 1866.
Mary Eleanor Russell, "   Mar. 2, 1869.
Angeletta Russell, "   Nov. 3, 1870, "   June, 1875.
Carrie Churchill Russell, "   Sept. 18, 1872.
Emily Howe Russell, "   Feb. 24, 1874.
Harry Wallace Russell, "   Aug. 26, 1876, "   Nov., 1878.
Jennie Edith Russell, "   Apr. 6, 1880, "   "   1882.

9.   **Emily Alden Little** married **John Newton Russell,** October 22d, 1862.

CHILDREN:

John Newton Russell, Jr., born June 5, 1864.
Frank Churchill Russell,   "   Apr. 28, 1867, died 1872.

9.   **William Cyrus Little** married **May Rose Simon,** October 16th, 1878.

CHILDREN:

Edith Hall Little,   born Mar. 21, 1880, died Mar. 26, 1880.
Alden Howe Little,   "   June 22, 1881.

William C. Little was brought up in the banking business in St. Louis, afterwards in business for himself, and then went to New York in 1883, where he is now in the same line, and of the firm of Kelley & Little, Wall Street.

9. **Harry Joseph Carver Alden Little** married **Nellie Maud Bulliam**, September 13th, 1883.

8. **Charles James Alden** married **Alice Maria Peckham**, November 24th, 1853.

CHILDREN :

Caroline Jones Alden, born Aug. 27, 1854, died Aug. 31, 1880.
Mary Alice Alden, " Mar. 9, 1856.

9. **Mary Alice Alden** married **David K. Snell**, June 3d, 1874.

CHILDREN :

Charles Alden Snell, born Apr. 29, 1875.
Carrie Jones Snell, " Oct. 12, 1882.

8. **Caroline Perkins Alden** married **Edward Dodge** (then of Philadelphia), May 3d, 1836.

CHILDREN :

Clinton Alden Dodge, born Feb. 28, 1837.
Caroline Jones Dodge, " Sep. 29, 1841.
Harry Eugene Dodge, " Jan. 14, 1844.

Edward Dodge was one of the firm of E. W. Clark & Co., and E. W. Clark, Dodge & Co., in Philadelphia and New York, in the exchange brokerage and banking business, his partner being Enoch W. Clark, formerly of Providence, his brother-in-law. He afterwards went to New York and continued in the same business under the firm name of the well-known Clark, Dodge & Co. He retired from business but afterwards resumed it with the well-known Jay Cooke, and as principal partner in the New York firm of Jay Cooke & Co. He subsequently retired from that firm, before their failure, and lived without the cares of business at his home in Brooklyn, until his death. He had married the second time, Ellen, daughter of J. T. and E. M. Daugherty, and she survives him.

9. **Clinton Alden Dodge** died in Venice, Italy, in June, 1852, aged 15. His mother also died in a foreign land, at St. James' Hotel, London, May 6th, 1855, at the age of 38.

9. **Caroline Jones Dodge** married **Theodore M. Morgan,** of Philadelphia, October 8th, 1862.

CHILDREN:

Caroline Alden Morgan,   born Nov. 7, 1863.
Theodore Hanson Morgan,   "   June 16, 1865.
Alice Carey Morgan,   } b. May 10, 1867, died July 20, 1867.
Jeannie Campbell Morgan,   } born May 10, 1867.
Edith Dodge Morgan, born Mar. 29, 1870, died Dec. 9, 1876.
Charlotte Sherwell Morgan, born Dec. 31, 1871, died Jan. 8, 1872.
Gertrude Clinton Morgan,   "   Jan. 6, 1878.

9. **Harry Eugene Dodge** married **Jeannie M. Hall** (born June 4th, 1847), October 8th, 1866, the same month and day his sister was married.

CHILDREN:

Edward Dodge, 2d, born Aug. 25, 1867.

Harry E. Dodge succeeded his father in the firm of Clark, Dodge & Co., New York, and the business as bankers and brokers still continues. It is said that he intends his son Edward to enter the house, looking forward to the time when there will have been three generations in the family as partners in the firm of Clark, Dodge & Co.

8. **Jane Frances Alden** married **Walter Chaloner Durfee** (born February 24th, 1816), March 23d, 1841.

CHILDREN:

Frances Eudora Durfee,   born Dec. 28, 1841, died Jan. 14, 1844.
Eliza Chaloner Durfee,   "   Jan. 31, 1845.
Walter Sherwood Durfee,   "   Aug. 4, 1847, "   Aug. 21, 1848.
Mary Hannah Durfee,   "   June 19, 1849, "   Sep., 1853.
Caroline Clinton Durfee,   "   July 22, 1852.
Jeannie Farquhar Durfee,   "   Apr. 13, 1855, "   Mar., 1872.
Winthrop Carver Durfee,   "   Apr. 23, 1858.
Annie Marvel Durfee,   "   June 6, 1860.
Harriet Alden Durfee,   "   Apr. 4, 1863.
Randall Nelson Durfee,   "   Oct. 13, 1867.
Margaret Russell Durfee,   "   Nov. 3, 1871.

Walter C. Durfee has been a manufacturer in Fall River for many years, being stockholder and treasurer of the Wampanoag Mills.

9. **Caroline Clinton Durfee** married **Edward Otis Stanley,** October 16th, 1879.

CHILDREN:

Marjorie Alden Stanley, born Jan. 22, 1882.
Robert Whitney Stanley, " Apr. 26, 1884.

9. **Winthrop Carver Durfee** married **Sylvie Whitney,** October 18th, 1881.

CHILDREN:

Walter Chaloner Durfee, 2d, born January 29th, 1883.

Sylvie Whitney's father and Edward O. Stanley's mother were brother and sister.

9. **Annie Marvel Durfee** married **David Foster Slade,** October 25th, 1883.

8. **Eliza Wood Alden** married **Edward Chase,** April 21st, 1847.

CHILDREN:

Edward Julius Chase, born Feb. 10, 1848, drowned June 13, 1861.
Nellie Farquhar Chase, " July 17, 1850, died Oct. 4, 1852.
Clinton Alden Chase, " Sep. 23, 1852.
Hattie Sherwood Chase, " Dec. 7, 1854, " Mar. 7, 1857.
Julia Crawford Chase, " Feb. 7, 1857.
Jane Frances Chase, " Feb. 22, 1859.
Lillian Chase, " June 7, 1861, " July 25, 1862.
Bertha Chase, " Aug. 1, 1863.
Eunice Leslie Chase, " Feb. 4, 1869.

9. **Clinton Alden Chase** married **Sallie Margaret Harmon,** March 20th, 1879.

CHILDREN:

Alden Chase, born Jan. 9, 1880.
Ednah Chase, " Mar. 4, 1882.

8. **Harriet Farquhar Alden** married **Joseph Petit, Jr.,** June 11th, 1851.

Edward Alden Petit,   born July 26, 1852.
James Van Nostrand Petit, " Aug. 5, 1854.

9. **Edward Alden Petit** married **Isabel Berrian**, June 6th, 1878.

CHILDREN:

Berrian Petit,   born June 12, 1879.
Jane Winifred Berrian Petit, " Nov. 24, 1881.

9. **James Van Nostrand Petit** married **Sarah Smith**, in Philadelphia, March, 1876.

CHILDREN:

Charlotte Alden Petit, born Dec. 18, 1876.
Emma Sherwood Petit, " Apr. 20, 1879.

Cyrus Alden, Esq., husband of Mrs. Mary Margaret Alden, was born May 20th, 1785, in Bridgewater, Mass. From "The Bristol County Book" I take the following: He was the fifth in descent and direct line from John Alden, the first one of the Plymouth colony to step upon the famous rock of that name at the landing of the Mayflower pilgrims in 1620. His father was Captain Joseph Alden, his mother and grandmother being members of the Carver family. He was one of nine children, of whom five were sons, two of whom, himself and a younger brother, were graduates from Brown University; the one to follow the profession of law, and the other that of divinity.

His own graduation took place in 1807, his education having been delayed by a severe and protracted illness. He studied law at Lichfield, and also read with Judge Whitman, of Marshfield, and Judge Baylies, of Taunton. He began the practice of law in Wrentham, marrying, soon after his entrance upon his profession, Mary Margaret, daughter of Mr. Alexander Jones, of Providence. After a short residence here, he removed with his family to Boston, where, in 1819, he published "An abridgment of the law, with practical forms," in two parts, a book of which he was the author and editor. It proved useful and acceptable, but has been superseded by other works of the same purpose.

In 1827 he once more removed his family and business, this time to Fall River, then known as Troy. He served the town as member of the State Legislature, and the Church (Ascension) as senior warden. His death occurred in March, 1855.

In addition to legal and judicial qualities of mind, which, with a marked and refined wit, he possessed to a great degree, he had poetic and inventive talent. He amused his leisure with the former and employed the latter to some practical results. An obituary, written by a fellow lawyer, says, for several years he did a considerable portion of Fall River's judicial business, his promptness and tenacity of memory being remarkable. He rarely took notes of testimony, and it was very seldom that a law book was required by him for reference in any decision. So thoroughly imbued was his mind with the essential principles of our laws, that his errors in stating them from memory merely were most infrequent, and I have heard it said, not without point, that more reliance could be place upon the opinion of Cyrus Alden, Esq., without books, than upon the opinions of many men with both books and laws. He was an author as well as a practitioner, and has left a volume as a memento to his brethren in the department of his profession. He died March 29th, 1855, aged 70 years.

OBITUARY NOTICES OF MRS. MARY MARGARET ALDEN.

From the Fall River and Providence papers.

Death of a Venerable and Well-known Lady.

Mrs. Mary Margaret Alden, the venerable and highly esteemed relict of the late Cyrus Alden, Esq., died this morning, April 14th, 1879, at the residence of her son-in-law, Walter C. Durfee. Mrs. Alden was born in Charleston, S. C., January 30th, 1795, and was, consequently, a little over 84 years old at the time of her death. Her father, Mr. Alexander Jones, was a merchant in Charleston, but removed to Providence, R. I., in 1805, where he continued for many years in mercantile business.

Mrs. Alden was an interesting and agreeable old lady, and possessed of many accomplishments, which made her a great favorite in the large circle of relatives and friends in which she moved, and by whom her loss is now sincerely mourned. She was an esteemed member of the Episcopal Church for more than half a century. She came to this city from Roxbury, Mass., with her husband in 1827, and has resided here ever since, a period of about 52 years. Her husband preceded her to the spirit land about 24 years ago. She leaves four children, daughters, all married, and a large number of grandchildren.

The funeral of the late Mrs. Cyrus Alden took place this afternoon (Thursday, 17th) at the residence of Walter C. Durfee. The Rev. Mr. Fitch, of the Church of the Ascension, read from the burial service, commencing with: "I am the resurrection and the life," which was followed by an anthem from the choir. The reverend gentleman then read from the first of Corinthians, 15 chapter, after which he made a few remarks applicable to a person who has reached the remarkable age of over four-score years, and who for 50 years had been a faithful member of the Church of Christ. He said she was taken from us just at Easter-time, when we were celebrating the resurrection of our Saviour, when our hearts were more than usually impressed with a realizing sense that all who go hence, relying on the Saviour's promises, will reap the reward laid up for them in Heaven. Then let us think of the dear departed one as having entered upon a blessed immortality, and that we, one by one, like a funeral procession, shall in due time pass on and join the loved ones gone before. On the top of the coffin of the deceased was a sheaf of ripe wheat, and upon one side a sickle formed of flowers, while over the foot was gracefully festooned some English ivy. At the head stood a crown, supplemented by a cross, both formed of flowers.

One closely connected with her by ties of fraternal love, writes: She had a gentle, lively and sociable disposition. A loving mother, grandmother, sister and aunt. There was a warm place in her heart for all her relatives and friends. All coming within her influence felt her gentleness, her kindness of heart, her pleasant, friendly ways. They were charms that did not fail to secure to her all who knew her as warm friends. Even as years increased upon her, her lively interest in everything did not diminish, but she enjoyed friendly visits and social gatherings as much as when the weight of years was far lighter. With an active mind, a remarkably retentive memory, and blessed with comparatively good health, she seemed to enjoy the pleasures of social life to the full, and gave pleasure and enjoyment to those around her. For many long years a follower of the Saviour, His disciple from early womanhood, a member of His Church, and living a consistent Christian life, she was prepared for the summons to depart and be with Christ, and is now at rest, with the hope of a joyful resurrection and "an inheritance that fadeth not away."

Rev. Alexander Jones, Jr., married **Ann Northey Churchill,** daughter of Captain Benjamin Churchill, of Bristol, R. I., November 3d, 1819. (The ceremony was performed by Bishop Griswold, and Samuel B. Shaw and Caroline F. Jones were groomsman and brides-maid.)

CHILDREN:

Clara Churchill Jones,	born May 31, 1820, died Dec. 29, 1881.	
Alexander Jones, 3d,	" Aug. 5, 1822.	
Benjamin Churchill Jones,	" Aug. 23, 1824, " July 19, 1863.	
Mary Farquhar Jones,	" July 26, 1826.	
George Wardwell Jones, } Twins. Joseph Jones, }	born June 11, 1828.	
Charles Christian Jones,	born Jan. 26, 1830, died Nov. 25, 1847.	
William Marlborough Jones,	" Jan. 28, 1832.	
Rebecca Churchill Jones,	" Dec. 11, 1833.	
Ann Northey Jones,	" Sept. 26, 1835.	
Loraine Farquhar Jones,	" Nov. 9, 1837.	
Henry Holman Jones,	" Mar. 26, 1839, " Oct. 15, 1859.	
Margaretta Brown Jones,	" Dec. 22, 1840, " Jan. 10, 1841.	

8.   **Clara Churchill Jones** married **Alexander Parker Crittenden,** April 24th, 1838.

CHILDREN:

Laura Crittenden,	born Mar. 22, 1839.	
Churchill Crittenden,	" May 17, 1840, died Oct. 4, 1864.	
James Love Crittenden,	" Dec. 15, 1841.	
Annie Churchill Crittenden,	" Jan. 19, 1843.	
Howard Crittenden,	" Nov. 17, 1844, " Oct. 23, 1871.	
Clara Crittenden,	" Aug. 2, 1846, " June 2, 1847.	
Blanche Crittenden,	" Mar. 25, 1848, " May 24, 1848.	
Parker Crittenden,	" Feb. 27, 1849.	
Mary Crittenden,	" Aug. 25, 1852, " Aug. 3, 1854.	
Edmund Randolph Crittenden,	" Mar. 26, 1854, " July 27, 1854.	
Carrie Campbell Crittenden,	" June 18, 1855.	
Thomas Turpin Crittenden,	" Apr. 4, 1857.	
Florence Alexander Crittenden,	" June 18, 1858, " Jan. 11, 1862.	
Henry Crittenden,	" Sept. 15, 1859, " May 16, 1863.	

NOTE.—Alexander Parker Crittenden was a lawyer of ability and considerable eminence in San Francisco, where he and his family had lived for many years. On the 5th of November, 1870, in the presence of his wife and daughter (who had just returned from a visit to the Eastern States), and a son who had come to meet them, he was shot and killed on the ferry boat by the celebrated and notorious Laura Fair. She was tried and acquitted. He was a nephew of Senator Crittenden, of Kentucky, and was originally from that State. His wife died December 29th, 1881.

9. **Laura Crittenden** married **Ramon Bernardo Sanchez**, December 6th, 1859; no children.

9. **Churchill Crittenden** was unmarried. The fate of this fine-looking young man was a sad one. He had entered the Confederate army, and joined himself to what was termed by our Government "*The Guerillas.*" By the rules of war, and the orders of our Generals, they were proscribed and considered in a different light from the soldiers of the regular Confederate armies. He was captured during an engagement or skirmish, and by the rules of war, was condemned and ordered to be shot, and the order was carried out the next day. Thus, in the days of his early manhood, he perished—cut off in the flower of his youth. He was a manly, splendid and promising young man.

9. **James Love Crittenden** married in 1879 **Nina Duval**, who was born Nov. 5th, 1851.

CHILDREN:

Thomas Piper Crittenden, born June 14, 1880.
Alfred Duval Crittenden, " Oct. 5, 1882.

9. **Annie Churchill Crittenden** married **Sidney M. Van Wyck**, November 8th, 1862.

CHILDREN:

Henry Van Wyck,	born Jan. 9, 1864, died June 23, 1864.
Clara Van Wyck,	" July 1, 1865.
Frances Akers Van Wyck,	" Nov. 20, 1866.
Sidney M. Van Wyck, Jr.,	" May 28, 1868.
Crittenden Van Wyck,	" Feb. 19, 1870.
Nannie Crittenden Van Wyck,	" Aug. 11, 1874.
Carolyn Barney Van Wyck,	" Nov. 10, 1875, died Aug. 3, 1877.
Laura Sanchez Van Wyck,	" Sept. 5, 1879.

9. **Howard Crittenden** married **Lucy Fisher**, July 6th, 1870.

CHILDREN:

Twins, who were born dead, July, 1871.
The mother died at the time, July 9th, 1871, and the father, Oct. 23d, 1871.

9. **Parker Crittenden** married **Elizabeth Clara Reed Henry** (who was born January 4th, 1851), February 17th, 1869.

CHILDREN:

Gertrude Clara Crittenden, born Dec. 26, 1869.
Grove Adams Crittenden,   "   Aug. 5, 1872.
Laura Churchill Crittenden, "   Sept. 16, 1874.
Florence Page Crittenden,   "   Sept. 5, 1881.

9. **Thomas Turpin Crittenden** married **May Esther Clark**, March 15th, 1881.

CHILDREN:

William Alexander Crittenden, born Jan. 21, 1882.

9. **Carrie Campbell Crittenden** married **Francis Pratt** (born June 18th, 1848), in October, 1880; no children.

8. **Alexander Jones, 3d,** married the widow of John Musgrave (maiden name **Mary Hay Lee**, born January 5th, 1830), in Grenada, Nicaragua, August 12th, 1856.

CHILDREN:

Alexander Jones, 4th, born Apr. 18, 1857, died May 26, 1870.
Annie Gilmour Jones,   "   Dec. 8, 1858.
Rennie Lee Jones,   "   Oct. 15, 1860.
Clara Churchill Crittenden Jones, born Dec. 23, 1863.

Alexander Jones, son of the Rev. Alexander Jones, graduated as a physician from the Jefferson Medical College, Philadelphia. He afterwards joined the expedition of General Walker, in Nicaragua, and was wounded in the leg in one of the battles or skirmishes. While there he married, and some years later settled in California with his family, where he now is practicing his profession.

9. **Rennie Lee Jones** married **Minnie Elizabeth Urquhart** (who was born August 24th, 1864), October 13th, 1882.

CHILDREN:

Alexander Irving Jones, born Dec. 21, 1883.

9. **Clara C. C. Jones** married **Alexander Frazer Urquhart** (who was born April 14th, 1860), January 23d, 1883.

CHILDREN:

Elizabeth Somerville Urquhart, born Oct. 13, 1883.

8. **Benjamin Churchill Jones** married **Josephine Eletha McGreal** (who was born October 2d, 1834), April 17th, 1853, in Texas.

CHILDREN:

Alexander Patrick Jones, born Feb. 5, 1854, died Sept. 20, 1854.
Churchill Thornton Jones, ( ) " Aug. 30, 1855, " July 20, 1863.
Francis William Jones, (Twins) " Aug. 30, 1855, " Oct. 20, 1859.
Ernest Jones, " Jan. 29, 1858, " Sept. 14, 1859.
Emily Josephine Jones, " July 25, 1861, " July 6, 1863.
Benjamine Churchill Jones, " Aug. 18, 1863.

B. Churchill Jones died July 19th, 1863, and his wife, Josephine, October 6th, 1875.

This record of his family is painfully sad, the youngest child being the only survivor of father, mother, sons and daughters. In forty-four days, in the year 1863, there were three deaths and one birth. The death of the father, the death of a daughter, the death of a son, and the birth of a daughter, after her father's death. Such a series of troubles and trials in one family, and in such a short time, is but seldom known.

BENJAMIN CHURCHILL JONES.

From the *Galveston News*, Texas.

Died, in Bienville parish, Louisiana, July 19th, 1863, Captain B. Churchill Jones, Quartermaster Eighth Texas Infantry, C. S. A., aged 38 years and 11 months. Captain Jones was born in Jefferson County, Virginia, and came to Texas in 1844, became a member of Wood's regiment of Texas Rangers in 1846, and settled in Brazoria in 1848, where for many years he filled the office of district clerk with great credit to himself and the satisfaction of the public. He afterwards

6

practiced the profession of the law, of which he was an honored member, in the city of Galveston.

But on the breaking out of this war for our liberties, he arranged his affairs to become an early and lasting participant in its arduous labors and in the duties to which he was assigned, devoted his whole soul, time and abilities, to the great approbation of the departments with which he was connected. So severe were his labors, his health gradually sunk under them, until he was not only forced to resign his duties to his country, but his life also.

Shortly previous to his death his only daughter, Emily Josephine Jones, died at Munroe, Louisiana, July 6th, 1863, which greatly preyed upon his mind, and shortly after, but without his knowledge at the time of his death, he lost his only son then born, Churchill Thornton Jones, who died at Bienville, July 20th, 1863. We can but trust that they now constitute a happy little family in the great place of rest beyond the grave.

We can but say, and without eulogy, that Captain Jones, in all the departments of life, whether as the kind and affectionate husband and father, the unswerving and faithful officer of the law, the brave and unflinching soldier, or the ever upright and honest man, commanded and received the affection, admiration and respect of all those who knew him.

Another noble man has gone to swell the host above, another noble and devoted wife is left to mourn a husband lost, and the country can sympathize with her in her tears.

8. **Mary Farquhar Jones** married **Amos Joliffe**, November 16th, 1848.

CHILDREN:

Charles Christian Joliffe,   born Aug. 22, 1849.
Lavinia Hopkins Joliffe,   "   Mar. 29, 1851, died Oct. 2, 1862.
Clara Crittenden Joliffe,   "   Apr. 3, 1853, "   Oct. 16, 1862.
Annie Churchill Joliffe,   "   Apr. 6, 1855, "   Oct. 8, 1862.
Harriet Tyson Joliffe,   "   Apr. 14, 1857, "   Oct. 5, 1862.
Lizzie Louise Joliffe,   "   May 18, 1860, "   Oct. 5, 1862.
Alexander Victor Joliffe,   "   May 26, 1862.
Rebecca Churchill Joliffe,   "   Nov. 22, 1864.
Churchill Crittenden Joliffe, "   May 12, 1866, "   May 17, 1866.

What a sad record those five deaths of those five little girls, aged 11, 9, 7, 5 and 2 years, and all of them within the space of fourteen days! An unusual, remarkable and terrible affliction. With war raging around her (in the Valley of the Shenandoah), this afflicted and agonized mother passed through an ordeal of trial almost too heavy for the heart to bear.

9. **Charles Christian Joliffe** married **Sallie T. Merryman**, August 18th, 1870.

CHILDREN:

Mary Farquhar Joliffe, born Sept. 13, 1871.
Edward Philpot Joliffe, " Jan. 14, 1873.
Grace Merryman Joliffe, " July 27, 1874.
Sallie Merryman Joliffe, } " Mar. 4, 1876, died May 26, 1876.
  and twin, born dead. }
Sallie Merryman Joliffe died March 9th, 1876.

Charles Christian Joliffe married, second, **Elizabeth Corbin Jennings,** June 5th, 1877.

CHILDREN:

William Jennings Joliffe, born Mar. 26, 1878.
Mittie Frank Jennings Joliffe, " Apr. 18, 1880.
Marlborough Churchill Joliffe, " Apr. 26, 1882, died Apr. 17, 1884.

8. **George Wardwell Jones** married **Louisa Adams Carrington** (born May 5th, 1836), May 15th, 1856.

CHILDREN:

Louisa Carrington Jones, born Feb. 20, 1857.
Richard Carrington Jones, " May 1, 1858, died Sept. 22, 1866.
Annie Churchill Jones, " June 1, 1859.
Joseph Courtenay Jones, " Oct. 18, 1861.
Mary Adams Jones, " Sept. 29, 1863.
George William Jones, " Jan. 26, 1866, " Sept. 20, 1866.
Rebecca Christian Jones, " May 21, 1867, " July 5, 1867.
William Marlborough Jones, " Feb. 13, 1870.
Alexander Jones, 5th, " July 5, 1871, " July 9, 1872.
Loraine Peterkin Jones, " Aug. 25, 1874.
Emily Page Jones, " Feb. 9, 1876.
Margaret Heron Jones, " Sept. 26, 1879.

George W. and Joseph Jones, twin brothers, married Virginia ladies, and have always lived in that State. The former is a successful dentist, practicing his profession in Richmond, living with his large family in Ashland, not many miles distant. The latter, the Rev. Joseph Jones, is settled in Millwood, Clarke County, having charge of the parish there and two other churches in that vicinity.

8. **Joseph Jones** married **Courtney Bowdoin Byrd** (born August 29th, 1833), September 20th, 1860. Her grandmother was Ann Randolph Meade, sister of Bishop Meade, of the Diocese of Virginia. She married Matthew Page, of Clarke County, and had two daughters. The oldest married Rev. C. W. Andrews, D.D., and the other John W. Byrd, Esq.

CHILDREN:

Charles Andrews Jones,	born Aug. 23, 1865.
Robert E. Lee Jones,	" June 17, 1867.
Churchill Crittenden Jones,	" July 20, 1868, died ——, 18—.
Mary Frances Page Jones,	" Oct. 29, 1869, " ——, 18—.
Matthew Page Jones,	" Feb. 6, 1872, " ——, 18—.
Joseph Churchill Jones,	" Sept. 1, 1873.
George Loraine Jones,	" Aug. 18, 1874.
Courtney Byrd Jones (boy),	" Sept. 2, 1876.

8. **William Marlborough Jones** married **Mary Lambert Macmurdo**, August 18th, 1863. She was born August 17th, 1837.

CHILDREN:

Charles Macmurdo Jones,	born July 25, 1864, died June 23, 1865.
Parker Crittenden Jones,	" Feb. 20, 1866.
William Churchill Jones,	" Feb. 23, 1868, " June 23, 1870.
Maggie Macmurdo Jones,	" Nov. 23, 1870.
Annie Churchill Jones,	" Dec. 26, 1872.
Alexander Jones, 6th,	" July 26, 1874, " May 18, 1875.
Mary Pickett Jones,	" July 12, 1876.
Walter Martin Jones,	" Aug. 19, 1882.

William M. Jones resided in Richmond a number of years, and carried on business there, but being unsuccessful (as nearly ninety-nine out of one hundred business men are), he afterwards came to Baltimore, where he is assistant in the office of Col. Craighill, United States Engineering Department.

8. **Rebecca Churchill Jones** married **Col. Wm. P. Craighill**, U. S. A. (who was born July 1st, 1833), September 22d, 1874; no children.

Colonel Craighill has charge of the United States Engineering Department for the District of Maryland, Virginia and North Carolina. His office is in Baltimore and he resides in Charlestown, Jefferson County, West Virginia.

8. **Annie Northey Jones** married, in California, **Dr. Johnson Price**, April 28th, 1859.

CHILDREN:

Alexander Jones Price, born Feb. 14, 1860.

Dr. Price was born February 27th, 1822, and died February 8th, 1868.

8. **Loraine Farquhar Jones** married **Matilda Fontaine Berkley**, daughter of Rev. Mr. Berkley (born March 13th, 1849), November 9th, 1870.

CHILDREN:

Annie Maury Jones,	born Aug. 25, 1871, died Aug. 11, 1873.
Edward Fairfax Berkley Jones,	" Jan. 11, 1874.
Mary Churchill Jones,	" May 13, 1877.
Charlotte Thornton Jones,	" Jan. 15, 1879.
Loraine Farquhar Jones, Jr.,	" Jan. 7, 1881.
Fontaine Maury Jones,	" Mar. 13, 1883.

Captain Loraine F. Jones was, with *fire* of his brothers, in the late Civil war, and on the Southern or "Confederate" side. His father, however, the Rev. Alexander Jones, remained loyal to his country and government, although six of his sons were in the rebel army. Capt. Jones was an active participant throughout the war, and, although he was engaged in forty different actions or battles, he escaped without wound or injury of any kind. Since the war he has been engaged in active business in the city of St. Louis, which he has made his home.

MRS. ANN NORTHEY (CHURCHILL) JONES,

Wife of the Rev. Alexander Jones, died early in the year 1855, leaving behind her the record of a fond and faithful wife, a loving and devoted mother, and a strong and sincere friend. With a large family of children, her family and household cares were no small burden to bear, and were constant and pressing upon her with no light weight. But she bore them all bravely, and with an unfaltering devotion to her many duties. Her character was marked by energy, strength and determined purpose, and these qualities were made manifest in her being indeed a help-meet to her husband and an excellent mother to her children. Nearly all of her children were born in Charlestown, where her husband was Rector of Zion Church for twenty-seven years. Receiving but a small salary, it was no easy task to this father and mother to rear and educate such a large family, but she was faithful in the performance of her duties, and in the care of her children, untiring and persevering. She was upheld and sustained by an active faith in her Lord and Saviour, and in the religion which she professed for so many years, and she died in that faith and with the blessed assurance that she would receive the Christian's reward.

REV. ALEXANDER JONES, D.D.

From the *Southern Churchman*, February, 1874.

We cannot permit the loving tribute of our venerable Presiding Bishop to be inserted without a word. Thirty years ago the writer of this saw him for the first time in all his gigantic proportions. He was then Rector of the church in Charlestown, Jefferson County, Virginia. A man of learning and decided ability, genial and pleasant in his manners and eminently Christian in his life. He had a large family, all of whom, sons and daughters, are following in the footsteps of their dear old father. A hard struggle he had to maintain them all and educate them all, but now in their useful lives they speak for him, for his education and for the lessons they learned from him, both by precept and example. Some of them have had to pass through deep afflictions, but they have not been without the consolations they first learned in the rectory at Charlestown.

A few lines from one of his sons (the Rev. Joseph R. Jones, of Milwood), may well conclude this brief notice of our dear old friend.

"My father died a quiet, peaceful death, ready for the summons and with a hope full of immortality. For several years he had been preparing for the great change and was patiently abiding the Lord's will. He had done his work as faithfully as God vouchsafed him strength. He preached His gospel earnestly and eloquently, and I believe has many souls as his reward. And now he rests from his labors, for God has taken him, and blessed be His holy name."

Written by Right Rev. Benjamin Bosworth Smith, D.D. and L.L.D.

That were much too brief a memoir of a cultivated, laborious and faithful minister of Christ, to enter only this short record:

"*Born*, Charleston, S. C., November 8th, 1796. *Died*, Perth Amboy. February 15th, 1874, aged nearly 78." Yet it often happens that the more useful such a life has been, the less it is marked by incidents worthy of record, or gratifying to the curious. "He walked humbly with his God," and his record is on high.

Facts in his history well known to the writer, his early companion in study and his life-long friend, and which went very far to mould his character and shape his destiny, are of interest and worthy of record.

A profound interest in sacred things, especially among young people, under the ministry of that man of God, Bishop Griswold, aided by lay services by Mr. Henshaw (afterwards Bishop of Rhode Island), beginning in Bristol, R. I., in 1812, were witnessed even on a larger scale in Providence, in 1814–15, a power attending the preaching of the Rev. Mr. Crocker, after his first awakening to the responsibilities of his sacred office, the fruits of which—*abundant fruits*—remain until this day. They were called "Revivals," and were not altogether free from some irregularities afterwards regretted, but it was long before, in less judicious hands, that the very name of "revivalist" was avoided as a term of reproach.

In the case of Mr. Jones and other members of his family, it was a memorable and blessed season. It determined him to change a gay and thoughtless life into one devoted to his Saviour, and to the improvement and salvation of his fellow-creatures. And the first step he took in order to repair the deficiencies of a college life, begun too early (he graduated when only eighteen), he devoted a year or two to the review of his classics, thus securing the broad basis of that accurate scholarship which rendered him for more than twenty years one of the most popular and successful of that class of clerical teachers in Virginia, from under whose hands, for several generations, the young men of that State passed to various colleges often to win their highest honors.

In the winter of 1816–17 there were daily assembled in an upper room, in Bristol, four young men, candidates for holy orders, under the oversight of Bishop Griswold: James W. Eastburn, Benj. B. Smith, J. J. Robertson and Alexander Jones. So great was the want of clergy, that Smith, who was graduated at Brown University only the Fall before, was ordained Deacon, April 17th, 1817. Soon after his ordination, Eastburn, scholar, poet and devoted missionary, closed a short ministry in Accomac County, Va., by an early and lamented death.

In the winter of 1873–4, within a radius of 100 miles from the city of New York, after having been widely separated in the Master's service, the other three: Smith, Robertson, and Jones were all living, restored almost to the scenes of their earliest years. And now, the youngest of the three is taken, and the others left. Oh! what dangerous voyages, what weary journeys, what arduous labors, what heavy sorrows, during all these fifty-seven years, have we been carried through; not wholly, it is hoped, without benefit to others, or without some little growth in the divine life!

In the case of Dr. Jones, my dear friend, having, from increased infirmities, laid aside his armor three years ago, he has since been calmly waiting for his last summons, and it came suddenly, as he had long expected, affording no opportunity of uttering words of comfort, but leaving behind a character and a life-work much more full of hope and consolation, than any which words, however precious, could ever afford.

Between 1817 and 1825, the supply of clergy in the Eastern diocese was beyond the demand, and in Virginia the demand far beyond the home supply. So it came to pass that all these four fellow-students had some years' experience in that most inviting field of labor. Dear Eastburn! his whole life-work a year or two; two others, from four to five years, and Dr. Jones, the greater part of his long life, having succeeded Smith, in Charlestown, Jefferson County, in 1823, where he labored most faithfully until 1849, when he accepted a call to St. Paul's, Richmond.

It is difficult to transplant a mountain oak to a city sidewalk, and the older it is, the more doubtful that it will kindly take root. In the course of five years, Dr. Jones became convinced that a more retired and rural parish would better suit him, and God, in his good providence, kindly provided for his declining years, in the delightful old parish and rectory of St. Peter's, Perth Amboy, N. J. Here it will not be altogether irrelevant to mention that Virginia, along these early years, was largely indebted to New England for some of her most distinguished clergy: Professors Keith, Lippitt, Dr. Hatch, of Charlottesville; Dr. Dana, of Alexandria; and the only survivor of them all, Dr. Andrews, of Shepherdstown. "The Fathers! where are they? The Prophets! do they live forever?" If none were raised up to take their places, we should be apt to think that "God's mercies were clean gone forever." But lo! His love for his Church, and His faithfulness to His promises are unchangeable. Successors are sure to be provided. Stronger in talent and in holy purpose cannot be found; but men of like ability and holy zeal, with much higher culture and better adaptation to the age, God has raised up in such noble bishops as Randall, and such living bishops and missionaries as we have in the far West, in China, in Japan, and in Africa. And so it will ever be, until God has gathered in his elect, from the four quarters of the habitable globe.

A CHURCHMAN.

FROM THE PROVIDENCE JOURNAL.

The Rev. Alexander Jones, D.D., class of 1814, Brown University, died at Perth Amboy, N. J., February 15th, 1874, aged 77 years, 3 months and 7 days. He was the son of Alexander and Mary (Farquhar) Jones, and was born in Charleston, S. C., Nov. 8th, 1796. His father was a graduate of the University in 1782, and was for many years engaged in mercantile pursuits in Charleston, though he returned to Providence in 1805, and here spent most of his life. The son pursued his early studies at Kent Academy, East Greenwich, under the charge of Joseph L. Tillinghast, and afterwards at the Academy in Bristol, under the tuition of Abner Alden (B. U., 1787). On leaving College, he studied theology under the direction of Bishop Griswold, then residing there. Before entering the ministry, however, he spent several years in charge of a school or academy in Bardstown, Kentucky, and returning to New England, was ordained a Deacon in the Episcopal Church by Bishop Griswold in 1822.

In 1825, he was ordained a Presbyter by Bishop Moore, in Richmond, Virginia, having in the year preceding become Rector of Zion Church, Charlestown, Jefferson County. He remained there 27 years, during which period he frequently had under his instruction students preparing for the Christian ministry. He subsequently become Rector of St. Paul's Church in Richmond, where he remained five years. Finding the charge of so large a parish too burdensome, he resigned his charge in Richmond and was soon after settled as Rector of St. Peter's Church, Perth Amboy, N. J. At this post of clerical service he spent 17 years, where, at the age of 75 years, he was smitten with paralysis and compelled to abandon his labors. He was an invalid for the last three years of his life, and suffered much from the prostration with which he was afflicted, but he bore his infirmities with great Christian fortitude and submission.

He held a high rank among the clergy of the Episcopal Church for scholarship and useful services, and was a gentleman of genial manners and refined tastes. He received the Honorary Degree of Doctor of Divinity at Kenyon College, in 1844. He was twice married, first to Ann Northey, daughter of Captain Benjamin Churchill, of Bristol, R. I., and second, to Annie, daughter of James H. Kearney, of Perth Amboy, N. J. His wife and nine children by his first wife survive him.

Brother Alexander was a man of fine personal appearance and splendid physique. He was well-built and fully six feet in height. He once told me, that while he was in Bardstown, Ky. (then a much wilder and rougher region than it now is), a man who was called the bully of the place, daily stopped him while on his way to the Academy, and wanted to have a trial of strength with him. He would say: "Parson! you are a strong, well-built fellow, and I've whipped everybody round here, and I want to try you." At first he spoke pleasantly and good-naturedly to him, but this daily annoyance become almost unbearable. One morning it was repeated, and with some taunts of cowardice, and his patience and temper gave way, and with one blow from his right arm, the bully was prostrated at his feet. Afterwards he was never again annoyed, but on the contrary, was always spoken to and of with the greatest respect. A clergyman of our church once said that Dr. Jones' sermons were remarkable for their clearness and directness. His analysis of any subject was excellent, his manner of delivery earnest, and his faithfulness as a preacher of God's Holy Gospel was almost remarkable. There were, no doubt, many "seals to his ministry" who were turned from their ways and brought to acknowledge and believe "the truth as it is in Jesus." That truth he ever preached, that Saviour he ever held up before his hearers as "the way, the truth and the life," and in the blessed presence of his Lord and Master, he inherits his reward.

DEATH OF JOSEPH JONES.

Died at Tampico, Mexico, November 12th, 1831, of fever, Joseph Jones, Esq., counsellor-at-law, son of Alexander Jones, Esq., of Providence, R. I., aged 32 years. All who knew the deceased must long cherish the remembrance of his many endearing qualities, and while they bow with submission to the mandate of the Eternal, deeply deplore the untimely exit of one, who, to a brilliant intellect, united great conversational powers and a playfulness of wit with much vivacity, a suavity of manner, a kind heart and a frank and generous disposition, which not only endeared him to his friends, but led them to cherish the fondest anticipation of future usefulness.

That he was called to meet his last summons while distant from the home of his youth, and far away from the soothing attentions of parental affection, must add bitterness to the grief of his afflicted family; but they should cherish resignation to the Divine will, reflecting that, as the dealings of Providence are often mysterious, this dispensation, which is to them so afflictive, may with regard to him have been ordered in mercy. C. H. D.

Lines selected by his sister Frances.

Brother! we parted on an Autumn day,
Fair was the sky, and bright the sunbeams fell.
Oh! little did I think, when hands were grasped,
And tears were dropping free,
That thus, should sever our fraternal link.
Soft fall ye dews—gild bright ye morning beams
The tufted hillock, where my brother lies;
Though distant far, I'll visit it in dreams,
And to the south wind, give my mournful sighs!
Methinks e'en now—he's standing by my side:
I turn to grasp—Lo! Death our hands divide!

Brother Joe, as he was familiarly called by us, was never married, though twice "engaged." He was ever the life of the circle in which he moved, and his wit, his fun, his imitations of words, looks and acts were irresistible, moving all who saw and heard him to bursts of great laughter. He was very fond of fishing and shooting, being expert in both, and his success with a rifle or shot gun was somewhat remarkable. In the social circle he was a general favorite, and his pleasing and graceful manners were observed by all. His musical talents were also marked, and his performances on the flute were as perfect and finished as those of any professionals the writer has ever heard. With a fine ear for music and a manly voice, he sang with remarkable and the most touching expression His recitations also of prose or poetry were always appreciated for their clearness and cultivated force, and whether it was some humorous story, some funny anecdote, or a sad and touching tale, he excited his hearers to immoderate laughter, or melted them to tears. He was a man of fine manly physique, with handsome and expressive features, and a form and movement that was grace itself. He was truly handsome, graceful and accomplished and a universal favorite. Cut down by death long ere he had reached the prime of manhood, his early departure caused poignant grief among all his friends and acquaintances, who mourned the loss of one so gifted with attractions of the person, mind and heart. G.

Caroline Flagg Jones married **Rev. Samuel Brenton Shaw** (who was born December 29th, 1799), August 1st, 1822.

An affectionate nature, a gentle disposition and a quiet spirit, were marked characteristics of my sister Caroline. She was a beautiful girl, a lovely woman and in her later years was spoken of by all as a lovely old lady.

She gave herself early in life to the service of her Lord and Saviour, and throughout that life, extended to more than eighty years, she maintained the character of her Christian profession. Her health was never robust, but she continued to have a bright color in her face even in her last years. With a large family she was ever the loving mother to her children, the devoted wife and helpmate to her husband, and faithfully performed all the duties that fell to her lot, quietly, gracefully and in the fear and love of God. The faith she professed in her early days was ever a comfort and support to her in the many hours of sickness that were hers, and in the time of her declining years when the infirmities of age came upon her. Cheerfully and uncomplainingly she bore sickness and those infirmities, and with the full hope of an immortality beyond the grave, she passed quietly away and entered into rest exactly at noon on Sunday, October 1st, 1882, aged 80 years and 8 months. She and her husband were together in the married life 60 years and 2 months to a day.

Rev. Samuel B. Shaw, D.D., is now living and in his 85th year. He was a graduate of Brown University, and was ordained a minister in the Episcopal Church more than sixty years ago. And with one short exception (on account of trouble with his eyes, which rendered an operation necessary), he has continuously and faithfully preached the Gospel and performed the duties of his sacred office. He was Rector of a church in Guilford, Vermont, for several years, then of St. Luke's parish, Lanesboro, Mass., where he served for thirty-four years, then at East Greenwich, R. I., and his last charge as Rector was at St. John's, Barrington Centre, for about fourteen years.

In his long and honored life he secured the good will, esteem and affection of all among whom he moved, whether as a faithful minister of Christ, or as a man, an associate or a friend, and he will have an eternal reward.

THEIR CHILDREN:

8. William Alexander Shaw,	born June 11, 1823, died Nov. 5, 1824.
George Jones Shaw,	" Aug. 25, 1824.
Samuel Brenton Shaw,	" Oct. 16, 1826, " July 4, 1842.
Caroline Jane Frances Shaw,	" Mar. 18, 1829.
Ellen Maria Shaw, { Twins }	" Nov. 28, 1830. *1831*
Emily Matilda Shaw,	
Mary Elizabeth Shaw,	" Oct. 24, 1832, " Mar. 21, 1882.
Anna Louisa Shaw,	" Feb. 1, 1834.
Edward Newton Shaw,	" Dec. 15, 1836, " Mar. 13, 1866.
Abby Greene Shaw,	" May 31, 1838.
Eliza Wood Shaw,	" May 26, 1840, " Mar. 27, 1841.

OBITUARY.—"BRENTON SHAW."

The following was in a newspaper published at that time, July, 1842:

"In Lanesboro, Massachusetts, by the explosion of a small cannon, Samuel Brenton, Jr., son of the Rev. Samuel Brenton and Caroline F. Shaw, and grandson of Alexander Jones, of Providence, R. I., was suddenly killed at early dawn of July 4th, 1842, aged 15 years, 8 months and 8 days."

The above is an inscription on a beautiful obelisk of clouded marble, thirteen feet high, erected by the liberality of the friends of the deceased, as a memorial of his worth and early death. On another side of the monument are the following words:

"This monument is the voluntary and honorable testimonial of numerous friends, to the memory of one whom all loved, and whose virtues, talents and acquirements were some indications of future usefulness and eminence."

8. **George Jones Shaw** married **Anne Dooley**, October 27th, 1867.

CHILDREN:

Samuel Brenton Shaw, 3d, born Aug. 11, 1868.
Caroline Anne Shaw,	" Mar. 15, 1872.
Mary Edith Shaw,	" May 10, 1875.
Katherine Shaw,	" July 28, 1880.

8. **Caroline Jane Frances Shaw** married **Dr. William Cushing**, of Cleveland, Ohio, December 25th, 1852; no children.

8.   **Ellen Maria Shaw** married **William A. Arnold**, of Providence, December 6th, 1853; no children.

8.   **Emily Matilda Shaw** married **William A. Howard**, of Providence, December 25th, 1852. (Three sisters married in December, and their husbands all named William.)

CHILDREN:

Caroline Brenton Howard,	born Sept. 30, 1853.	
William Augustus Howard,	" Apr. 7, 1856, died Sept. 6, 1861.	
Ellen Howard,	" Aug. 23, 1861, " " 8, 1861.	
Mabel Howard,	" Feb. 12, 1864.	
Henry Tyler Howard,	" Aug. 27, 1865.	

8.   **Mary Elizabeth Shaw** married **James T. Clark**, November 26th, 1856.

CHILDREN:

Brenton Shaw Clark, born Oct. 16, 1857.
Edith Mary Clark,   "   Jan.   7, 1860.
Rose Barrington Clark, " Dec. 15, 1871.
Mary Elizabeth Clark died March 21st, 1882, in her 50th year.

8.   **Edward Newton Shaw** married **Julia Betts**, October 21st, 1863; no children.
Some 16 or 17 years after Edward N. Shaw's death, March 13th, 1866, his widow married again.

"THE GOLDEN WEDDING"

Of the Rev. Dr. Samuel B. Shaw and his wife (taken from the newspapers), at Barrington Centre, R. I., August 1st, 1872.

Last Thursday a large number of the relatives of the Rev. Dr. Shaw and Caroline, his wife, assembled at the rectory of St. John's Church, Barrington, to celebrate their golden wedding. Mrs. Shaw was the fourth daughter of Alexander Jones, late of Providence, and fifty years ago, August 1st, 1822, was married to Samuel Brenton Shaw, at St. John's Church, Providence, by the late Rev. Dr. Crocker. In her quiet home on this eventful day she received, with gentle dignity, the congratulations of a large number of her and her husband's relatives. Bishop Clark was present (and later in the day Bishop Howe), and after all were assembled he conducted a short and impressive religious service, and for the second time a heavy wedding ring, presented by one of her daughters, was placed on Mrs. Shaw's finger, thus renewing the contract made a half century ago. Two poems were then read, the first a beautiful one selected by one of the daughters, and well delivered by the Bishop, and the second a humorous one written by the brother of the wife, Mr. George F. Jones, of Philadelphia, which was extremely interesting, as it contained so many witty and touching allusions to the different members of the family.

After the good things generously provided by the congregation had been enjoyed, many presents were given to the bride and groom, and the golden acknowledgments amounted to more than five hundred dollars. One especially gratifying circumstance was the gift of the parish in Lanesboro, Mass., where Mr. Shaw had labored for 34 years, of $181 in gold, accompanied by a letter testifying their personal regard. Their first groomsman in 1822, Mr. William S. Patten, of Providence, and a bridesmaid, Mrs. Resolved Waterman, were also present with changed but still beautiful countenances, and memory turned back the leaves of a half century of time, and recalled the day when they, the bride, the groom and all were in the first bloom of manhood and womanhood.

There were three distinct gatherings during the day. First came the relatives from Philadelphia, New York, Brooklyn, Jersey City, Providence, Fall River, Bristol, Warren, East Greenwich, etc.; then the friends, the congregation and others, and last, the children of the church and parish. The occasion was from first to last a deeply interesting one to all concerned, and especially to the family and relatives, as it brought together so many who for years had been widely separated. It was a lovely summer day, and one long to be remembered, as it proved to be the only golden wedding in the Jones' family for more than two hundred years.

GENEALOGY OF REV. SAMUEL B. SHAW, D.D.

From Roger Williams.

2. **Freeborn Williams**, daughter of Roger Williams, married Governor Walter Clark.

3. **Mary Clark**, their daughter, married Gov. Samuel Cranston.

4. **Frances Cranston**, daughter of Samuel and Mary Cranston, married Jahleel Brenton, grandson of Gov. William Brenton.

5. **Samuel Brenton**, son of Jahleel and Frances Brenton, married Susan, daughter of Silas Cook.

6. **Elizabeth Cook**, daughter of Samuel and Susan Brenton, married Dr. William Gorham Shaw.

7. **Samuel Brenton Shaw**, their son, born December 29th, 1799.

From William Brenton.

1. **Governor William Brenton** came from Hammersmith, England, in the year 1634, to Boston, colony of Massachusetts. After a short time he left Boston and went to Rhode Island in the year 1638, and was among the first settlers of Newport, R. I. He was president under the first charter—lieutenant-governor and governor from 1660 to 1668 under the second, and died about 1674.

2. **William Brenton, Jr.**, son of William Brenton.

3. *****Jahleel Brenton**, son of William, Jr., married Frances Cranston.

4. **Samuel Brenton**, their son, married Susan Cook, and died about 1797.

5. **Elizabeth Brenton**, their daughter, married Dr. William G. Shaw.

6. **Samuel Brenton Shaw**, their son, born December 29th, 1799.

The name and fame of Roger Williams are so well known in our country it would be useless to make further mention here. In the annals of Rhode Island the name of Brenton occupies a prominent position, as he was a large landholder, and held the highest offices among his fellow-citizens.

SEVENTH GENERATION.

Jane Sherwood Jones married **Dr. William W. Valk**, of Charleston, S. C., July 16th, 1829.

CHILDREN:

Eugene William Valk, born	May 5, 1830, died	Dec. 17, 1849.
Sarah Maria Valk,	"	Apr. 14, 1833,	"	May 23, 1833.
Sarah Mary Valk,	"	Dec. 14, 1835,	"	July 19, 1837.
Lawrence Bolton Valk,	"	Nov. 17, 1837.
Ada Virginia Valk,	"	Aug. 19, 1839,	"	Mar. 23, 1843.
John Reginald Valk,	"	July 28, 1841,	"	Mar. 18, 1843.
Henry Valk, { Twins }	"	Jan. 13, 1844.
Albert Valk, { }	"	Jan. 13, 1844,	"	Nov. 3, 1846.
Francis Valk, baptized	Oct. 28, 1846.

---

* Jahleel was married twice, and was the father of twenty-two children.

8.   **Lawrence Bolton Valk** married **Ellen E. Childs** (born September 28th, 1840), January 6th, 1862.

CHILDREN:

Eugene Reuben Valk,   born Jan. 31, 1863, died April 18, 1863.
Arthur Lawrence Valk,   "   Apr. 27, 1865.
Frank Rudolph Valk,   "   Oct. 15, 1866.
Louis Valk,   "   Aug. 20, 1867,   "   Sept. 15, 1867.
Ada Virginia Valk,   "   Dec. 31, 1869,   "   Sept. 20, 1870.
Caroline Louisa Valk,   "   Feb. 4, 1872,   "   June 21, 1872.
Nellie May Valk,   "   Aug. 6, 1873.
Mabel Ellen Valk,   "   Nov. 7, 1874,   "   June 28, 1875.

L. Bolton Valk is an architect and has built numerous churches and other buildings in many parts of this country. Besides his plans and drawings he acts as a building architect. His business has proved successful, and is an instance of perseverance and success from one's own unaided efforts.

8.   **Henry Valk** married **Louisa Barton Easby**, November 2d, 1871, Washington, D. C.

CHILDREN:

William Horatio Nelson Valk, born July 26, 1872.
Ada Valk,   "   Dec. 5, 1873, died Dec. 8, 1873.
George Sherwood Valk,   "   May 13, 1875, " July 14, 1875.

8.   **Francis Valk** married **Marion C. Easby**, August 2d, 1874, Washington, D. C.

CHILDREN:

Francis Marion Valk, born May 2, 1875.
Elizabeth Barton Valk, "   Mar. 18, 1879.
Jane Sherwood Valk,   "   Aug. 9, 1883.

Dr. Francis Valk is a physician in good practice in New York City, secured also by his own unaided efforts.

Dr. Wm. W. Valk was Assistant Surgeon in the navy about the year 1836. His wife with two children on their voyage to Pensacola, where he had been assigned for duty, was shipwrecked, but their lives were saved. After he resigned from the navy he practiced his profession in various places, at one time in Bridgeport, Conn., and at another in Flushing, L. I. During the late war he was Assistant Surgeon in the army, serving in a regiment from Maryland and one from New York, besides being in the army hospital in Washington, D. C. He married the second time.

MRS. JANE SHERWOOD VALK.

Died in Flushing, Long Island, on the first day of February, 1854, Mrs. Jane Sherwood Valk, wife of Dr. William W. Valk, and daughter of Alexander Jones, Esq., of Providence, R. I.

The lovely character, the consistent Christian life, the patient suffering and the peaceful end of a follower of the Redeemer should always be recorded, not so much as an eulogy on the departed, but as an incentive to those who survive. And in the life and death of this lovely woman there is much to be admired and much for all to reflect upon, as both present the true Christian character in the most attractive form.

Brought up in the fear of God by her father and mother (who for many years were pious members of the Episcopal Church), and in answer to their prayers she in early womanhood chose the better part, and gave herself unreservedly to the service of Christ, her Lord and her God. For a period of more than twenty years she "lived the life of the righteous," and it is now ours to record the fact that her "last end was like His." It pleased God to visit her with affliction, five of her children being taken from her by death in their young life, and thus to purify her in the furnace of trial until she became "as fine gold, purified in the fire." The dross was removed and the pure metal shone brighter in the eyes of all. She wept the loss of her children as God took them to Himself, and one, her eldest son, just entering on manhood, was also mourned with all the sorrow that a mother's loving heart can feel; but still she trusted in God, and always said (not only in words, but in acts of daily life), "Thy will be done." For the last few months of her stay on earth she was called to suffer great bodily pain, and although the frail tenement writhed under the agony of the disease which destroyed her life, her soul was filled with "the peace of God, which passeth all understanding." Here was *the life* of the Christian, bringing forth its fruit *in death*. Here was the proof that Christ is precious to the soul of the believer, for He was now her stay, her comfort, her support in going "through the dark valley of the shadow of death." With faith in God and with hope through Christ only, as her Saviour, did she give up all on earth and resign herself submissively to death. Her three little boys were confided by her to the spiritual care of her pastor, earnestly asking him to watch over and care for their souls' health, and thus giving them up she at last "fell asleep in Jesus." At her funeral, which was attended by a large number of those who knew and loved her, all felt that for her to die was great gain. They could mourn their loss, for she was, to all who associated with her, the lovely woman, the kind friend, the humble Christian, but she had exchanged the sorrows of her mortal life for a never fading immortality in heaven. She "being dead, yet speaketh" to each and to all, reminding us, in her religious life, her firm and unshaken faith in the dark hour of death and her strong hope of eternal life, that we, "to die the death of the righteous," *must live their life* and become "reconciled to God, through Jesus Christ our Lord."

March, 1854. G.

SEVENTH GENERATION.

Frances Nelson Jones married **Theodore P. Bogert**, of New York, April 15th, 1828.

CHILDREN:

Theodore P. Bogert, Jr., born Oct. 22, 1830.
Mary Benezet Bogert,　　" Sept. 14, 1832, died Feb. 14, 1880.

8.　**Theodore P. Bogert, Jr.,** married **Sarah Bull Wilkins** (born December 24th, 1833), February 17th, 1853.

CHILDREN:

Frances Nelson Bogert, born Feb. 1, 1854.
William Benezet Bogert, " Oct. 2, 1860.
Theodore P. Bogert, 3d. " Nov. 14, 1862.

9.　**Frances Nelson Bogert** married **Robert E. O'Brien**, of Portland, Oregon, September 27th, 1883.

CHILDREN:

Frances Hope O'Brien, born June 19, 1884.

8.　**Mary Benezet Bogert** married **Dr. S. Conant Foster**, of New York (who was born October 24th, 1816), September 23d, 1857.

CHILDREN:

Theodore Bogert Foster, born Aug. 10, 1858.
Conant Foster,　　　　" July　6, 1860, died July 13, 1870.
Mary Conant Foster,　　" Nov. 22, 1862.
Francis Nelson Foster,　" June 19, 1865.
James Reginald Foster,　" Nov. 23, 1867.

Mrs. Mary B. Foster was one of my favorite nieces, and deserved the esteem and love of a large circle of relatives and friends, which she enjoyed to a great degree, for she was a favorite with all. Her husband was a practicing physician in the city of New York and of marked ability and skill. His health became delicate and obliged him to relinquish his practice and devote himself to its restoration, but the dread disease, consumption, was too deeply seated. He traveled to Lake Superior and afterwards sailed for Spain. In the Fall of 1872, he, as a last resort, sailed for Nassau, in the Bermudas, but while there death claimed its victim, and he died leaving his wife and four little children, the oldest but fourteen, "strangers, in a strange land." Seven years afterwards, February 4th, 1880, his wife, who had suffered with the same fearful malady, was called away by death, but with a firm and sustaining faith and a sure hope of a blessed immortality. And here it is not irrelevant to state, that the death of her mother by consumption was one of only four cases in eight generations of the Jones family of Milford. The oldest of Mrs. Foster's children has since her death graduated from the General Theological Seminary, New York, been ordained Deacon and Priest, and was for one year assistant minister in St. James' parish in that city. He is now first assistant at St. Luke's Church, Brooklyn, with the Rev. Mr. Vandewater. May his work and labors ever help to advance the cause of Christ and His gospel, and "bring many to righteousness."

DEATH OF MRS. FRANCES N. BOGERT.

" At her residence in Geneva, New York, July 19th, 1848, Frances Nelson, wife of Theodore P. Bogert, and daughter of Alexander Jones, Esq., of Providence, R. I., departed this life, aged 42 years and 6 months."

After years of failing health and much suffering, the loved one passed away. During these many weary months, she was sustained by a strong faith in Him, whom, at the early age of 14, she had professed to love. She was a beautiful example of patient endurance, of sweet submission, and of cheerfulness under trials and great suffering. She possessed a highly cultivated intellect, and a loving, sympathizing spirit. Dignity and grace, intellectual superiority, independence and a true modesty and firmness, united with gentleness, were some of the traits of her character.

Sister Frances was of a peculiarly refined and delicate temperament, and with a vivid and earnest imagination. Accomplished, intelligent

and very bright, she was ever striving to improve her mind and store
her memory with the thoughts given to the world by the best writers
of the day. Her constant aim seemed to be to gain knowledge and
acquire information. And in this pursuit and in her intercourse with
the best authors, she acquired, with her natural genius for it, a peculiar
power and grace in conversation, which was always a delight for her
friends. Having also an excellent voice for singing, and a cultivated
ear, this accomplishment added much to the enjoyment of those who
knew her, and she was always an intelligent, pleasant and most agreeable companion. As a professing Christian, and from quite an early
age, she was ever mindful of her duties and her vows, and endeavored
to "live as becometh the gospel of Christ." She could only be sustained, in her painful and prolonged sickness, by faith in her Saviour
and a trust in His merits, and this faith and trust did sustain her until
the time when God called her and took her to Himself.

Mr. Bogert was in the business of banking and brokerage in Wall
Street, New York, and for some time in partnership with Col. J. B.
Wood, his brother-in-law, the firm being Wood & Bogert. He was
subsequently in a bank in Geneva. He married (a second time) Miss
Eliza Howe, of Bristol, and had a number of children. Receiving a
handsome fortune from his father's estate, he purchased a fine house
and property in Bristol, R. I., and settling his family there, became a
prominent citizen of that town. He was elected to the General Assembly of the State, and only recently died at an advanced age.

SEVENTH GENERATION.

George Farquhar Jones, of Philadelphia (born in Providence,
R. I., February 11th, 1811), was married by the Rev. N. B. Crocker,
D.D., to **Lorania Carrington Hoppin,** on his birthday, Wednes-
day, February 11th, 1835.

CHILDREN:

Mary Farquhar Jones,	born Dec. 21, 1835.		
Amy Hoppin Jones,	" Jan. 18, 1838.		
Lorania Carrington Jones,	" " 10, 1841,	died Aug. 24, 1884.
George Farquhar Jones, Jr.,	" Dec. 17, 1843,	" April 29, 1853.
Frances Ellen Jones,	" " 18, 1845.		
Maria Hoppin Jones,	" Jan. 13, 1848.		
Emily Matilda Jones,	" " 7, 1852.		
Annie Hoppin Jones,	" Mar. 14, 1854.		

Mrs. Lorania C. Jones died on Thursday morning, January 10th, 1884, at ten minutes past 10 o'clock.

It is not fitting for me to speak in eulogy of my faithful and devoted wife for 49 years, but it is appropriate that I use the words of others, which are as follows:

"When I first saw your wife, I was at once attracted by her quiet dignity, her intelligence and affectionate kindliness of manner, and I liked her better at each subsequent meeting; and (this is a precious thought) she is in Paradise at this moment, and henceforth and for-forever, free from pain and sickness and sorrow.

"From her early life, your wife has loved and followed her Blessed Redeemer, who has prepared a place for all those who love Him—*and she is there.*

"She was a good and loving friend to all your relations, as if they were her own, and was ever kind to me whenever I was under your hospitable roof.

"You have, from her fulfilment of all the duties incumbent on the wife, the mother, and the disciple of Christ, the assurance that she has gone to the blessed peace and rest of heaven."

"The few times that I have been a guest in your household, were enough to cause me to hold my dear Aunt in most affectionate and revered remembrance.

"Her gentle, quiet manner, her great love and anxiety for her children, her calm and humble trust in her Saviour, all impressed me with a sense of her real worth, and the certainty that she had chosen the better part and had found the pearl of great price."

8. **Mary Farquhar Jones** married **Robert Maxwell Green,** of Charleston, S. C., on her birthday, December 21st, 1859.

CHILDREN:

James Farquhar Green, born Oct. 15, 1860.
George Farquhar Green, " Dec. 2, 1861, died May 28, 1880.

THE DEATH OF GEORGE FARQUHAR GREEN,

At the University of the South, May 28th, 1880.

The unlooked for and unexpected illness and death of this noble and promising boy must not be allowed to pass without special notice. He had but a short time before entered at Sewanee College, Tennessee,

to study for a profession, but in those few short months had secured
the respect and regard of the authorities, as well as of his fellow-students. Bright, genial and withal studious, he at once, by strictly ob-
serving the rules of the institution and the fulfilment of his duties,
gained the good will of all the officers and professors. His short illness of but two days was soon pronounced to be a fatal one, and when
one of the professors told him of his condition, and afterwards asked
him not to be afraid, the brave and noble boy, away from all those he
loved, and dying among comparative strangers, replied, "*I have no
fear.*" How impressive, how touching, to see one so young prepared
to meet death.

Unusual respect and honors were paid to him in taking his body to
the chapel for religious services, thence to the station, attended by the
officers, professors, students, cadets and ladies of the place, all uniting
in their appreciation of his early and sad death, and showing their testimony to his manly, noble and winning qualities. His almost broken-
hearted father waited at the railroad station to receive his precious
body, and bore him to his last home in Magnolia Cemetery, Charleston, South Carolina.

8. **Amy Hoppin Jones** married **William Erwin Hoy**, December 2d, 1862.

CHILDREN:

Lorania Carrington Hoy, born Aug. 24, 1863.
James Hoy, 3d,   " July 19, 1867, died Feb. 3, 1873.
William Erwin Hoy, Jr., " May 5, 1875.

8. **Lorania Carrington Jones** married **Frederick Augustus
King**, of Providence, April 7th, 1870.

CHILDREN:

Lorania Carrington King, born Mar. 27, 1871.
Frederick A. King, Jr.,   " Aug. 2, 1872.
Lorania Carrington (Jones) King died Sunday evening, August
24th, 1884.

This lovely woman, the fond, devoted wife and mother, the beloved
daughter and sister, the affectionate relative, the sincere and pleasant
friend, was called away from earth to the eternal world, and left many
sad and lamenting hearts to mourn her departure. In the dispensa-

tion of God's Providence, she was seized with a long and painful illness in September, 1883, and the disease baffled the skill of her physicians, and for many long and weary months excited the deep interest
of all who knew her and loved her. Alternate hope and fear pre-
vailed, but with a care, skill, devotion and attention almost unprecedented, that was incessant and hourly lavished on her, a decided improvement was apparent, and strong hopes were cherished of an
entire recovery. Soon after entering on the twelfth month of her
sickness, when all her loved ones were joyously anticipating a perfect
restoration, the dread summons went forth, and the pure, chastened
spirit was called from "things temporal to those that are eternal."
Her faith was so child-like, simple and unquestioning, that we are assured
of its now blessed fruition. But the tear of sorrow must fall, the
loving heart must ache with grief at the death of one so lovely and so
loved. She was to all, within the circle of relatives and friends where
she moved, the sweet, graceful, loved woman, the cherished friend, the
pleasant companion. A void is left among them that never can be
filled, a home is made cheerless and desolate, but her gain is unspeakable and eternal joy.

8. **Frances Ellen Jones** married **Charles Goodrich King**,
of Providence, April 26, 1866.

CHILDREN :

Charles G. King, Jr.,   } Twins { born May 15, 1867.
George Jones King,   }
Mary Jones King,   "   Jan. 13, 1870.

Two sisters married two brothers, and they were third cousins.
Charles G. King died in Bristol, R. I., August 27th, 1881.

8. **Annie Hoppin Jones** married **Charles Herbert Yarnall**,
June 9th, 1881.

CHILDREN :

Helen Farquhar Yarnall, born June 19, 1882.

DEATH OF CHARLES G. KING.

From the Providence papers, August, 1881.

The death of Charles G. King, Esq., of the firm of William J.
King & Sons, and the second son of Deacon Wm. J. King, which occurred

at an early hour on Saturday morning, was an event that became immediately known throughout business circles, and was a great shock to all, although his intimate friends were aware of the great suffering he had endured for the past six months. He had for a long time been afflicted with Bright's disease of the kidneys, and by advice of his physicians, had retired to his and his brother's farm in Bristol, early in May, where he had since remained, and had been much benefited by a quiet and rural life. Though absent from the city, he still retained an active interest in events transpiring here. He was one of our leading business men, and one who, had his life been spared, would unquestionably have been most prominently identified in the future with our leading and central mercantile interests. At the time of his death he was a director in the First National Bank, a prominent member of the Board of Trade, being one of the Executive Council, and also upon the Finance and Floor Committees. He had always taken a deep interest in all the affairs of the Board and in furthering its prosperity. This is affectingly manifested in a letter which we have seen, written to a personal friend in this city, only Friday, which does not at all indicate that his strength was declining.

For a long time during the rapid fluctuations in the cotton market, he sustained a leading part in the conduct of the extensive enterprises in which his house was engaged, and his was a well-known face on the Cotton Exchange, in New York, during its stormiest days. He had been identified with the cotton business almost from his early boyhood.

He graduated at Amherst College in 1861, and afterwards went to Philadelphia to study for the profession of medicine. He, however, found that his nature could not endure the strain which the practice of that profession called for. He embarked in business with Mr. George F. Jones of that city, whose daughter, Fanny, he afterwards married. In 1865 he returned to Providence, and with his brother Edward, and their father, in October of that year, formed the partnership of Wm. J. King & Sons, of which firm he continued a member till his death.

Though of a retiring disposition, which made his true worth known only to his associates, his friendly attachments were uncommonly strong to those who had once gained his confidence, and he would do anything in his power for those whom he knew would appreciate him. He was born in Providence, January, 1840, and was consequently in the 42d year of his age. The Right Rev. M. A. DeWolf Howe, who united Mr. King and his wife in marriage, officiated at his funeral, which was largely attended, the cotton dealers closing their places of business as a token of respect. His sad and sudden demise has cast a marked gloom over our community.

SEVENTH GENERATION.

Ellen Maria Jones married **Charles Henry Dabney**, of Providence, April 27th, 1830.

CHILDREN:

Ellen Maria Jones Dabney, born Mar. 2, 1831.
Emily Matilda Dabney,   " Jan. 9, 1833.
Charles Henry Dabney, Jr., "   " 20, 1836, died Aug. 5, 1837.
Theodore Bogert Dabney,   "   " 27, 1838, "   " 24, 1839.
Frances Elizabeth Dabney, " Feb. 17, 1840.
Mary Farquhar Dabney,   " Aug. 3, 1844.

8. **Ellen Maria Jones Dabney** married **James Francis D'Wolf**, of Bristol, R. I., September 28th, 1847.

CHILDREN:

Francis LeBaron D'Wolf, born Aug. 21, 1848, died June 17, 1877.
Infant daughter,   " Nov. 22, 1850, " Dec. 15, 1850.
James Francis D'Wolf, Jr., " Oct. 30, 1852.
Ellen Post D'Wolf,   " Aug. 19, 1854.
Infant son,   " May 28, 1859, " June 3, 1859.
Henry Dabney D'Wolf,   "   " 1, 1861, "   " 5, 1881.
Nelson Sherwood D'Wolf, " Nov. 16, 1864.
Infant son,   " Sept. 14, 1865, " Sept. 30, 1865.

James Francis D'Wolf, born April 16th, 1823, was an officer in the army during the late civil war, and served with honor. His health suffered from his exertions and exposures. He died February 15th, 1870. His widow married second, Major Raymond H. Perry (who was born October 2d, 1835), also of Bristol, R. I., September 9th, 1875.

9. **Ellen Post D'Wolf** married **Archibald Walthall Archer** (born February 21st, 1847), of Richmond, Virginia, February 23d, 1877.

CHILDREN:

Ellen Dabney Archer,   born Dec. 31, 1877.
Archie Walthall Archer,   " Feb. 13, 1880.
Henry Dabney Archer,   " July 11, 1882.
James D'Wolf Archer,   " Oct. 8, 1884.

8. **Emily Matilda Dabney** married **Emil Heinemann**, of New York, December 12th, 1855.

CHILDREN :

Ellen Frances Heinemann, born Sept. 26, 1856.
Emil Dabney Heinemann,   "   Feb. 28, 1859.
Walter Dabney Heinemann,   "   June 9, 1861.
Robert Dabney Heinemann,   "   Mar. 25, 1863.
Emily Farquhar Heinemann, "   June 26, 1865.
Lillie Heinemann,   "   Apr. 4, 1867, died Apr. 7, 1867.
Arthur Blake Heinemann,   "   "   6, 1871.
Clara Cecilia Heinemann,   "   Mar. 26, 1873.
Spencer Oswald Heinemann, "   June 3, 1875.

Mr. Heinemann was engaged in the importing business in Pine Street, New York, in partnership with his brother-in-law, Mr. Payson. He retired from the business, and some ten years ago removed to England with his family, and has settled there.

GENEALOGY OF EMIL HEINEMANN.

1. **Ernest Kristoft Von Heinemann**, colonel in the Brunswick army, was born in 1710, and died in 1781.

2. **Friedrich Von Heinemann**, captain in the Netherland army, and fought at Waterloo. He died in 1818. (From this time the Dutch branch dropped the " Von " from the name.)

3. **Johann Jacob Heinemann**, born in Friesland (Holland), on the 17th of March, 1797, died in Hanover, Sept. 2d, 1854.

4. **Emil Heinemann**, born in Osterode, March 2d, 1832. Lived in the city of New York and Bristol, R. I., from 1854 to 1874, now a banker in London, and senior partner of Blake Brothers & Co. He sold his estate in Bristol to Charles and Frederick King, and their families occupy it as a Summer residence. It is now called Kingsthorpe.

9. **Ellen Frances Heinemann** married (at Ratton, England), June 9th, 1880, **Rev. Francis Clyde Harvey**, of Hailsham, England.

CHILDREN :

Catharine Clyde Harvey, born at Hailsham, Mar. 26, 1881.
Edith Clyde Harvey,   "   "   Apr. 4, 1882.
Hilda Clyde Harvey,   "   "   Mar. 29, 1883.
Marjory Clyde Harvey,   "   Eastbourne, Mar. 21, 1884.

The above is a somewhat remarkable record. In the great number of the records of our families which I have examined (running back some 280 years), I have not found a similar case. Four children born in less than four years, and the birth dates all comprised in fourteen days.

The Rev. Francis Clyde Harvey is Vicar of Hailsham, Sussex, England, and his father was also Vicar before him.

8. **Frances Elizabeth Dabney** married **Julius M. Rhett**, of South Carolina, January 12th, 1881 ; no children.

8. **Mary Farquhar Dabney** married **Francis Payson**, of New York, April 8th, 1862.

CHILDREN:

Francis Lithgow Payson, born Feb. 19, 1863.
Mary Dabney Payson, " Oct. 31, 1865.
Charles Arthur Payson, " Dec. 18, 1868, died Aug. 19, 1881.
William Farquhar Payson, " Feb. 18, 1876.
Harold Payson, " May 3, 1884.

9. **Francis Lithgow Payson** married **Jane Crocker**, of Taunton, Mass., October 6th, 1883.

The Dabneys have been so closely connected with our family, William Dabney marrying the sister of Alexander Jones, and his son, Charles Henry Dabney, marrying his daughter, it seems appropriate to record some particulars of their ancestors. The original name was d'Aubigné, and it is believed by some of the descendants that the Chevalier d'Aubigné was their ancestor, and by some that they are descended from the celebrated Madame de Maintenon. As this is not susceptible of proof, it must be considered as a tradition. Mr. William H. Dabney (who has devoted much time to his family record, and to whom I here and now desire to acknowledge my obligations and to thank him for the information given) has kindly furnished me with a very full statement, from which I make the following selections.

All the Dabneys, north and south, now living in these United States, have come from the same stock, viz.: from three brothers named d'Aubigné, who were French Huguenots, and who fled from France to England and thence to America at the time of Revocation of the Edict of Nantes, in 1685. They must have been of tender age at the time, and have gone with their parents or relatives from France to England.

Robert and **Elizabeth d'Aubigné** came to Boston previous to 1717, and must have changed their name to Dabney very soon after coming, as in that year Robert appears in Court Records in a suit, and his name is there spelled "Daubiney *alias* Dabney." They had two sons, viz., Charles, supposed to have been born in England previous to their coming over to this country, and John, born in Boston, as per records of State or city and of Kingschapel, Boston, August 17th, 1723.

Charles Dabney (1st) married **Elizabeth Gardner**, daughter of Nathaniel and Mary Gardner, Boston, December 13th, 1739, as per record in archives.

CHILDREN:

Charles (2d), Nathaniel, John and Mary.

The father died in December, 1756, and his widow married Dr. Eleazor Hurlow, of Boston, March 23d, 1758, and in 1765 they removed to Duxbury. In that same year their house in Duxbury was burned, and her daughter, Mary Dabney, aged 11, and Mary Hurlow, his daughter, aged 13, perished in the flames. Mrs. Hurlow died in 1807, aged 90 years, and Dr. Hurlow in 1812.

Charles Dabney (2d) married **Mary Bass**, daughter of the **Rev. John Bass**,* of Ashford, March 6th, 1766.

---

* The Rev. John Bass, it should be remembered, was called to be pastor of the new church in Mill River that was organized by Elder John Jones and others at his house on "The Dale Farm," but declined for some reason to accept the call. This Rev. John Bass was an ancestor of Charles Henry Dabney on his father's side, as well as Elder John Jones, who was his ancestor on his mother's side. He must have been a bright, witty individual, for it is related of him that he came to preach for the Rev. Amariah Frost, who was ordained and took charge of the new church, to which the Rev. John Bass was invited, just referred to. On this occasion the two walked out to see the pretty stream of water called Mill River. Mr. Frost called his brother clergyman's attention to it, but he, looking at it a moment, said, "This may do for *Frost fish*, but not for *Bass*."

The Rev. John Bass was born in Braintree, Mass., in 1716. He was the son of John Bass, Sr., who was born in 1688, was married in 1716, and died in 1762. The Rev. John married Mary Danielson, of Killingly, Conn., November 24th, 1743. They had six children, Mary, who married Charles Dabney (2d), being the second child and oldest daughter.

CHILDREN:

John Bass Dabney, born Dec. 13, 1766, married Roxa Lewis,
died Sept. 2, 1826, in Fayal.

Mary Dabney, born Dec. 15, 1768, died in 1775, in Providence.

Charles Dabney, born Dec. 20, 1770, married Dorcas Gilbert,
died July 10, 1825, in Brooklyn, Conn.

William Dabney, born July 6, 1772, married Hannah Jones,
died July 11, 1858, in Lynchburg, Va.

Mary Dabney, born Dec. 26, 1779, married Charles Young,
died Sept. 24, 1813, in Philadelphia.

James Dabney, born Mar. 3, 1782, died in 1820, in London.

Eliza Dabney, born Oct. 2, 1783, married John Spaulding,
died Apr. 12, 1853, in Wisconsin.

Charles Dabney (2d) died in Providence in 1785, aged 44 years, being born in 1741.

John Bass Dabney was in business in Alexandria, Virginia, at an early age, under the firm name of Rogerson & Dabney. In 1794 he went to France and remained there ten years, and was in business in Bordeaux. In 1804 he went to Fayal, Azores Islands, and in 1806 was made Consul for the Azores, which office he held until his death, September 2d, 1826. He was the first United States Consul appointed by the government, and filled the office for twenty years.

Charles William Dabney, who was born in Alexandria March 19th, 1794, held the office of consul from the death of John B. Dabney in 1826 until 1869, a period of forty-three years. He married Frances Alsop Pomeroy, a daughter of Samuel Wyllys Pomeroy, who was a descendant of Pomeroy, of Devon, England, who came to Hartford in 1633, and by collateral descent from Miles Standish and also John Alden.

Charles William and Frances (Pomeroy) Dabney had seven children, and the fourth was Samuel Wyllys Dabney, born in Fayal, January 6th, 1826. He was appointed United States Consul for the Azores in 1872, which office he now holds and resides in Fayal with his family.

It will therefore be seen that for *seventy-five years* the Dabneys have been United States consuls for the Azores, and consecutively, with the exception of three years, when President Grant appointed a Western editor in 1869 until 1872. The office was held by the Dabneys thus:

John B. Dabney,   from 1806 to 1826, 20 years.
Charles William Dabney, " 1826 to 1869, 43 "
Samuel Wyllys Dabney, " 1872 to 1884, 12 "

           Making 75 "

In this connection I copy from a newspaper extract in Mr. C. H. Dabney's Family Record, which is as follows:

The Dabney family in Fayal have, with only one brief interval of time, held the office of American Consul for several generations. "By their fidelity and integrity they made the office respected and honored, while they have rendered substantial service to their country. Their courtesy, dignity and hospitality, united with high intellectual culture and noble benevolence, have given a grace and charm to their homes, and these have spread like rays of sunlight to gladden and brighten the social life of Fayal. They remind us of one of the Roman patrician families in the palmiest days of that commonwealth, when patriotism, social virtues and devoted public service passed from father to son, making the name of the house illustrious."

Wm. Henry Dabney, recorded in another place as born at Fayal, May 25th, 1817, and married to Mary Ann Dabney Parker, was in the year 1862, appointed U. S. Consul of the Canary Islands, and held that office for twenty years, resigning in 1882. He removed with his family to the United States, and is now with his children residing in Boston. He has kindly furnished me with a long detailed account of the various branches of the Dabney family, but though it contains much that is of interest, it would spread out items that belong only to a connection of a collateral branch of our family, and must therefore be omitted. Suffice it to say, that the two brothers, John and Cornelius d'Aubigné, came to Virginia from Wales, and settled on the Pamunkey River, the one on the north and the other on the south side, at the spot known as "Dabney's Ferry" and about eighteen miles from Richmond. In the course of time the descendants of these two brothers spread down and up into the various neighboring counties, and some are to be found in Georgia and Mississippi. One from the latter State is now living in the city of Baltimore, hale and hearty, at the advanced age of eighty-seven years.

The Rev. Edward Fontaine, a descendant of the Dabneys, writes: "There is hardly an aristocratic Huguenot or cavalier family in the Old Dominion which is not impregnated with the prolific blood of that

brave, conscientious and highly accomplished confessor of the Protest-
ant faith, from whom the Dabneys of Gloucester, King William,
Hanover and all the tidewater counties of Virginia are descended.
They are connected with the Fontaines, Millers, Henrys (Patrick),
Winstons, Armisteads, Lewis, Lees, of Lowdon, Seldens, Carys, Alex-
anders, Nelsons, Moores, Carters, Stewarts, of Chantilly, Pollards, of
King William, Shirleys, Carrs, Walters, Taylors, Pendletons, Robin-
sons, Beverleys, etc."

IN MEMORIAM OF CHARLES HENRY DABNEY.

From the *Churchman.*

On the 15th of December, 1879, died at Hastings, England, after a
long and distressing illness, Charles Henry Dabney, aged 72 years.
On the 20th of July, 1880, his remains were returned to his native
country, and laid to rest in the beautiful cemetery at Swan Point,
Providence, R. I.

Immersed in business in Providence and New York for many years,
he never, amid his worldly cares, forgot the Master and His poor.   On
Sundays when most business men feel justified in taking some hours to
rest (after the services of the church), this "good and faithful servant"
went about doing good, visiting the sick and dying and the aged poor
wherever he could follow the footsteps of his Lord.   Even in his last
and mortal illness in a foreign land, his great loving heart still remembered the needy and aged pensioners of his charity, and he directed
his sorrowing and devoted wife (and helpmeet indeed to him in all
good works), to do as they had ever done, for all to whom they had
ministered.

In business his unflinching rectitude and high principles were bul-
warks of strength to his younger associates.   The great day alone will
disclose all this good man was in his generation to the world, to the
church, and especially to the poor and afflicted.   To his own large
family of relations he was the beloved and wise counselor and ever
helpful friend.   He leaves to his wife, his children and grandchildren
the blessed heritage of a spotless Christian name here, and a perfect
assurance of his present blessed and holy state, in the presence of his
adorable Lord and Saviour.   "G."

When a noble oak which has withstood the storms of many years
falls to the ground, it shocks all who have seen it in its glorious prime,
and awakens the regrets of all to see it lying prostrate on the earth.

So is it when a noble man lies prostrate in death and is carried to the grave. And the one to whose memory these few and feeble lines are written, was indeed like the noble tree, *a noble man*. With all the manly qualities he united the attributes of the real gentleman, and to those qualities of the man and the gentleman, those of the sincere Christian. Such a man, such a gentleman and such a Christian was *Charles Henry Dabney*.

He was the active and energetic secretary of the Blackstone Manufacturing Company, of Providence, R. I., and afterwards became its faithful and efficient treasurer. Its stockholders, principally the rich and influential house of Brown & Ives and the wealthy Cyrus Butler, witnessed his faithful and intelligent manner of conducting the large and important business of the company, and his ability and efficiency in the management of its large interests. These qualifications, combined with an undoubted integrity of character and conservative business views and opinions, caused his selection as a controlling partner in the large banking house and firm of Duncan, Sherman & Co., New York, in 1854. For several years he managed the affairs of this important house with marked ability, and in 1863, formed a new firm and house under the name of Dabney, Morgan & Co. After a successful career of several years, finding the cares and responsibilities of such a large business too heavy and onerous, he retired from business and removed with his family to Philadelphia, and here, with occasional visits to England to see his children and grandchildren, he passed the last few years of his life.

As a husband and father he was affectionate and devoted to a remarkable degree, but he yet had room in his large and generous heart for all who were connected with him by the ties of blood, and for pity and sympathy for the poor and distressed. His benevolence showed itself continually, and his benefactions often came to those who needed them, unasked and unsought. Cheerfully and freely did he give of the abundance with which God had blessed him, and his charities sprang from a loving and pitying nature as well as from a sense of duty as a follower of Christ. There are many left with grieving hearts to mourn his loss, who have tasted of his bounty and who have enshrined him in their memory with feelings of grateful love. He was an honest man, a just man, whose integrity was singularly strict and pure, ever looking on deceit with abhorrence and on falsehood with contempt. But it was as a Christian that his character was the most marked and shone the brightest. His aim was to do the will of God and "to live as becometh the gospel of Christ." With a strong and

8

an abiding faith he was an humble and devoted follower of his Lord and Master, Jesus Christ, and like Him he "went about doing good." This strong faith, which guided him when in health and life, upheld and cheered him when sickness and death came, and showed itself in the perfect calmness of spirit, in submissive resignation to God's holy will.

He lived beyond "the age of man, three-score years and ten," and has now gone to his reward, which we are assured is the inheritance of "the just made perfect;" full of years and leaving a record for all to imitate.

> "The sweet remembrance of the just
> Shall flourish while he sleeps in dust."

This feeble tribute to one, whose equal is but seldom seen, who possessed the rare combination of the just man and one with unaffected kindness of heart, I lay upon his grave with a loving memory and increasing regret, for—*I loved him.*   G. F. J.

SEVENTH GENERATION.

Emily Matilda Jones married **Joseph T. Daugherty, Esq.,** of Charlestown, Jefferson County, Virginia, July 7th, 1834.

CHILDREN:

Emily Matilda Daugherty, born Aug. 7, 1835, died
Ellen Maria Daugherty,   "   Mar. 27, 1837.
Joseph Jones Daugherty,   "   Dec. 22, 1838, died
Mary Josephine Daugherty, "   Nov.,   1840, died

Mr. Daugherty was a lawyer of ability, and with a good practice, and a refined, intelligent and courteous gentleman. He died December 13th, 1842.

Emily M. Daugherty married second, **Henry Marchant,** manufacturer, of Providence, and formerly of South Kingston, R. I., September 7th, 1848.

CHILDREN:

Mary Marchant,   born Dec. 26, 1850.
George Farquhar Marchant,   "   May 10, 1852.

8.   **Ellen Maria Daugherty,** daughter of J. T. and E. M. Daugherty, married **Edward Dodge** (his second wife, his first was her cousin, Caroline P. Alden), September 12th, 1860; no children.

8.   **Mary Marchant,** daughter of Henry and E. M. Marchant, married **Robert Little,** formerly of England, but in business and residing in Shanghai, China, April 29th, 1869; no children.

Mrs. Emily M. Marchant has presided over and managed "*The Teacher's Rest*," for a number of years. It is situated on high ground, on the west bank of the Hudson River, at Tomkin's Cove, Rockland County, New York, and quite near the House of the Good Shepherd, and the Rectory. The "Rest" was planned and intended for lady teachers, by Miss Clement, of Germantown, Pa., and is literally *a rest*, where those who are, or have been teachers, can take board for a few weeks, at a small expense. It has received ladies from all parts of the country, and has also received the praises of all who have dwelt under its roof, and has been termed by them a pleasant, refined, and delightful home. Its great advantages as to location (the views are always charming to the eye), the fine air to breathe, and above all, the excellence of its management, commend it highly and strongly to the benevolent, to carry it on successfully, and to the wearied teacher, who is desirous of summer rest and recreation.

RECAPITULATION.

The descendants of Alexander and Mary (Farquhar) Jones have been nearly four hundred in all. They had 11 children, 81 grandchildren, 196 great-grandchildren, and up to the present time, 84 great-great-grandchildren have been born. Therefore arranging them as follows:

Seventh generation, 11   Ninth generation, 196
Eighth   "   81   Tenth   "   84

the sum total is—372; of these 121 have died, leaving at the present time, 251 of the descendants living. These are widely scattered, and are to be found in Texas, New Mexico, Wyoming Territory, California, Wisconsin, Missouri, Iowa, Ohio, Virginia, West Virginia, Maryland, Pennsylvania, New York, New Jersey, Rhode Island and Massachusetts. One gratifying circumstance is, that in this large number there is no instance known of the arrest of any one of them, for the perpetration of any felony or crime. A large proportion of those who have arrived at maturity, are professors of the faith of Christ, as were their ancestors. May not this be the result of the prayers of those pious ancestors, who continually put up their petitions to God, that He would ever keep, bless, preserve and save their children and their children's children.

The following was received too late for insertion in its proper place on page 34:

Mr. Joseph M. Wilkinson died September 14th, 1884.

COLLATERAL BRANCHES.

FAMILIES AND THE DESCENDANTS
OF THE
Brothers and Sisters
OF
ALEXANDER AND MARY (FARQUHAR) JONES.

6. **David Jones**, second son of Joseph and Ruth (Nelson) Jones, married **Polly Strong**, of Williamsburg, Pa. (his first wife), in the year 1791.

CHILDREN:

Juliana Jones,   born Oct. 14, 1792, supposed died young.
Polly Strong Jones,   "   Jan. 22, 1794, died Sept. 14, 1798.
Joseph Strong Jones, "   Sept. 20, 1795, "   young.
Jane Wilson Jones,   "   "   1, 1797, "   June 23, 1798.
Nathaniel Jones,   "   Jan. 29, 1799, "   young.
David Nelson Jones, "   Apr. 4, 1803, "   Oct. 20, 1861.

David Jones married second, **Olive Sumner Chapin**, in October, 1833. He died September 29th, 1841, aged 74 years and 6 months.

He had lived many years in the interior of the State of New York (I think in Homer), but returned to Milford, his old home, married his second wife there, and died as above named at a good old age, leaving no children, but his youngest son, David Nelson Jones, who died unmarried at the age of 58 years.

Ballou, in his History of Milford, says of the father:

"David Jones was a man of good intellectual powers, well informed by books, travel and observation; a fluent and entertaining conversationalist, a pleasing letter writer and a gentleman of much enterprise." I well remember, when I was a boy, that where this uncle of mine then lived was thought to be a long and tiresome journey from Providence.

HANNAH JONES, WIFE OF WILLIAM DABNEY.
Born 1775.   Died 1836.

My father and my Uncle David could, therefore, see each other only at long intervals. In the list of births and deaths as recorded, all are said to have died young, with the exception of the youngest son. One or two members of our family have heard that a son or grandson lives in one of the Western States and in comfortable circumstances, and another son or grandson in the Adirondack region, N. Y. Not knowing how or where to address them (supposing this hearsay to be true), I am unable to record anything further or more definite.

6. **Nathaniel Jones,** third son of Joseph and Ruth (Nelson) Jones, married **Jane Field,** of Charleston, S. C., but no record of date is to be found. He died May 22d, 1808, and was buried in St. Philip's churchyard. No record whatever as to his wife's death has been discovered.

6. **Lucinda Sophronia Jones,** oldest daughter of Joseph and Ruth (Nelson) Jones, died, aged 5.

6. **Joseph Jones,** fourth son and fifth child of Joseph and Ruth (Nelson) Jones, died, aged 18.

6. **Hannah Jones,** sixth child and second daughter of Joseph and Ruth (Nelson) Jones, married **William Dabney,** August 24th, 1797.

CHILDREN:

William Dabney, Jr.,   born May 27, 1798, died June 8, 1798.
William Augustus Dabney,   "   Jan. 11, 1801,   "   July 9, 1830.
Robert Maxwell Dabney,   "   Apr. 6, 1802,   "   Sept. 12, 1802.
Nathaniel Jones Dabney,   "   June 18, 1803,   "   June 26, 1803.
Lucinda Eliza Dabney,   "   Sept. 24, 1804,   "   Feb. 19, 1880.
Charles Henry Dabney,   "   July 25, 1807,   "   Dec. 15, 1879.
Julia Sophia Dabney,   "   Sept. 16, 1809,   "   Sept. 27, 1863.
Emmeline Louisa Dabney,   "   June 3, 1811,   "   "   19, 1814.
Nancy King Dabney,   "   Feb. 4, 1813.

William Dabney, the father, died July 11, 1858, aged 87 years.
Hannah (Jones) Dabney, the mother, Aug 16, 1836, aged 61 years.

William Dabney was an amiable, intelligent man, a good husband and father, and one, who, throughout his long life, maintained the character of an honest man, a man of truth and integrity. All of his kindred stood high in the estimation of their fellow-men. His wife, my Aunt Hannah, was a superior woman. In early life, her beauty of person, her vivacity and pleasing manners, made her attractive to a great degree. In her early married life, all the qualities of mind and heart were rendered more beautiful by the influence of religion, which became the ruling power over her life. She was devoted to the service of her Redeemer, and showed her devotion by her marked influence on all who approached her. With her it was her life, her hope, her joy. In her conversation and in her letters (which were peculiarly marked in sentiment and expression), she ever showed that she was a disciple of the meek and lowly Jesus. Her influence for good was ever active, and is still felt, although she "sleeps in dust."

7. **Lucinda Eliza Dabney** married **Henry Monroe**, of Bridgewater, N. Y., in Providence, R. I., June 2d, 1829.

CHILDREN:

Julia Sophia Dabney Monroe, born March 15, 1830, died Nov. 30, 1830.
Emmeline Louisa Monroe,   "   Nov.   1, 1831.
James Henry Monroe,   "   July   6, 1835, "   Oct. 30, 1838.

8. **Emmeline Louisa Monroe** married **Charles M. White**, August 25th, 1852, in Cleveland, Ohio.

CHILDREN:

Henry Monroe White,   born Aug. 11, 1854, died Sept.   6, 1855.
Jesse Bishop White,   "   Aug. 15, 1856.
Emma Monroe White,   "   June   7, 1863,   "   Feb. 26, 1868.
William Dabney White,   "   Jan.   1, 1867.
Mary Keokee White,   "   Sept.   6, 1869.
Charles Nelson White,   "   April 9, 1872.

Charles M. White was the son of Moses White, of Warwick, Mass., and Mary (Andrews) White, of Providence, R. I., and was born in Cleveland, Ohio, May 21st, 1829.

Mrs. Lucinda Monroe lived for a great many years in Cleveland, Ohio, and with her only surviving child, Mrs. Charles M. White. She had reached her 76th year, and her death was without doubt, hastened by the tidings that her beloved brother, Charles Henry Dabney, had died in England, Dec. 15th, 1879. The writer had seen, only six months before, in Bristol, R. I., that brother with his two sisters enjoying a reunion, which proved to be their last. Mrs. Monroe died February 19th, 1880, two months after her brother's death.

7. **Charles Henry Dabney** married **Ellen Maria Jones,** April 27th, 1830.

Names of children among grandchildren of Alexander Jones.

7. **Julia Sophia Dabney** married **Albert Parker,** of Boston, July 12th, 1826.

CHILDREN:

Mary Anne Dabney Parker, born May 26, 1827, died Jan. 13, 1879.
Julia Lucinda Parker,   "   April 19, 1833, "   July 25, 1837.
Amanda Tarbell Parker,   "   April 10, 1835.

Julia Sophia (Dabney) Parker married second, **Pleasant Labbe,** of Virginia, February 7th, 1853. She was two years my senior in age, and I well remember what a beautiful girl she was. After her second marriage she lived in Lynchburg, Va., and died there September 27th, 1863, aged 54.

8. **Mary Anne Dabney Parker** married **William Henry Dabney** (who was born in Fayal, May 25th, 1817), September 3d, 1844. Mr. Dabney was from Fayal, Azores Islands, and son of the American consul Dabney.

CHILDREN:

Olivia Frederica Dabney, born Aug. 2, 1848.
Julia Parker Dabney,   "   Sept. 2, 1850.
William Dabney,   "   April 8, 1855.

When Mary Anne Dabney Parker married, her name was changed to Marianne.

8. **Amanda Tarbell Parker** married **Jeremiah A. Hunter,** of Lynchburg, Va., in that place, January 13th, 1859.

CHILDREN:

Henry Peter Hunter,   born Jan. 1, 1860.
Jerry Andrew Hunter,   "   Dec. 9, 1861.
William Dabney Hunter,   "   July 25, 1863.
Albert Pleasant Hunter,   "   June 16, 1866.
Mason Parker Hunter,   "   Sept. 4, 1868.
William Bishop Hunter,   "   Dec. 16, 1870.
Julia Noel Hunter,   "   Mar. 1, 1874.

Mr. Hunter carried on farming, in Virginia, and during the late war suffered inconveniences, privations and losses. A few years since he removed with his family to Massachusetts, on a farm in the neighborhood of Boston, and with his six boys, has been moderately successful in carrying it on. Mrs. Hunter must have inherited some of the sterling qualities of her grandmother, Hannah Dabney, bearing herself in sickness, adversity and trouble, with cheerful fortitude and courage.

7. **Nancy King Dabney** married **William W. Bishop**, of Providence, R. I., August 20th, 1840.

CHILDREN:

Fanny Winsor Bishop,	born May 28, 1841.	
Mary Josephine Bishop,	" April 20, 1843, died Jan. 8, 1865.	
Anna Jones Bishop,	" Jan. 10, 1845, " Jan. 8, 1865.	
Emma Franklin Bishop,	" Mar. 22, 1847, " Aug. 25, 1848.	
Ella Dabney Bishop,	" April 11, 1849, " Feb. 12, 1851.	
Ellen Bishop,	" Nov. 6, 1853.	

William W. Bishop at one time was manager of the Rhode Island Bleaching and Dyeing Company, but after a few years retired from it, engaging in no regular business pursuit afterwards. In January, 1865, a most sad and terrible calamity occurred, by which a fearful affliction fell upon this family. The father, with his two daughters, Mary and Anna, sailed from New York in a steamer bound for Port Royal, South Carolina, and on the second day out, about 50 miles from Cape May, she was lost. Sinking beneath them, as she had foundered, they were left (many of the passengers with life-preservers, floating on the ocean's broad surface), and for hours struggling with the winter's cold, and the swelling waters, until exhausted they sank into the dark depths of the sea. The father in the full prime of life, and the daughters only 22 and 20 years old. A fearful calamity and terrible affliction to the wife and mother and two daughters left.

8. **Ellen Bishop**, daughter of Wm. W. and Nancy K. Bishop, married **Wm. Alexander Cameron**, of England, November 7th, 1870; no children.

6. **Lucinda Jones** married **John King** (born October 29th, 1774), of Providence, R. I., September 21st, 1800.

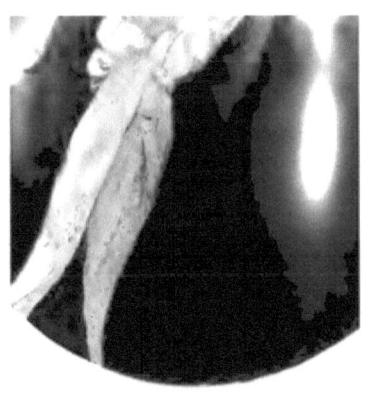

WILLIAM DABNEY.
Born 1772.　　　　Died 1858.

Harriet Jones King,	born	in	1803,	died	March 4, 1861.
Maria Cooke King,	"	Jan. 13, 1805,	"	May 23, 1837.
John William King,	"	Oct. 15, 1806,	"	April 23, 1852.
Hannah Louisa King,	"	Oct. 24, 1808,	"	Jan. 18, 1879.
Lucinda Sophronia King,	"	Nov. 4, 1811,	"	Oct. 7, 1868.
Mary Anne King,	"	May 31, 1815,	"	Mar. 12, 1850.
George Washington King,	"	July 18, 1816.
James Lawrence King,	"	Apr. 14, 1819.

John King was connected in business, in Charleston, with his brother-in-law, Wiswall Jones, under the firm of King & Jones, merchants, and for many years. John King died October 24th, 1847, and Lucinda, his wife, January 12th, 1852.

My Aunt Lucinda lived at the South, in Charleston, S. C., and we could not see her except at long intervals, when she could visit our home in the North. I well remember her when she came to visit my father and mother, and her two sisters, Aunts Hannah and Nancy. I think of her always as a sweet, motherly lady, fond of her relations and showing her attachment to them by the most gentle and loving ways. She, like her two sisters, had suffered afflictions, and, like them, had recognized in those visitations, the chastening and purifying love of God. She had given herself to the service of her Creator, and lived a Christian life, in peace with God, and in love and charity with mankind. With a meek and submissive spirit, she bore all her trials, and daily took up her cross and followed her Saviour as his faithful disciple. Many years have passed since she laid down life's burdens and sorrows, but she has left all who loved her a precious example of love, hope and trust, and a remembrance of a gentle and loving spirit that cannot fade.

7. **Harriet Jones King** married **Samuel N. Bishop**, in Charleston (who was born February 14th, 1797), January 8th, 1821.

Charles King Bishop,	born	1821.
Edward Augustus Bishop,	"	1828.
Adeline Amelia Bishop,	"	Jan. 29, 1831,	died	Jan. 4, 1872.

8. **Charles King Bishop** married three times. His first wife, **Anna Hester Lloyd**, October 22d, 1857; no children. She died

December 23d, 1859. His second wife, **Hannah Tilford Colloque,** in 1866; no children. She died the same year. His third wife, **Emmeline Melissa Colloque,** in 1870.

There were two children by this wife, their names and dates of birth unknown to me. In regard to Mr. Bishop's family, the foregoing is all I have been able to ascertain. Letters were written to him direct, and personal application used, but either no record has been kept, or a dislike felt to give names and dates. I am indebted to a relation for such information as I have given.

7. **Maria Cooke King** married **Horatio Leavitt,** in 1831.

CHILDREN:

Maria Leavitt,   born 1832.
Horatio Leavitt, Jr., " 1834.
The husband, wife and two children died May 23d, 1837.

The tragic end of this family was one of those unusual, startling and terrible events, which, happily at long intervals of time, occurs to shock and horrify relations, friends and the entire community. The husband and father took his wife and children to ride at Sullivan's Island, near Charleston, and drove into the water, as many were daily in the habit of doing. The beach is a beautiful one and very gradual in its descent into the sea, and for a long distance out. But there was one place where there was an abrupt declivity, steep and deep, and to that spot Mr. Leavitt drove with his lovely wife and their two children. It is believed (but this could only be conjecture), that they saw and felt their danger, but he, bent upon his own and their destruction, kept on until all were engulfed in the swelling and rushing waters. It was a fearful tragedy, and almost unique in its conception and accomplishment.

I well remember this lovely cousin of mine, first seeing her when she visited her relations in Providence. She was then in the full bloom of maidenhood, when her personal and mental charms, united to an amiable, graceful and pleasing deportment, won all hearts.

She became a devoted, earnest Christian, and in her love for her Saviour, grew a love for those "without God in the world." I have been told, that in company with a friend (Miss Holmes, a sister of Senator Holmes, of South Carolina), she would go out into the highways and by-ways of the city searching out the sin-stricken, suffering and afflicted poor. Those two earnest Christian women would strive to bring them into the fold of the blessed Master. Universally respected and esteemed, they were called "Paul and Barnabas." The one was taken in early womanhood by a sudden and fearful ending of her beautiful life, and the other lived to a good old age, having died but a few years since, more than 80 years old.

7.   **Hannah Louisa King** married **William Lloyd**, in Charleston, May 16th, 1826.

CHILDREN:

Louisa Jones Lloyd,	born Nov. 5, 1827, died Nov. 23, 1850.
William Grenville Lloyd,	" Dec. 1, 1829.
Theodore Whittemore Lloyd,"	July 22, 1831, " June 26, 1855.
Horatio Bishop Lloyd,	" Mar. 15, 1833, " Aug. 22, 1833.
Anna Hester Lloyd,	" " 12, 1836, " Dec. 23, 1859.
Julius Smith Lloyd,	" Apr. 5, 1838.
Angus McNeil Lloyd,	" Jan. 29, 1840.
Maria Harriet Lloyd,	" July 17, 1841, " Nov. 3, 1846.
Malvina Elvira Lloyd,	" Jan. 31, 1843, " Mar. 3, 1862.
Francis Porcher Lloyd,	" Oct. 20, 1847, " Sept. 3, 1849.

William Lloyd (born December 10th, 1804), died August 10th, 1856, aged 52 years.

Hannah Louisa (King) Lloyd, his wife, died January 18th, 1879, aged 71 years. She lived to see seven of her ten children die, before she was called away. Of an amiable, affectionate disposition, a fond and loving mother, who, in her long life's journey, had borne many trials and afflictions with true resignation, she at last "passed through things temporal, to those that are eternal."

8.   **Louisa Jones Lloyd** married **J. L. Yates**, February 3d, 1846; no children.

8.   **William Grenville Lloyd** married **Adeline Amelia Bishop**, in Baltimore, by Rev. Dr. Burnap, January 29th, 1852.

CHILDREN:

Ida Adeline Lloyd,	born Apr. 16, 1853.
Louisa Adelaide Lloyd,	" July 19, 1854, died Sept. 11, 1854.
Florence Augusta Lloyd,	" Sept. 4, 1856, " Aug. 23, 1859.
Clara Augusta Lloyd,	" Aug. 5, 1859, " " 8, 1860.
Charles Grenville Lloyd,	" Nov. 20, 1867.
Adeline Amelia Lloyd, } Twins {	" Jan. 4, 1872, " Jan. 11, 1872.
Emily Adeline Lloyd, } {	" " " " " " "

Adeline Amelia (Bishop) Lloyd, died January 4th, 1872.

8. **William Grenville Lloyd** married second, **Ellen Louisa Claggett**, in Brooklyn, N. Y., May 1st, 1876, by Rev. E. B. Claggett; no children.

8. **Julius Smith Lloyd** married **Adeline Emma Paddon,** December 28th, 1865.

CHILDREN:

Henry Grenville Lloyd, born Sept. 11, 1868.

8. **Angus McNeil Lloyd** married **Marietta Warner,** August 30th, 1865.

CHILDREN:

William Angus Lloyd, born June 7, 1866, died Apr., 1871.
Henry McNeil Lloyd, " June 7, 1869.
Mrs. Marietta (Warner) Lloyd died 18 .

8. **Angus McNeil Lloyd** married second, **Sallie W. Jones,** June 2d, 1880; no children.

7. **Lucinda Sophronia King** married **William W. Whittemore, Jr.,** May 20th, 1831. He was born in West Cambridge, Mass., April 27th, 1802.

CHILDREN:

Lucinda Elizabeth Whittemore, born Apr. 1, 1832, died Sept. 18, 1850.
Julia Adelaide Whittemore, " Feb. 10, 1834.
William Whittemore, 3d, " Oct. 26, 1836, " Dec. 15, 1861.

William Whittemore, Jr., died at Astoria, Oregon, December 15th, 1849.

Lucinda Sophronia Whittemore, died at New York City, October 7th, 1868.

William Whittemore, 3d, was a member of the Washington Light Infantry, and in "Hampton's Legion." He was in the battle of Manassas, but was unhurt, and died of typhoid fever a few months afterwards.

Well do I remember the bright, handsome cousin, Lucinda King, who came to make us a visit at Bellevue (my father's house in Providence), from Charleston, I think it was in 1828, when she was nearly 17. Her beauty attracted the young men, and she received much attention from those who visited at the house. Lucinda King was a belle and quite a favorite. But in later years there was a greater brightness about her, and that was her Christian faith and her Christian graces. The girlhood was lovely and bright, but far brighter and far better was the womanhood, when she had taken religion as her choice, and showed her faith by her works. In the family she was a peacemaker, and the Saviour said, "blessed are the peacemakers, for they shall be called the children of God." That is a glorious reward, and as a child of God, we have the blessed assurance that they shall become "an inheritor of the Kingdom of Heaven."

8. **Julia Adelaide Whittemore** married **Robert Alexander Young**, of Camden, S. C., in Charleston, S. C., March 12th, 1856.

CHILDREN:

Julia Adelaide Young,	born May 3, 1857.	
Robert Alexander Young, Jr.,	" May 12, 1860.	
Florence Whittemore Young,	" Mar. 3, 1863,	died July 10, 1863.
Marion Kershaw Young,	" Dec. 28, 1864.	
Lillian May Young,	" May 18, 1868.	

Mr. Young is a civil engineer, and has resided in Brooklyn, N. Y., many years.

7. **Mary Anne King** married **Elijah A. King**, of Providence, R. I., in the year 18 ; no children.

She died March 15th, 1850, and he died in New Orleans, some time in 1851.

7. **George Washington King** married **Frances Mary Porter**, in Charleston, August 1st, 1848; no children.

She was born April 1st, 1826, and died January 15th, 1852.

He married second, **Hannah Gray Cook**, of Lebanon, Tennessee, July 15th, 1856; no children.

7. **James Lawrence King** married **Sarah Ann Stubbs**, Bibb County, Ga., April 30th, 1843. He married second, **Martha A. E. Anderson**, of Va., May 8th, 1855.

CHILDREN:

Six by first wife.

Eudora Ann King,	born Mar. 21, 1844,	died May 28, 1845.
Horatio Leavitt King,	" Mar. 12, 1846.	
Maria Eugenia King,	" Dec. 24, 1847,	" Jan. 31, 1873.
John Angus King,	" Nov. 24, 1849,	" Nov. 24, 1877.
George E. King,	" Nov. 3, 1851.	
Chas. Lawrence King,	" July 22, 1853,	" Aug. 20, 1853.

Lulu King,	born Feb. 24, 1856, died Sept. 16, 1857.
Ella Gertrude King,	"	Mar. 9, 1858,	"	May 17, 1866.
Annie Lou King,	"	Dec. 6, 1860.
Charlie Jordan King,	"	Feb. 27, 1863,	"	Mar. 2, 1866.
James Lawrence King, Jr.,	"	July 22, 1866.
Clifford Anderson King,	"	Sept. 12, 1868,	"	July 16, 1873.
Eula May King,	"	Sept. 6, 1871.
Clyde Laurie King,	"	Aug. 31, 1874.
Eva Ethel King,	"	Aug. 21, 1879.

In the eight generations of the Jones family of Milford, Mass., this family of the Rev. James Lawrence King, shows the largest number of children. The family of Clara Churchill (Jones) Crittenden numbered fourteen children, and that of her father, the Rev. Alexander Jones, thirteen. There are also several families of twelve children, but this family, just recorded, of fifteen, outnumbers all the rest.

Mrs. Sarah Ann (Stubbs) King died in Atlanta, Ga., July 31st, 1853.

Martha A. E. Anderson, second wife of Rev. James Lawrence King, was the daughter of Major H. R. and M. R. Anderson, born in Nottoway County, Va., May 3d, 1837.

8. **Horatio Leavitt King** married **Josie Langford**, in Texas, "*about* 1875."

CHILDREN:

Angus Dallas King, born, date not given, died in infancy.
Lawrence King, " 1880, the date not given.

8. **George E. King** married **Iola Simmons**, daughter of Colonel Joseph P. Simmons, of Norcross, Ga., October 21st, 1874.

CHILDREN:

Jessie Eugenia King, born, date not given, died in infancy.
Lucille King, " Nov. 24, 1877.
Lillian King, " Sept. , 1879.
Christian King, " 1882.

The Rev. James Lawrence King is a Presbyterian minister, and has been in Georgia for a number of years. At present he resides in La Fayette, Walker County. Eight of his fifteen children have died.

6. **Nancy Jones** married **Elijah King,** of Providence, R. I., May 24th, 1802.

CHILDREN:

William Jones King, born June 14, 1803.
James King, " probably in 1805, ⎞
George King, " " " 1807, ⎬ died young.
Alexander King, " " " 1809, ⎠
Elijah A. King, " " " 1810, " in 1851.
Louisa King, " Feb. 28, 1814.
Mary Jones King, " Mar. 3, 1816.

It is much to be regretted that the above record is necessarily imperfect, and that the dates of some of the births and deaths cannot be had in detail. In a letter that I received from the eldest daughter, Mrs. Louisa Claggett, she writes: "I was the possessor of the family Bible, which contained all the necessary items, and it was accidentally destroyed, many years ago. I regret very much that I cannot give you the information you desire." As the memories of the other surviving members of the family cannot supply the information wanted, the record must, of course, remain imperfect.

Capt. Elijah King was a brother of John King, and they married two sisters, Nancy and Lucinda Jones. Capt. Elijah King went to sea from Providence, just before " The great gale," as it was called, in September, 1815. This extraordinary storm extended throughout the New England States, and far out in the Atlantic Ocean. Capt. King was never heard of after he sailed.

I have made efforts to discover the ancestry of John and Elijah King, but without success.

Mrs. Nancy (Jones) King died July 25th, 1845, aged 62 years.

7. **William Jones King** married **Lydia Coit Gilbert** (who was born April 4th, 1807), October 20th, 1832.

CHILDREN:

Elizabeth Gilbert King, born Feb. 13, 1835.
William Jones King, Jr, " Oct. 14, 1837.
Charles Goodrich King, " Jan. 3, 1840, died Aug. 27, 1881.
Edward Gilbert King, " Nov. 20, 1841, " Sept. 18, 1872.
Frederick Augustus King, " Jan. 17, 1844.
Lydia Gilbert King, " June 15, 1846,
Theodore Gilbert King, " May 28, 1850.

And here I would stop to pay a tribute to the memory of Mrs. Nancy Jones King. From my early childhood to the age of 18 years I was much and often under her hospitable roof, being intimate with and fond of my cousin, Elijah King. A warm welcome was always ready for me from Aunt Nancy, and I can recall many happy hours and days passed there in my boyhood.

She was eminently a Christian woman, energetic and untiring in advancing the cause of the Redeemer, and ever striving to bring the thoughtless and imprudent to a sense of their folly and sin and their absolute need of a Saviour. Taking perhaps rather a sombre view of a religious life and its duties, she strove to bring others to Christ by "the terrors of the law" rather than by the great and boundless love of God, as shown in the life and death of His Son. But she was "instant in season and out of season" in her endeavors "to bring souls to Christ," and no question of her sincerity can for a moment be entertained. She was resolute and determined to work for Him who had redeemed her from sin and death, and she did work and pray even to the end.

She was an affectionate and devoted mother, a loving relative and a consistent member of the Church of Christ. One of the many in the line of her family who had chosen the better part, one more added to the great company of the redeemed in Heaven.

8.   **William Jones King, Jr.**, married **Jeannie Pratt**, of Buffalo, N. Y., June 27th, 1860.

CHILDREN:

Samuel Pratt King,	born Feb. 12, 1863.
William Jones King, 3d,	" Oct. 13, 1864.
Daisy Fletcher King,	" Mar. 12, 1872.

Jeannie (Pratt) King died September 24th, 1872.

8.   **William Jones King, Jr.**, married second, **Nellie Augusta Gould**, May 4th, 1877; no children.

8.   **Charles Goodrich King** married **Frances Ellen Jones**, April 26th, 1866.
List of the children under the head of George F. Jones' family.

8.   **Edward Gilbert King** married **Mary Atwater**, daughter of Charles Atwater, of New Haven, May 31st, 1865, by Rev. Dr. Harwood.

CHILDREN:

Edward Gilbert King, Jr., born Feb. 19, 1867.
Frederica Augusta King,   "   Apr. 5, 1868.
Gilbert Montgomery King,   "   Sept. 15, 1871.
William Jones King, 4th,   "   Jan. 1, 1873.

Edward Gilbert King died September 18th, 1872, aged 31 years.

Mary (Atwater) King died January 22d, 1873, aged about 25 years

The early deaths of this husband and wife in their early manhood and womanhood were sad and touching—cut off as they were in their young lives. This young and beautiful wife and mother left four young children, the eldest barely six years old, the youngest only three weeks, fatherless and motherless. But He "who ordereth all things right," raised up one, who has for years devoted herself to their welfare, and by her care for their physical and moral culture, has filled the place of their lost mother. Their father's sister has given herself to the sacred and responsible duties which have devolved upon her, and is endeavoring to "bring them up in the nurture and admonition of the Lord."

8. **Frederick Augustus King** married **Lorania Carrington Jones,** April 7th, 1870.

List of the children under the head of George F. Jones' family.

8. **Lydia Gilbert King** married **Edmund Furse,** of Rome, Italy (born March 30th, 1841), October 25th, 1871.

CHILDREN:

Lydia Coit Furse,   born Sept. 28, 1872, died Aug. 26, 1873.
Elizabeth Gilbert Furse, "   Jan. 31, 1874.
Emilie Ronald Furse,   "   Nov. 17, 1875.
Edmund William Furse,   "   Aug. 17, 1877.
George Armand Furse,   "   Feb. 21, 1880.
Charles Francis Furse, "   Mar. 16, 1882.
William King Furse,   "   June 26, 1883.

8. **Theodore Gilbert King** married **Anna Rebecca Barry,** of New York, October 24th, 1877, by Rev. John Cotton Smith, D.D.; no children.

7. **Louisa King** married **Rufus Claggett** in Providence, October 25th, 1834.

9

CHILDREN:

Mary Louisa Claggett,	born Apr. 10, 1835.
Charles Clifton Claggett,	" June 12, 1837.
Henry Austin Claggett,	" Oct. 14, 1839.
Cornelia Jones Claggett,	" Jan. 29, 1842.
Ellen Louise Claggett,	" Dec. 28, 1844.
Augustus King Claggett,	" Aug. 4, 1846.
Eugene William Claggett, } twins {	" Nov. 28, 1848.
Clarence Duroy Claggett, } twins {	" Nov. 28, 1848, died Aug. 28, 1849.

8. **Charles Clifton Claggett** married **Anna Matilda Burke,** October 4th, 1867.

CHILDREN:

Annie Louisa Claggett, born July 4, 1868.
John Bagley Claggett, " Apr. 18, 1870, died June 4, 1875.
Florence May Claggett, " Mar. 1, 1875.

8. **Cornelia Jones Claggett** married **Oliver Wilcox Marvin,** April 22d, 1865.

CHILDREN:

Cornelia Marvin,	born Jan. 17, 1866.
Ida Louisa Marvin,	" Jan. 3, 1868.
Augusta Wilcox Marvin,	" Sept. 2, 1869.

8. **Ellen Louise Claggett** married **William Grenville Lloyd,** May 1st, 1876; no children.

WILLIAM JONES KING.

The following communication I insert with great pleasure:

William Jones King, born June 14th, 1803, is now in his eighty-second year, and though borne down with the weight of severe physical troubles, preserves the strong, well-balanced mind which has made him successful beyond his fellows, and the earnest faith, dating from his boyhood, still sustains his declining years.

Captain Elijah King, his father, sailed from Providence five days before the great September gale of 1815, and the vessel, in which all but a trifling portion of his property was invested, was never again heard from. Thus at 12 years of age the oldest son was obliged to abandon his school and work for his mother and family, which he did heartily and lovingly. He filled one position after another with credit, gradually gaining for himself the confidence and respect of all. Ill health obliged him to give up his position as cashier of the Union Bank of this city, and in 1836, he rented the office No. 8 Westminster Street, where, with the exception of one or two years, he has since remained. His success as a merchant soon became assured, and he passed unhurt through all the troubles that are incident to a long mercantile career, and now retires from all business with abundant prosperity as the crown of an upright business life.

He was never willing to accept any political office, however pressing the demand, and not seeking the honors most men crave, he peremptorily declined the Presidency of his old bank, where he had served as cashier. But he willingly gave his time and best thoughts as trustee of the Reform School for twenty-five years; and many of the boys there have come to him in after years, to thank him for the words of advice which found a place in their hearts and bore fruit. He was also deeply interested in the Young Ladies' Seminary at Norton, Massachusetts, being one of its trustees for forty years. The following from a late letter of the present principal shows how good a work under his Master's guidance he accomplished there: "The thought of opening school at the beginning of another year without having your presence to lead us in our first Friday evening devotions, is indeed a very painful thought. I cannot bear to think that you may not come again to the school which has ever been so dear to you and for which you have done so much. How many good, noble women there are, who hold you in grateful remembrance for the help you have given them!"

Early in life he became an enthusiastic worker in the Sunday School, and was superintendent of that of the Beneficent Church for eighteen years, and again of the Central Church for twenty-eight years, doing much to advance the attractiveness and effectiveness of their teachings. Who that has heard Deacon King in his Sunday School addresses, will ever forget his apt illustrations and clear expositions of Bible truths?

"They that be wise, shall shine as the light, and they that turn many to righteousness, as the stars, forever and ever."

"Diligent in business, fervent in spirit, serving the Lord."

6. **Wiswall Jones,** youngest son of Joseph, Jr., and Ruth (Nelson) Jones, was married by Rev. Dr. Pope to **Martha W. Price** at Savana, La Mar Island, Jamaica, in Grace Church, April 19th, 1817.

CHILDREN:

Mary Price Jones, born Oct. 17, 1818.
Frances Susan Jones, " Aug. 11, 1820.
Augustus Horatio Jones, " Sept. 9, 1823.
Alexander David Jones, " Sept. 3, 1825, died April 17, 1866.
Caroline Augusta Jones, " Jan. 24, 1828.
Lucius Manlius Jones, " Oct. 10, 1829, " July 26, 1879.

7. **Mary Price Jones** married **Dr. Albert H. Nagel**, of Columbia, S. C., November 3d, 1841.

CHILDREN:

William Percival Nagel, born in Columbia, Dec. 11, 1843.

He lost his life in the late civil war at James' Island, February 10th, 1865. The only hope of his mother, and aged 21 years and 2 months.

7. **Frances Susan Jones** married **William B. Smith** in Charleston, November 11th, 1840.

CHILDREN:

Fanny Rosa Smith, born Feb. 22, 1843.
Helen Smith, " Jan. 21, 1847.
Pauline Smith, " June 26, 1850.

8. **Fanny Rosa Smith** married **Andrew Hasel Heyward** at Grace Church, Charleston, March 1st, 1866.

CHILDREN:

Wm. B. Smith Heyward, born Jan. 10, 1867,
Georgiana Hasel Heyward, " Dec. 23, 1869.
Andrew Hasel Heyward, Jr., " Dec. 22, 1871, died Oct. 13, 1872.
Frances Smith Heyward, " Sept. 22, 1873.
John Ashe Heyward, " Feb. 22, 1875.
Lillie Williman Heyward, " Feb. 17, 1877.
Catharine Lechmere Heyward, " Sept. 8, 1879.
Pauline Heyward, " Sept. 21, 1881.
Andrew Hasel Heyward, 3d, " Jan. 11, 1883.

8. **Helen Smith** married **W. B. Whaley** in Pendleton, S. C., August 29th, 1865.

CHILDREN:

William Burrows Smith Whaley, born May 24, 1866.
Helen Smith Whaley, " Aug. 18, 1868.
Thomas Prioleau Whaley, " July 12, 1870.
Richard Smith Whaley, " July 15, 1874.
Francis Percival Whaley, " Apr. 29, 1879, d. Feb. 20, 1882.

8. **Pauline Smith** married **Irvine Keith Heyward** in Grace Church, Charleston, April 23d, 1873.

CHILDREN:

Irvine Keith Heyward, Jr., born Nov. 9, 1875.
Irvine Keith Heyward, the father, died at Sullivan's Island, September 21st, 1880.

7. **Augustus Horatio Jones** married **Julia Ann Fitch**, of Columbia, S. C., January 30th, 1851.

CHILDREN:

Julia Augusta Jones, born June 9, 1853.
William Mosely Jones, " Sept. 14, 1856.
Frederick Augustus Jones, " Oct. 19, 1858.
Francis Fitch Jones, " Mar. 18, 1860.
Wiswall Price Jones, " Jan. 16, 1862.
Leila Sumter Jones, " Aug. 21, 1864.
Annie Vane Jones, " Oct. 14, 1866.
Caroline Smith Jones, " June 4, 1869.

8. **Julia Augusta Jones** married **Dr. James Henry Parker** in Charleston, April 26th, 1877; no children.

Dr. Parker was engaged in business pursuits in Charleston, and afterwards removed his home and business to New York City, where he is now actively engaged, with branch houses in two other cities.

8. **William Mosely Jones** married **Sallie Fell** at Mount Pleasant, October 16th, 1881.

CHILDREN:

Augustus Horatio Jones, 2d, born Sept. 17, 1882, died Sept. 29, 1883
A daughter, not yet named, " Feb. 13, 1884.

8. **Leila Sumter Jones** married **Walton Storm,** of New York, in Charleston, November 15th, 1883.

Walton Storm, Jr., born Sept. 17, 1884.

7. **Alexander David Jones** married **Mary E. H. Whilden,** December 10th, 1850.

Mary Katharine Jones, born Apr. 18, 1854.

Mrs. Mary E. H. Jones died in Charleston, November 23d, 1857.

8. **Mary Katharine Jones** married **Edward Fisher Holmes** in Charleston, June 17th, 1874.

James Gadsden Holmes, born Feb. 13, 1876, died Nov. 8, 1881.
Julia Augusta Holmes,   "   Sept. 26, 1879.
Amelia Levering Holmes, "   Mar. 8, 1881.
Anna Wilcox Holmes,   "   May 28, 1883.

7. **Alexander David Jones** married second, **Fanny Mather Fitch** at Williamsburg, S. C., December 23d, 1862.

Edith Mather Jones, born Aug. 13, 1866.

Alexander David Jones died in Charleston, April 17th, 1866, in his 41st year.

7. **Caroline Augusta Jones** married **George Edward Gibbon,** of Charleston, February 2d, 1848.

Mary Elizabeth Gibbon,   born Apr. 21, 1850.
George Edward Gibbon, Jr., "   Jan. 24, 1853.
Albert Henry Gibbon,   "   Aug. 29, 1858.
Caroline Agusta Gibbon,   "   Feb. 3, 1863.
Lucia Jones Gibbon,   "   May 29, 1866.
Charles William Gibbon,   "   Jan. 20, 1871.

8. **Mary Elizabeth Gibbon** married **William Webb**, of Charleston, November 21st, 1878.

CHILDREN:

Caroline Augusta Webb, born Oct. 31, 1879.
Susan Waring Webb, " Oct. 10, 1881.

Mrs. Caroline Augusta Gibbon died in Charleston, June 3d, 1875.
Mr. George E. Gibbon also died in Charleston, October 31st, 1881.

I had never seen my cousin Caroline until about a year before her death, when she came to my house in West Philadelphia while on a visit to the North. I was strongly reminded of her mother (Aunt Martha, as we used to call her), and her pleasing manners were very much the same.

I was impressed with her unaffected, sincere and winning address, and hoped, though living so far apart, that our acquaintance would be increased. But death comes at times very unexpectedly, taking away from us those we cherish, admire and love, and in less than one short year this lovely woman was numbered with the dead. Her charm and grace of manner, speaking so plainly of her lovely character, will remain in our memory. Seldom has one been called away from a circle of loving friends and relatives so sweet in disposition, so lovely in her character and manner, as Caroline Augusta Gibbon.

7. **Lucius Manlius Jones** married **Letitia Laidler King** (born April 16th, 1835), of Charleston, January 8th, 1857.

CHILDREN:

Arthur Laidler Jones, born Sept. 15, 1858.
Mary Price Jones, " Nov. 9, 1859, died Apr. 24, 1860.
Ella Florence Jones, " Dec. 7, 1860.
Letitia Adeline Jones, " Feb. 8, 1863.
Rosa Lillian Jones, " July 12, 1864.
Jesse King Jones, " Aug. 7, 1866, " Oct. 24, 1876.

Lucius Manlius Jones died at Saluda, N. C., July 26th, 1879, in his 50th year.

Augustus H. and Lucius M. Jones, the oldest and the youngest brother, sons of Wiswall Jones, were for many years partners in business with Wm. B. Smith, their brother-in-law, in Charleston, and under the firm name of W. B. Smith & Co. This firm has been in existence

I think, about or perhaps over fifty years. I understand that it still exists, but instead of dealing in cotton or general goods, the business is principally banking. It has been one of the few successful houses, and it is without doubt owing to watchful attention, wise management and good business abilities.

8. **Ella Florence Jones** married **Basil Wallace Jones**, of Williamsburg, S. C., April 13th, 1882.

CHILDREN:

Basil Wallace Jones, Jr., born Jan. 16, 1883.
Arthur Laidler Jones, 2d,   "   Apr. 23, 1884.

8. **Letitia Adeline Jones** married **Stonewall Jackson Huggins**, of Williamsburg, S. C., November 7th, 1883.

My uncle, Wiswall Jones, was the youngest son of Joseph, Jr., and Ruth (Nelson) Jones, and my father's youngest brother. He and his brother Noah were named by their father for an intimate friend and connection, Noah Wiswall. I find in Ballou's history of Milford, that he was born in the year 1741. He was of the family of Elder Thomas Wiswall, who came from England in 1635, and settled in Dorchester. His father was Thomas Wiswall, his grandfather Lieut. Thomas, his great-grandfather, Captain Noah, and his great-great-grandfather, Elder Thomas. He, Noah Wiswall, was of the fifth generation of Wiswall, and married Susanna Tenney, widow of Isaac Tenney, and daughter of Jonathan and Lydia (Jones) Whitney, and a granddaughter of Elder John Jones. It is said that the Wiswalls were men of distinction.

Between my father and his brother Wiswall, there existed a strong and enduring attachment, a fond brotherly love. I vividly recall his appearance, address, manners and conversation, when he came to Providence from Charleston, to make his almost yearly visits in summer, at his brother's house and to see his two sisters, Hannah and Nancy, who lived in Providence.

Bright, genial, affable, and withal the perfect gentleman, he won the praise of friends as well as relatives, who all admired and loved him. Integrity, honesty and ability were his to a marked degree, and these qualities shone brightly throughout his life. He lived with an endeavor to "do unto others, as you would they should do unto you," and "thus to fulfil the law of Christ." He died on his brother Alexander's birthday, August 8th, 1842.

MATERNAL ANCESTORS

OF

LORANIA CARRINGTON HOPPIN,

Wife of George F. Jones.

FIRST GENERATION.

The Austerfield Church in Yorkshire, England, has the following:

William Bradford—First.

Thomas Bradford, baptized Mar. 9, 1558.
Robert Bradford, " June 25, 1561.
Elizabeth Bradford, " July 16, 1570.

William Bradford married, June 28th, 1584, **Alice Hanson.**

THEIR CHILDREN WERE:

Margaret Bradford, born Mar. 8, 1585.
Alice Bradford, " Oct. 30, 1587.
William Bradford (the Pilgrim), " Mar. 19, 1589.

William Bradford, first, death unknown as to the month and day, but his burial took place, as on record, January 11th, 1596.

Alice (Hanson) Bradford's date of death is not on record.

William Bradford came to this country with the "Pilgrim Fathers" in the "Mayflower," landing at Plymouth, December 21st, 1620.

He married, for his second wife, **Alice Southworth** (whose name has been often mentioned in poetry and romance), August 14th, 1623. Her maiden name was Carpenter, and she was born in Lincolnshire, England, in 1590, arriving in Plymouth in the schooner "Ann" in 1623. She died March 26th, 1670.

SECOND GENERATION.

William and **Alice** (**Southworth**) **Bradford.**

THEIR CHILDREN WERE:

William Bradford, 3d, born June 17, 1624.
Mercy Bradford,   "   in 1626.
Joseph Bradford,   "   in 1630.

William Bradford died May 9th, 1657.

THIRD GENERATION.

William Bradford, 3d, married, in 1652 (month and day not known), **Alice Richards.**

(Here are three wives in succession named Alice.)

CHILDREN:

John, born in 1653; William, 1655; Thomas, 1657; **Samuel,** 1659; Alice, 1661; Hannah, 1663; Mercy, 1665; Melatiah, 1667; Mary, 1669; Sarah, 1671; Israel, 1673; Ephraim, 1675; David, 1677, and Hezekiah, 1679.

William Bradford, 3d, died Feb. 20th, 1703; his wife's death not recorded.

FOURTH GENERATION.

Samuel Bradford married **Hannah Rogers,** at Duxbury, Mass., in July, 1688.

CHILDREN:

Hannah, born in 1689; Gershom, 1691; **Perez,** 1693; Elizabeth, 1696; Jerusha, 1699; Wealthea, 1702; Gamaliel, 1704.

Samuel Bradford died April 11th, 1714; his wife's death not known.

FIFTH GENERATION.

Perez Bradford married **Abigail Belcher,** at Attleboro, Mass., in the year 1715.

CHILDREN:

Perez, born in 1716; Joel, 1717; George, 1718; John, 1719; Joseph, 1720; **Abigail,** May 15th, 1721; Mary, 1723, and Elizabeth, 1724.

The deaths of Perez Bradford and his wife were not found recorded.

SIXTH GENERATION.

Abigail Bradford married **Samuel Lee, Jr.**, at Swansey, December 31st, 1740.

CHILDREN:

Charles, born September 15th, 1742; Abigail, 1744; Samuel, 1746; Elizabeth, 1748; Margaret, 1750; Mary, 1752; Bradford, 1754; Mary, 1756; William, 1758; Rebecca, 1760, and Belcher, 1763.

Neither the death of Abigail (Bradford) Lee or that of her husband is known.

SEVENTH GENERATION.

Charles Lee (born September 15th, 1742) married **Amy Harris,** at Johnston, R. I., in the year 1765.

Their only child was Abigail Lee, born Oct. 29th, 1766.

The date of death of Charles Lee was August 22d, 1813, and that of his wife, Amy Lee, is not known.

EIGHTH GENERATION.

Abigail Lee, daughter of Charles and Amy (Harris) Lee, married **Samuel Bourse Bowler** in Providence, R. I., early in the year 1786.

CHILDREN:

Charles Lee Bowler,   born Dec. 9, 1786.
Amy Harris Bowler,   "   Mar. 10, 1789.

Samuel Bourse Bowler died May 13th, 1790, and his wife, Abigail (Lee) Bowler, died February 15th, 1840, aged 74 years.

NINTH GENERATION.

Amy Harris Bowler, daughter of Samuel B. and Abigail (Lee) Bowler, married **Henry Hoppin** in Providence, R. I., November 26th, 1810.

By this marriage, Henry Hoppin of the *sixth* Rawson generation, and Amy Harris Bowler of the *ninth* Bradford generation, united the two, one being a lineal descendant of Edward Rawson, first Secretary of Massachusetts Colony, and the other of William Bradford, the first Governor of the same.

The children of Henry and Amy H. Hoppin will be found recorded under the head of the Paternal Ancestors of Lorania Carrington Hoppin.

In the historical and State papers many facts and occurrences are to be found, but a much larger space than we have at our disposal, would be required to put them on record. A few may be named.

The Bradfords originated in Austerfield, England, and Mr. L. B. Hoppin when in England visited the place and examined the records in the old church there. He has in his possession a picture of the church. Governor William Bradford's first wife was *Dorothy May*, who was drowned December 7th, 1620, before the Pilgrims landed at Plymouth. His second wife was the widow, "Sweet Alice Southworth," as she was called, and they were married in Plymouth, August 14th, 1623. It is stated that she was highly respected by the whole colony. Major William Bradford was commander-in-chief of the Plymouth forces in the King Philip war. He often exposed himself to all its perils, and on one occasion received a bullet into his body, which he carried with him the rest of his life. Samuel Bradford was a prominent man in the community, and his son Perez was a member of the General Council, Selectman, etc.

PATERNAL ANCESTORS

OF

LORANIA CARRINGTON HOPPIN,

Wife of George F. Jones.

FIRST GENERATION.

Edward Rawson was born in Gillingham, Dorsetshire, England, April 16th, 1615.

Rachel Perne, his wife, date of birth unknown.

She was a daughter of Thomas Perne, and granddaughter of John Hooker, whose wife was a Grindall, sister of Archbishop Grindall, of London, York and Canterbury in the time of Queen Elizabeth.

THEIR CHILDREN WERE 10:

Edward, born in 1638; Rachel, 1641; David, 1644; Perne, 1646; William, 1651; Susan, 1654; Rebecca, 1656; Elizabeth, 1657, and John and **Grindall**, 1659.

Edward Rawson was Secretary of the Colony of Massachusetts many years, and was spoken of as the Honorable Edward Rawson. The writer has in his possession a document recording the verdict of " The Court of Assistants," dated in Boston, September 5th, 1671.

Edward Rawson died August 27th, 1693, date of his wife's death unknown.

SECOND GENERATION.

Grindall Rawson was born January 23d, 1659.

Susannah Wilson, his wife. They were married (month and day not given) in the year 1682.

THEIR CHILDREN WERE 11:

Edmund, 1684; John, 1685; Susannah, 1686; Edmon, 1689; **Wilson,** July 23d, 1692; John, 1695; Mary, 1699; Rachel, 1701; David, 1703; Grindall, 1707, and Elizabeth, 1710.

Grindall Rawson died February 6th, 1715, and Susannah, his wife, July 8th, 1748.

THIRD GENERATION.

Wilson Rawson and **Margaret Arthur**, his wife, were married May 4th, 1712, her date of birth being unknown, or not on record.

THEIR CHILDREN WERE 9:

Wilson, 1713; **Thomas**, 1715; Mary, 1717; Grindall, 1719; Edward, 1721; Stephen, 1722; Paul, 1725; John, 1727, and Priscilla, 1733.

Wilson Rawson died December 1st, 1736, and Margaret, his wife, November 14th, 1757.

FOURTH GENERATION.

Thomas Rawson and **Anna Waldron**, his wife, were married in the year 1737, month and day not known, and her birth date not on record.

THEIR CHILDREN WERE 12:

William Rawson,	born Nov. 11, 1738,	married	Mary Aldrich.
Priscilla Rawson,	" May 22, 1740,	"	Ephraim Walker, Providence, R. I.
Stephen Rawson,	" Mar. 2, 1743,	"	Silence Ward.
Nathaniel Rawson,	" July 9, 1745,	"	Elizabeth Nelson.
Rachel Rawson,	" Mar. 6, 1747,	"	Stephen Chapin.
Anne Rawson,	" May 8, 1749,	"	Col. Benj. Hoppin, Providence, R. I.
Persis Rawson,	" May 6, 1751,	"	Joseph Carpenter.
Margaret Rawson,	" Apr. 7, 1753,	"	Benjamin Walker.
Thomas J. Rawson,	" May —, 1755, died young.		
Catharine Rawson,	" May 20, 1757,	" in 1761.	
Pernell Rawson,	" July 12, 1760,	" October, 1761.	
Francis Rawson,	" Jan. 8, 1763,	" April 3, 1811.	

Anna (Waldron) Rawson died in 1783, and her husband married, second, Hannah Nelson in 1784. He died July 10th, 1802 and she in 1803.

In the first part of this book, relative to the fifth generation of G. F. Jones' Paternal Ancestors, there are notes of Ruth Nelson's family. By reference to them it will be seen that she was the daughter of Nehemiah Nelson and Hannah (Sheffield) Nelson. The second wife of Thomas Rawson, as above named, was Nehemiah Nelson's widow. Thomas and his wife lived a long time on "The Nelson Place," in

Milford, both being members of the Congregational Church, and were highly respected by the entire community.

It will also be seen by looking at the two records of G. F. Jones and his wife's *paternal* ancestors, that G. F. Jones' grandmother was a sister of Nathaniel Rawson's wife, and that he (the fifth in descent from the Honorable Edward) was the brother of L. C. Jones' grandmother, or, that Nathaniel Rawson and his wife were great-uncle and aunt to George F. Jones *and the same* to his wife, Lorania C. Hoppin. Therefore in the seventh generation the two families were brought into one.

FIFTH GENERATION.

Anne Rawson married **Colonel Benjamin Hoppin**, of Providence, R. I., January 24th, 1770.

Their Children were 8:

Davis Ward Hoppin,	born May	6, 1771.
Candace Hoppin,	" Sept.	11, 1772.
Lorania Hoppin,	" July	19, 1774.
Benjamin Hoppin, 4th,	" May	26, 1777.
George W. Hoppin,	" Aug.	19, 1779.
Thomas Coles Hoppin,	" Oct.	3, 1785.
Levi Hoppin,	" July	3, 1787.
Henry Hoppin,	" Sept.	13, 1789.

Anne (Rawson) Hoppin died January 1st, 1794, and in about six months, May 28th, 1794, he married, second, Mary Whitney.

Col. Benjamin Hoppin died November 30th, 1809.

The Hoppin families in this country are supposed to be descendants of Thomas Hoppin (or Hoppen), of Northumberland, England. Mr. Lloyd B. Hoppin, who was in England some ten or eleven years ago (I think in 1873), states that in his examination of books, annals and registers he only found one of the name of Hoppin. The conclusion, therefore, that he was the progenitor of the Hoppins in this our land, seems to be correct. Thomas Hoppin, whose name is recorded in Northumberland, *Liber Feoder*, page 24, and in the time of Elizabeth, Queen of England, must be the first of that name that can be traced, and his son Stephen must have come to and settled in the colony of Massachusetts and perhaps among the later Pilgrims.

Thomas Hoppin, the father of Stephen, lived in a place called

Hoppin, a township in Bamborough parish, and about 320 miles from London. He at one time held large estates, but a son of his, in combat with a knight named Orde, slew him and then fled to Flanders, and for this those estates were confiscated.

Stephen was born in 1626, and probably was quite young when he crossed the ocean. He settled in Dorchester, Mass., and married there **Hannah Makepeace** in the year 1647. They had nine children as follows:

Deliverance,	born in Dorchester,		in 1648.
John,	"	"	in 1649.
Stephen,	"	"	in 1651.
Hannah,	"	"	in 1652.
Sarah,	"	"	in 1654.
Thomas,	"	Roxbury, Nov. 21, 1655.	
Opportunity,	"	"	Nov. 15, 1657.
Joseph,	"	"	in 1659.
Benjamin,	"	"	in 1666.

Stephen, the father, died December 1st, 1677.

One account states that they settled in Gloucester, and afterwards removed to Attleboro, Mass., a township about eight miles from Providence, R. I., and near the boundary line dividing Rhode Island and Massachusetts. But another states that it was another generation that made this change of residence. It is not absolutely important. And here a question arises, whether Stephen was the son or the grandson of Thomas Hoppin. The latter, as before stated, was living "in the time of Queen Elizabeth," and she died March 24th, 1603.

Her reign lasted about forty-five years. Had our ancestors in the fifteenth and sixteenth centuries, kept carefully written records, a vast amount of trouble would have been avoided by their posterity.

Benjamin Hoppin, born in 1666, and son of Stephen, married **Elizabeth** (surname not known), probably in the year 1702.

THEY HAD THREE CHILDREN:

Benjamin, 2d, born Apr. 12, 1703.
Hannah, " Oct. 15, 1705.
John, " " 17, 1707.

Benjamin Hoppin died Apr. 11th, 1732, aged 66 years.

Benjamin Hoppin, 2d, married **Mary Day,** April 22d, 1731.

Benjamin, 3d, born May 16, 1732, died Apr. 26, 1733.
Mary,   "   Apr. 17, 1736.
Betty,   "   Nov. 5, 1741.

Mary (Day) Hoppin died in the year 1743, and her husband married second, **Phœbe Davis**, June 27th, 1745.

THEY HAD ONLY ONE CHILD:
Benjamin, 4th, born May 12th, 1747.

He is generally called the third Benjamin, but by the foregoing record, he must be the fourth Benjamin Hoppin. It may have been the third, because his brother of that name only lived about a year. His father having been lost at sea, he was living, in 1764, in the town of Providence, with his widowed mother. In 1772, two years after he had married, he occupied a house in Broad Street, next to "The Congregational Church of Christ," the Rev. Mr. Snow, pastor, commonly called in the succeeding generation, "Mr. Wilson's church."

1776, a regiment of 750 men was called for by the General Assembly of the State, and he was captain of a company in that regiment, which was under the command of Colonel Lippitt. He was afterwards an officer in Colonel John Topham's regiment, and distinguished himself at Princeton, Red Bank, etc. He was collector of taxes after leaving the army, and in 1782 was appointed as "vendue master," making him the first auctioneer in Providence.

That same year he entered into business with a Mr. Smart, and their advertisement was found in the *Providence Gazette* of December 13th, 1782. In 1785, he was named as one of the corporators of "The Beneficent Congregational Society." In 1790 business was carried on under the firm name of Hoppin & Snow. In the year 1799, he was elected Representative to the General Assembly. On the 30th of November, 1809, he died at the age of 62. At the time of his death, he and his son Benjamin were partners in the auction business, which was afterwards carried on by his two sons, Benjamin and Thomas, under the firm name of B. & T. C. Hoppin

The various families of the Hoppins have continued for many years to be prominent citizens of Providence, and have maintained their position in each succeeding generation.

In January, 1794, the following obituary notice of the death of Mrs. Annie Rawson Hoppin appeared in the *Providence Gazette:*

10

"On Wednesday morning last, January 1st, departed this life, deservedly lamented, the amiable consort of Colonel Benjamin Hoppin, aged 45 years. Through life she sustained a virtuous and exemplary character. By her death her children have lost a tender and endearing parent, her husband a most affectionate companion, and the church, also, of which she was a respected member, must mourn the untimely stroke."

With regard to the progenitor of the Rawson family, some facts, which I take from a book entitled, "The Rawson Family," are of interest. This book contains the names of 5,450 persons, and there were others who were not reported to the committee that managed the matter for publication. There were two gatherings of the descendants at Worcester, Mass., and at the last, the venerable Jared Rawson, then past 90 years, addressed them. Edward Rawson, "the honored Secretary of the Massachusetts Colony," traced his ancestry back to Richard Rawson, in the year 1380, during the reign of Richard II, and the coat of arms of the family is described in the book referred to.

He (Edward Rawson) was a grantee of the town of Newbury, also town clerk, selectman, commissioner and attorney. He also represented the town in the General Court. Afterwards he was chosen to be Secretary of the Colony. He was also one of twenty-eight persons who first organized "The Old South Church" in Boston.

SIXTH GENERATION.

Henry Hoppin married **Amy Harris Bowler**, in Providence, Rhode Island, Nov. 26th, 1810.

CHILDREN:

Maria Aborn Hoppin,	born Feb. 28, 1812.	
Lorania Carrington Hoppin,	" Jan. 15, 1814,	died Jan. 10, 1884.
Henry Hoppin,	" Mar. 15, 1816.	
Samuel Bowler Hoppin,	" " 23, 1818,	
Abby Bowler Hoppin,	" " 1, 1820.	
Lewis Tiffany Hoppin,	" Apr. 16, 1822,	" Jan. 14, 1846.
Lloyd Bowers Hoppin,	" Mar. 16, 1824.	
Amy Bowler Hoppin,	" Apr. 12, 1826,	" May 2, 1855.
Charles Bowler Hoppin,	" Nov. 6, 1829,	" Dec. 6, 1852.
Anne Rawson Hoppin,	" Feb. 18, 1833.	

Henry Hoppin died February 15th, 1835. He was the eighth and youngest child of Benjamin and Annie (Rawson) Hoppin. At the age of 10 he attended school kept by the Rev. Mr. Wilson, and here he met and knew a little girl about his own age, Amy Bowler, and an attachment grew and continued to grow between them until they arrived at manhood and womanhood, when they became husband and wife. At the age of 15 he joined the church of which Mr. Wilson was pastor. In 1804 he was a clerk in his father's store. At that time he displayed a talent for sketching with pen and pencil, and some of those sketches are still preserved in the family.

May 26th, 1809, he sailed on a voyage to Canton in the ship "Baltic," Capt. Jonathan Aborn, to enter the employ of General Edward Carrington, who had married his sister, Lorania Hoppin, but on arriving at Canton he found that General Carrington had concluded to return to the United States.

And here I would record something rather singular, if not somewhat extraordinary. The day before I was married, Mr. Hoppin handed me a paper, which was an invoice of four bales of cotton, with a letter of instructions from my father to Mr. Hoppin, on the eve of his sailing for the East Indies. It was what was called an adventure, and Mr. Hoppin was requested to order and purchase, with the proceeds of the cotton, a very full and large dinner and dessert set of china, decorated with a deep blue and gold border, each piece (both large and small) to have the monogram *A. M. J.* The cotton was sold and the order filled. In due time it arrived in Providence, and now, after nearly seventy-five years, many pieces are still in possession of different members of our family. How little did my father, when he gave this invoice to that young man, think that a son of his, yet unborn, would marry the daughter of Mr. Hoppin, and how would Mr. H. at that time even dream of such an event.

To resume, Mr. Hoppin returned from Canton in the ship "Vancouver," Capt. Whittemore, June 6th, 1810, on both voyages having a record of every day's sailing and occurrences, which is now in the possession of his son Lloyd.

November 26th, 1810, Henry Hoppin and Amy Harris Bowler were married, and by this connection, the lineal descendants of two distinguished men, in and among the early New England colonists, and whose names are among those most prominent in history, were united. On the side of the bride, **William Bradford**, Governor of the Colony of Massachusetts, and on the side of the bridegroom, **Edward Rawson**, the honored and honorable Secretary of the Colony.

In 1812, Mr. Hoppin joined in business with his step-brother, Hercules Whitney, and started the callendering, bleaching and dyeing of cotton goods. In the course of years it became a large and prosperous business, and the establishment has become widely known as *The Providence Dyeing, Bleaching and Callendering Company*. It became an incorporated and stock company under that title, and a part of the shares are now held by some of Mr. Hoppin's children and grand-children.

Mr. Hoppin died at six o'clock Sunday morning, February 15th, 1835, after an illness of but four days, and on the fourth day after his daughter's marriage, leaving ten fatherless children. Mrs. Hoppin afterwards removed to Philadelphia, and subsequently, after her children had married, resided with her oldest daughter, Mrs. Knight, in Brooklyn. There she lived to the good old age of 82 years, until December 24th, 1870, and then, in peace with all the world, she gave up her life to God who gave it, and entered into eternal rest and with the hope of everlasting life.

It is difficult to speak of this lovely old lady in any but the most exalted terms, for her character was remarkable for its unaffected simplicity, purity and great loving kindness. With an intimate knowledge of her, and affectionate intercourse with her, the writer can truly say that he has seldom known any one who more completely filled all the duties incumbent on the wife, the mother, or the friend, than did this truly good and pure-minded woman. One characteristic was very marked—she never would speak ill or harshly of any one. Quiet, gentle, affectionate and charitable in thought, speech and feeling, she exemplified throughout her life the true spirit of the real Christian. Full of years, and leaving a record of a well-spent life, hers was an example that the young and the old might profitably imitate and follow. Her end was peaceful, her inheritance bright.

OBITUARY NOTICE OF HENRY HOPPIN.

From the *Providence Journal.*

On Sunday morning last (February 15th, 1835), Mr. Henry Hoppin died, in the 46th year of his age. Mr. H. was the first person who established and put into successful operation the Providence Dyeing, Bleaching and Callendering Company's establishment in this city.

He was always a friend to the poor, and "his hand was as open as the day to melting charity." His memory will long be cherished by those who have received from him acts of kindness. He was a kind husband, an affectionate father, and a sincere friend. We trust that he now reposes in the bosom of his Father and his God.

Maria Aborn Hoppin married **Nehemiah Knight**, in Providence, November 14th, 1837, and by the Rev. Mark Tucker.

CHILDREN:

Lucina Comstock Knight,	born Aug. 23, 1838.	
Henry Hoppin Knight,	" Jan. 6, 1843, died Oct. 22, 1882.	
Maria Hoppin Knight,	" Nov. —, 1846, " Mar. 4, 1851.	
Amy Trowbridge Knight,	" Sept. 14, 1853.	

Nehemiah Knight was born in Centreville, Warwick, R. I., February 5th, 1812. His great-grandfather, Nehemiah Knight, was a representative in Congress, and, more than eighty years ago, was nearly a fortnight in making the journey to Washington. His great-uncle (also Nehemiah Knight) was elected Governor of Rhode Island in 1817, and in 1821 United States Senator to succeed the Hon. James Burrill, who had died. He was elected to fill a two years' vacancy in that office, and afterwards for three full terms in succession, making twenty years' service. Mr. Knight's father was Dr. Sylvester Knight, and his mother Lucina Comstock, of Connecticut, who was a granddaughter of William Greene, of Warwick. He fitted for college under Charles Henry Alden, and entered Brown University in 1829, I think. Henry B. Anthony, afterwards Governor, and then elected United States Senator for four terms of six years each in succession, was his "chum" throughout their college course. In 1833 he went to New York, and was a clerk with Eugene Bogart (afterwards Hoyt & Bogart) for some years. Then Hoyt, Tillinghast & Co., Mr. Knight being a partner, then Hoyt, Spragues & Co., thus being associated with Edwin Hoyt for forty years in the domestic dry goods commission business. The correspondence and financeering of their very large business was ably carried on and managed solely by Mr. Knight.

Of his character, one can say, without eulogy, it was marked by its candor, amiability, uprightness and gentlemanly bearing. He had a deep interest in the woes of suffering humanity around him, and during the late war his time, money and efforts for our sick and wounded soldiers were spent for their benefit and welfare. Knowing him intimately for more than forty years, I cheerfully place on record this short sketch of his life, adding that he was ever a fond husband and father and a strong friend. Many there are who still mourn his loss and love his memory. He died May 30th, 1876. His funeral took place from Christ Church, and the Rector, Rev. Dr. Bancroft, spoke in an address in eloquent terms of the graces of mind and person which the deceased

possessed, and of the virtue and charm of his domestic life. Many
friends attended the solemn service, and to look with deep regret and
for the last time on one they had so long respected and loved.

He had held many positions of trust and honor, being a director in
the Atlantic Insurance Company, the Continental Bank, vice-presi-
dent of the South Brooklyn Savings Institution, and served as director
in several insurance companies in New York. Candid, straightforward
and honest in business, genial, hearty and amiable in social life, his
death left deep regrets in the hearts of all who knew him.

Lucina Comstock Knight married **Livingston Satterlee**, of
New York, May 9th, 1861.

CHILDREN:

Florence Satterlee,	born Mar.	1, 1862.
Edith Livingston Satterlee,	" Dec.	15, 1865.
Livingston Knight Satterlee,	" Feb.	27, 1871.
Maude Le Roy Satterlee,	" Mar.	8, 1873.
Ernest Mostyn Satterlee,	" Jan.	3, 1878.

Henry Hoppin Knight married **Amy Comstock**, of East
Hartford, Conn., June, 1867.

CHILDREN:

Mabel Knight, born July, 1871, died Mar. 15th, 1881.

Amy (Comstock) Knight died February 2d, 1879.

Henry Hoppin Knight married second, **Helen T. Williams,**
of Manchester, N. H., January 19th, 1881.

CHILDREN:

Henry Hoppin Knight, Jr., born Nov. 4, 1882, died June 29, 1884.

Henry Hoppin Knight died Oct. 22d, 1882.

Amy Trowbridge Knight married **Joseph Judson Dimock,**
of Brooklyn, N. Y., June 19th, 1879.

CHILDREN:

Joseph Judson Dimock, Jr., born July 24, 1880.		
Ernest Knight Dimock,	" June 30, 1884.	

Lorania Carrington Hoppin married **George Farquhar
Jones,** of Philadelphia, February 11th, 1835.

The children are among those of the Jones family.

Henry Hoppin, Jr., married **Mary Ann Conrad** (born December 2d, 1821), of Philadelphia, daughter of Matthew and Christiana (Beck) Conrad, October 25th, 1842.

CHILDREN:

Mary Christiana Hoppin, born Aug. 22, 1843.
Henry Hoppin, 3d,   "   Sept. 9, 1844.
Matthew Conrad Hoppin,   "   Feb. 21, 1847.
Amy Bowler Hoppin,   "   Jan. 10, 1852.
Elizabeth Wells Hoppin,   "   Mar. 10, 1861.

Henry Hoppin came from Providence to Philadelphia in 1838 or 1839, and went into business with his brother-in-law, George F. Jones. In a few years another partner, Milton Smith, joined with them under the firm name of Jones, Hoppin & Co., and the business, which was that of domestic goods, commission merchants, became changed to printing, dyeing and finishing of cotton and woolen goods.   It was at first very successful, but when the tariff of 1846 became a law, having a heavy stock of goods on hand, prices fell heavily, which produced large losses, and the firm was obliged to suspend and was dissolved.

Mary Christiana Hoppin married **Orray Taft Knight,** of Providence, June 15th, 1869.

CHILDREN:

Harry Hoppin Knight, born Sept. 9, 1870.
Orray Taft Knight, Jr.,   "   Mar. 12, 1872.
Edward Taft Knight,   "   Nov. 15, 1873.
Mary Catharine Knight, "   Aug. 12, 1875.

Orray Taft Knight is a son of Jabez C. Knight, ex-Mayor of Providence, and brother of Nehemiah Knight, who married Henry Hoppin's sister.   Mr. O. T. Knight lives in the State of California with his family and is superintending mining operations there.

Matthew Conrad Hoppin married **Annie Keith Knight,** of Providence, January 8th, 1879.

CHILDREN:

Matthew Conrad Hoppin, Jr., born Oct. 22, 1883.

Mrs. Annie Keith (Knight) Hoppin is a daughter of ex-Mayor Jabez C. Knight.

Matthew Conrad Hoppin is engaged in the wool business in New York.

Amy Bowler Hoppin married **William Fosdick Aldrich,** of Providence, October 10th, 1878.

CHILDREN:

    Amy Hoppin Aldrich,   born Nov. 10, 1879.
    William Fosdick Aldrich, Jr.,   "   Oct. 21, 1883.

Mr. Aldrich is engaged in business in Providence, R. I. as Whitford, Aldrich & Co.

Samuel Bowler Hoppin married **Mary Weed Wallace** (born December 1st, 1828), of Philadelphia, February 28th, 1855.

CHILDREN:

Amy Trowbridge Hoppin, born Dec. 20, 1855.
Thomas Wallace Hoppin,   "   Dec. 11, 1858.
Loraine Knight Hoppin,   "   Jan. 28, 1872, died Mar. 26, 1874.

Dr. Samuel B. Hoppin came to Philadelphia when quite young, and was first a clerk with his brother-in-law, G. F. J., and afterwards clerk and book-keeper with the firms of Jones & Hoppin, and Jones, Hoppin & Co. In 1847 he went to Mexico as Quartermaster's clerk. On his return he studied medicine and graduated at the Jefferson Medical College, and practiced his profession.

During the late civil war he received the appointment of Assistant Surgeon in the United States Navy, and afterwards was appointed to the same position in the army.

Abby Bowler Hoppin married **Marcus Morton, Jr.,** of Taunton, Mass., October 19th, 1843.

CHILDREN:

    Amy Morton,   born July 27, 1844.
    Charlotte Morton,   "   Nov. 4, 1845.
    Maria Hoppin Morton,   "   July 7, 1847, died July 5, 1848.
    Mary Hoppin Morton,   "   Dec. 15, 1849.
    Marcus Morton, 3d,   "   Jan. 27, 1855, "   "   27, 1855.
    Abby Hoppin Morton,   "   June 5, 1857.
    Lorania Carrington Morton, " Sept. 21, 1859.
    Marcus Morton, 4th,   "   Apr. 27, 1862.

Amy Morton married **William Charnley,** of New Haven, October 16th, 1866.

CHILDREN:

William Charnley, Jr.,   born Aug. 14, 1867.
Marcus Morton Charnley,   " Sept. 11, 1868, died Oct. 11, 1873.
Amy Elizabeth Charnley,   " Dec. 2, 1874, " May 26, 1875.
Lorania Morton Charnley,   " July 29, 1876.

Charlotte Morton married **Frank Ames Mullany,** of the U. S. M. Corps, son of Commodore Mullany, November 8th, 1869; no children.

Mary Hoppin Morton married **Clarence Whitman,** of New York, merchant, December 1st, 1875.

CHILDREN:

Clarence Morton Whitman,   born Feb. 14, 1877.
Arthur McGregor Whitman,   " Oct. 12, 1879, died July 9, 1880.
Harold Cutler Whitman,   " Aug. 3, 1883.

Mr. Whitman is in the domestic goods commission business, Leonard Street, New York.

Abby Hoppin Morton married **David Bates Douglass,** of Andover, Mass., December 2d, 1883.

CHILDREN:

Sarah Hale Douglass, born Aug. 30, 1884.

Marcus Morton, Jr., the father, and son of ex-Governor Morton, of Massachusetts, was born April 8th, 1819, in Taunton, Mass. He fitted for college at Bristol Academy, in Taunton, and entered Brown University, Providence, in 1834—graduated in 1838. Studied law in the law school of Harvard University for two years, and one year in the office of Sprague & Gray, Boston. Was admitted to practice in 1841, and continued it until 1858, about nineteen years.

He was elected a member from Andover, of the Constitution Convention of the State, 1853, and here an anecdote should be mentioned respecting "the member from Taunton" (his father), and "the member from Andover." In one of the discussions that took place, the father, who was a life-long Democrat, took decidedly adverse views of the question then under consideration, to those of the son, who had left the Democratic party and had become a " Free Soiler " or Republican. He attempted to show that certain propositions or statements advanced by the member from Andover were incorrect, untenable, and were only pardonable on account of a lack of judgment and experience on the part of the member from Andover. After the father had finished, the son rose to reply, and, as was stated, demolished the father *by quoting from his own writings,* which he could neither put aside or deny. Much amusement was caused among the members of the convention by this episode.

In 1858 he was elected to the House of Representatives of the State, and served one term. That same year he was appointed Associate Justice of the Superior Court of the County of Suffolk. This court was abolished, and he was made Judge or Associate Justice in 1859, of the Superior Court for the Commonwealth. In 1869 he was appointed Associate Justice of the Supreme Judicial Court, and in 1882 was made Chief Justice of the same.

From the Boston papers I extract the following:

Judge Morton's father, whose Christian name he bears, sat for fifteen years on the Supreme Bench of this State, and left the judge's chair for the governership, to which, as the Democratic candidate, he had been elected in 1839 by a majority of one vote.

The young lawyer, who was admitted to the bar in 1841, made his home in our city, where he lived some seven years, and then removed his home and family to Andover, where he has since resided. A judge by descent, Mr. Morton inherits the judicial temperament in a marked degree. He is one of the natural lawyers, born, not made. His mind easily grasps legal principles, and his opinions, which are models of good sense, show the workings of an intellect which pursues its way through the labyrinthine windings of the law as confidently as if the path were straight and the gate of exit in sight from the start. Not a book lawyer, not a delver into the "black letter" of the law, but rather a reasoning lawyer, one might say.

Judge Morton often seems to have worked out a case in this way: "This is the common sense of the matter, therefore it is good law to decide in this wise." He seems to have taken Sir John Powell's wise saying for his motto: "Let us consider the reason of the case, for nothing is law that is not reason."

The older lawyers find it pleasant to take their cases before him, and feel sure of courteous treatment and all the assistance the court can offer in the dispatch of litigation. A judge the greater part of his life, should he arrive at the dignity of the chief justiceship, he will creditably maintain the traditions of that great office, and the reputation for learning and efficiency of its incumbents, from John Adams to Horace Gray.

Lloyd Bowers Hoppin married **Arabella Frances Horne**, of Philadelphia, November 2d, 1853; no children.

L. B. Hoppin came to Philadelphia in 1839 or 1840, a boy of 15 or 16, and at first was clerk in one of the large auction houses, engaged in selling dry goods. After a long apprenticeship, he became expert in arranging goods for the sales and other matters connected with that business. He afterwards became an auctioneer himself. He also carried many large sales in New York and Brooklyn. For many years past, however, he has given almost sole attention to making models of celebrated buildings in this country and in Europe *in cork work*. His largest models were those of Windsor Castle, St. Peters at Rome, Lambeth Palace and Westminster Abbey. Besides these, he has produced a large number of the English cathedrals and castles, together with old and celebrated buildings and churches in this country.

It is believed that he is the only artist in this description of work, and with strict adherence to measurements, architecture, style, detail, etc., he produces an almost perfect *fac-simile* of the object. Throughout this city and the country he is well known, and his work has received the appreciation it so well deserves.

To the genealogy of his family he has devoted a large amount of time, effort and labor, and has produced a family record book that excites the admiration of all who have seen it. It is almost unique. I here once more acknowledge my indebtedness to him for much valuable information.

Amy Bowler Hoppin married **George A. Trowbridge**, of New York, April 30th, 1851.

CHILDREN :

Lewis Hoppin Trowbridge, born Mar. 29, 1852, died Apr. 25, 1856.
Charles Hoppin Trowbridge, " Oct. 14, 1854, " Apr. 7, 1856.

She died May 2d, 1855, only 29 years old.

The above is a sad record of a short married life. In the short space of less than five years she was married, had two children and died, the two children also following her to the grave. She was a beautiful girl, both in person and in character, and has left with all the members of the family, and with those who knew her, a memory ever bearing a most pleasant fragrance.

Anne Rawson Hoppin married **Henry A. Dunning,** son of Czar Dunning, of Brooklyn, June 8th, 1870; no children.

Lewis Tiffany Hoppin and **Charles Bowler Hoppin** died at 24 and 22 years of age, and unmarried.

The first died at the house of his brother, Henry Hoppin, January 14th, 1846.

The second at the house of his brother-in-law, George F. Jones, December 6th, 1852.

RECAPITULATION OF ANCESTRY.

PATERNAL ANCESTORS OF GEORGE F. JONES.

First Generation.

Thomas Jones,	born in say	1598.
Ann Jones,	" "	1600, maiden name unknown.

Second Generation.

Abraham Jones,	born in say	1638.
Sarah Jones,	" "	1640, maiden name unknown.

Third Generation.

"Elder" John Jones,	born in say	1670.
Sarah Jones,	" "	1668, maiden name unknown.

Fourth Generation.

Joseph Jones,	born	Dec. 27, 1709.
Mary (Whitney) Jones,	"	May 28, 1710.

Fifth Generation.

Joseph Jones, Jr.,	born	Sept. 29, 1737.
Ruth (Nelson) Jones,	"	Nov. 10, 1743.

Sixth Generation.

Alexander Jones,	born	Aug. 8, 1764.
Mary (Farquhar) Jones,	"	Dec. 24, 1773.

Seventh Generation.

George Farquhar Jones,	born	Feb. 11, 1811.
Lorania (Carrington) Jones,	"	Jan. 15, 1814, Hoppin.

Eighth Generation.

Mary Farquhar Jones,	born	Dec. 21, 1835.
Robert Maxwell Green,	"	May 28, 1827.

Ninth Generation.

James Farquhar Green, 4th,	born	Oct. 15, 1860.

MATERNAL ANCESTORS OF GEORGE F. JONES.

First Generation.

John Sherwood,	born in the year 1713.
Elizabeth Sherwood,	" Dec. 26, 1714, maiden name unknown.

Second Generation.

Elizabeth Sherwood,	born Oct. 15, 1746.
George Farquhar,	" Apr. 13, 1745.

Third Generation.

Mary Farquhar,	born Dec. 24, 1773.
Alexander Jones,	" Aug. 8, 1764.

Fourth Generation.

George Farquhar Jones,	born Feb. 11, 1811.
Lorania Carrington Hoppin,	" Jan. 15, 1814.

Fifth Generation.

Mary Farquhar Jones,	born Dec. 21, 1835.
Robert Maxwell Green,	" May 28, 1827.

Sixth Generation.

James Farquhar Green, 4th, born   Oct. 15, 1860.

ANCESTORS OF GEORGE F. JONES,

BY THE

Nelson Line, through his Grandmother, Ruth Nelson.

First Generation.

Thomas Nelson, born in England, probably 1597.
Joan Dummer,   "   "   "   1601.

Second Generation.

Thomas Nelson, born in England, probably 1638.
Ann Lambert,   "   America,   "   1640.

Third Generation.

Gershom Nelson,   born   July 11, 1672.
Abigail Ellithorpe,   "   probably 1680.

Fourth Generation.

Nehemiah Nelson, born   Oct. 4, 1716.
Hannah Sheffield,   "   Feb. 28, 1723.

Fifth Generation.

Ruth Nelson, born   Nov. 10, 1743.

Notes and remarks about the Nelson family are to be found in full under the marriage and births of the children of Joseph, Jr., and Ruth (Nelson) Jones.

PATERNAL ANCESTORS OF LORANIA CARRINGTON HOPPIN.

First Generation.

Edward Rawson,	born in England,	Apr. 16, 1615.
Rachel Perne,	" "	supposed 1618.

Second Generation.

Grindall Rawson,	born	Jan. 23, 1659.
Susannah Wilson,	"	probably 1668.

Third Generation.

Wilson Rawson,	born	July 23, 1692.
Margaret Arthur,	"	probably 1693.

Fourth Generation.

Thomas Rawson,	born	probably 1715.
Anne Waldron,	"	" 1719.

Fifth Generation.

Anne Rawson,	born	May 8, 1749.
Benjamin Hoppin,	"	May 12, 1747.

Sixth Generation.

Henry Hoppin,	born	Sept. 13, 1789.
Amy Harris Bowler,	"	Mar. 10, 1789.

Seventh Generation.

Lorania Carrington Hoppin,	born	Jan. 15, 1814.
George Farquhar Jones,	"	Feb. 11, 1811.

Eighth Generation.

Mary Farquhar Jones,	born	Dec. 21, 1835.
Robert Maxwell Green,	"	May 28, 1827.

Ninth Generation.

James Farquhar Green, 4th,	born	Oct. 15, 1860.

MATERNAL ANCESTORS OF LORANIA CARRINGTON HOPPIN.

First Generation.

William Bradford, of Austerfield, England.
No record of wife.

Second Generation.

William Bradford,	born in year 1589, "The Pilgrim."
Alice Southworth,	" " 1590.

Third Generation.

William Bradford, 3d,	born June 17, 1624.
Alice Richards,	" probably 1629.

Fourth Generation.

Samuel Bradford,	born in year 1659.
Hannah Rogers,	" probably 1665.

Fifth Generation.

Perez Bradford,	born in year 1693.
Abigail Belcher,	" probably 1694.

Sixth Generation.

Abigail Bradford,	born May 15, 1721.
Samuel Lee, Jr.,	" probably 1718.

Seventh Generation.

Charles Lee,	born Sept. 15, 1742.
Amy Harris,	" probably 1744.

Eighth Generation.

Abigail Lee,	born Oct. 29, 1766.
Samuel Bourse Bowler,	" probably 1763.

Ninth Generation.

Amy Harris Bowler,	born Mar. 10, 1789.
Henry Hoppin,	" Sept. 13, 1789.

Tenth Generation.

Lorania Carrington Hoppin,	born Jan. 15, 1814.
George Farquhar Jones,	" Feb. 11, 1811.

Eleventh Generation.

Mary Farquhar Jones,	born Dec. 21, 1835.
Robert Maxwell Green,	" May 28, 1827.

Twelfth Generation.

James Farquhar Green, 4th,	born Oct. 15, 1860.

ANCESTORS OF LORANIA CARRINGTON HOPPIN,

BY THE

Hoppin Line, through her Grandfather, Benjamin Hoppin.

First generation,	Thomas Hoppin,		born about	1590.
Second "	Stephen Hoppin, son of Thomas,	"	in	1626.
Third "	Benjamin Hoppin, son of Stephen,	"	"	1666.
Fourth "	Benjamin Hoppin, son of Benjamin,	"	"	1703.
Fifth "	Benjamin Hoppin, 3d, his son,	"	May 17,	1747.

COINCIDENCES

IN

DATES OF BIRTHS, MARRIAGES AND DEATHS.

Priscilla Jones,	married Jan.	1, 1756.
Annie (Rawson) Hoppin,	died	"	1, 1794.
Henry Peter Hunter,	born	"	1, 1860.
William Dabney White,	"	"	1, 1867.
William Jones King, 4th,	"	"	1, 1873.
Harriet Farquhar Jones,	"	"	3, 1791.
Charles Goodrich King,	"	"	3, 1840.
Ida Louisa Marvin,	"	"	3, 1868.
Wilmot Farquhar Wood,	"	"	3, 1869.
Ernest Mostyn Satterlee,	"	"	3, 1878.
Frances Nelson Jones,	"	"	7, 1806.
Emily Matilda Jones,	"	"	7, 1852.
Edith May Clark,	"	"	7, 1860.
Loraine Farquhar Jones, Jr.,	"	"	7, 1881.
Lorania Carrington Jones,	"	"	10, 1841.
Margaretta Brown Jones,	died	"	10, 1841.
Anna Jones Bishop,	born	"	10, 1845.
George Gideon Nichols,	"	"	10, 1846.
Amy Bowler Hoppin,	"	"	10, 1852.
Wm. B. Smith Heyward,	"	"	10, 1867.
Lorania Carrington Jones,	died	"	10, 1884.
Lucinda (Jones) King,	"	"	12, 1852.
Frances Elizabeth Dabney,	married	"	12, 1881.
Maria Cooke King,	born	"	13, 1805.
Henry Valk,	"	"	13, 1844.
Albert Valk,	"	"	13, 1844.
Maria Hoppin Jones,	"	"	13, 1848.
Amanda Tarbell Parker,	married	"	13, 1859.
Mary Jones King,	born	"	13, 1870.
Marianne Dabney,	died	"	13, 1879.
Harriet Ruth Wood,	born	"	15, 1813.
Lorania Carrington Hoppin,	"	"	15, 1814.
Edward Breck Bostwick,	"	"	15, 1848.
Charlotte Thornton Jones,	"	"	15, 1879.
Amy Hoppin Jones,	"	"	18, 1838.
Hannah Louisa Lloyd,	died	"	18, 1879.
Alexander Jones,	married	"	28, 1790.

Wm. Marlborough Jones,	born	Jan.	28, 1832.
Loraine Knight Hoppin,	"	"	28, 1872.
Mary Margaret Jones,	"	"	30, 1795.
Augustus Horatio Jones,	married	"	30, 1851.
Caroline Flagg Jones,	born	"	31, 1802.
Eliza Chaloner Durfee,	"	"	31, 1845.
Eugene Reuben Valk,	"	"	31, 1863.
Maria Eugenia King,	died	"	31, 1873.
Elizabeth Gilbert Furse,	born	"	31, 1874.
Anna Louisa Shaw,	"	Feb.	1, 1834.
Jane Sherwood Valk,	died	"	1, 1854.
Frances Nelson Bogert,	born	"	1, 1854.
Nancy King Dabney,	"	"	4, 1813.
Edith Adelia Nichols,	"	"	4, 1864.
Emma Leslie Chase,	"	"	4, 1869.
Caroline Louisa Valk,	"	"	4, 1872.
Mary Benezet Foster,	died	"	4, 1880.
Henry Hoppin,	"	"	15, 1835.
James Francis D'Wolf,	"	"	15, 1870.
Rev. Alexander Jones,	"	"	15, 1874.
Maria Aborn Hoppin,	born	"	28, 1812.
Clinton Alden Dodge,	"	"	28, 1837.
Samuel Bowler Hoppin,	married	"	28, 1855.
Emil Dabney Heinemann,	born	"	28, 1859.
Stephen Rawson,	"	"	2, 1743.
Joshua Crocker Wood,	died	"	2, 1820.
Ellen Maria Jones Dabney,	born	"	2, 1831.
Joshua Brackett Wood,	died	"	2, 1852.
Mary Eleanor Russell,	born	"	2, 1869.
Sarah Jones,	died	"	3, 1750.
Mary Jones King,	born	"	3, 1816.
Normand Knox Wood,	"	"	3, 1819.
Malvina Elvina Lloyd,	died	Mar.	3, 1862.
Florence Whittemore Young,	born	"	3, 1863.
Amy Harris Bowler,	"	"	10, 1789.
Leonard Jones,	"	"	10, 1791.
Samuel Breck Bostwick,	"	"	10, 1815.
Elizabeth Wells Hoppin,	"	"	10, 1861.
Samuel James Wood,	died	"	14, 1828.
Annie Hoppin Jones,	born	"	14, 1854.
Henry Hoppin, Jr.,	"	"	15, 1816.
Julia Sophia Dabney Monroe,	"	"	15, 1830.
Horatio Bishop Lloyd,	"	"	15, 1833.
Caroline Anna Shaw,	"	"	15, 1872.
Ruth Farquhar DeGraw,	"	"	15, 1876.
Mary Jones Alden,	"	"	18, 1814.
Charles James Alden,	"	"	18, 1816.

Caroline Jones Frances Shaw,	born	Mar.	18, 1829.
Josephine Howard Wood,	"	"	18, 1829.
John Reginald Valk,	died	"	18, 1843.
Francis Fitch Jones,	born	"	18, 1860.
Elizabeth Barton Valk,	"	"	18, 1879.
William Bradford,	"	"	19, 1589.
Alexander Jones,	died	"	19, 1840.
John Jones, 3d,	born	"	23, 1744.
Samuel Bowler Hoppin,	"	"	23, 1818.
Jane Frances Alden,	married	"	23, 1841.
Ada Virginia Valk,	died	"	23, 1843.
Ellen Maria Daugherty,	born	"	27, 1837.
Eliza Wood Shaw,	died	"	27, 1841.
Lorania Carrington King,	born	"	27, 1871.
Robert Maxwell Dabney,	"	Apr.	6, 1802.
Arthur Blake Heinemann,	"	"	6, 1871.
Jennie Edith Russell,	"	"	6, 1880.
James Farquhar Green,	died	"	6, 1882.
William A. Howard, Jr.,3	born	"	7, 1856.
Charles Hoppin Trowbridge,	"	"	7, 1856.
Lorania Carrington Jones,	married	"	7, 1870.
James Lawrence King,	born	"	14, 1819.
Harriet Farquhar Alden,	"	"	14, 1829.
Sarah Maria Valk,	"	"	14, 1853.
Harriet Tyson Joliffe,	"	"	14, 1857.
James Farquhar Wilkinson,	"	"	14, 1858.
Alexander Fraser Urquhart,	"	"	14, 1860.
Mary Margaret Alden,	died	"	14, 1879.
Frances Nelson Jones,	married	"	15, 1828.
Jennie Elizabeth Little,	born	"	15, 1851.
Mary Jones,	married	"	29, 1784.
George Farquhar Jones, Jr.,	died	"	29, 1853.
Charles Alden Snell,	born	"	29, 1875.
Richard Carrington Jones,	"	May	1, 1858.
Henry Dabney D'Wolf,	"	"	1, 1861.
Ellen Louise Claggett,	married	"	1, 1876.
George Farquhar Marchant,	born	"	10, 1852.
Alice Carey Morgan,	"	"	10, 1867.
Jeannie Campbell Morgan,	"	"	10, 1867.
Mary Edith Shaw,	"	"	10, 1875.
George Wardwell Jones,	married	"	15, 1856.
Charles Goodrich King, Jr.,	born	"	15, 1867.
George Jones King,	"	"	15, 1867.
Lizzie Louise Joliffe,	"	"	18, 1860.
Lillian May Young,	"	"	18, 1868.
Alexander Jones, 6th,	died	"	18, 1875.
Mary Jones,	born	"	28, 1710.

Benjamin Hoppin,	married	May	28, 1794.
Robert Maxwell Green,	born	"	28, 1827.
Fanny Winsor Bishop,	"	"	28, 1841.
Theodore Gilbert King,	"	"	28, 1850.
Sidney M. Van Wyck, Jr.,	"	"	28, 1868.
George Farquhar Green,	died	"	28, 1880.
Anna Wilcox Holmes,	born	"	28, 1883.
Clara Churchill Jones,	"	"	31, 1820.
Abby Greene Shaw,	"	"	31, 1838.
James Farquhar Wilkinson, 2d,	"	"	31, 1869.
Emmeline Louisa Dabney,	"	June	3, 1811.
Eliza Augusta Nichols,	"	"	3, 1844.
Mary Alice Alden,	married	"	3, 1874.
Caroline Augusta Gibbon,	died	"	3, 1875.
Spencer Oswald Heinemann,	born	"	3, 1875.
Abby Hoppin Morton,	"	"	5, 1857.
John Newton Russell, Jr.,	"	"	5, 1864.
Charles Christian Joliffe,	married	"	5, 1877.
Henry Dabney D'Wolf,	died	"	5, 1881.
Julia Augusta Jones,	born	"	9, 1853.
Walter Dabney Heinemann,	"	"	9, 1861.
Ellen Frances Heinemann,	married	"	9, 1880.
Annie Hoppin Jones,	"	"	9, 1881.
William Alexander Shaw,	born	"	11, 1823.
George Wardwell Jones,	"	"	11, 1828.
Joseph Jones,	"	"	11, 1828.
Harriet Farquhar Alden,	married	"	11, 1851.
William Bradford,	born	"	17, 1624.
Robert E. Lee Jones,	"	"	17, 1867.
Francis La Baron D'Wolf,	died	"	17, 1877.
Mary Hannah Durfee,	born	"	19, 1849.
Frances Nelson Foster,	"	"	19, 1865.
Edward Livingston Davis,	"	"	19, 1875.
Amy Trowbridge Knight,	married	"	19, 1879.
Helen Farquhar Yarnall,	born	"	19, 1882.
Frances Hope O'Brien,	"	"	19, 1884.
Jane Wilson Jones,	died	"	23, 1798.
Alexander Blodget Chace,	married	"	23, 1842.
Henry Van Wyck,	died	"	23, 1864.
Charles Macmurdo Jones,	"	"	23, 1865.
William Churchill Jones,	"	"	23, 1870.
Nathaniel Jones,	"	"	26, 1803.
Pauline Smith,	born	"	26, 1850.
Theodore Whittemore Lloyd,	died	"	26, 1855.
Emily Farquhar Heinemann,	born	"	26, 1865.
William King Furse,	"	"	26, 1883.
Ellen Maria Jones,	"	"	30, 1812.

Ernest Mostyn Knight,	born June 30, 1884.
Maria Hoppin Morton,	died July 5, 1848.
Rebecca Christian Jones,	" " 5, 1867.
Alexander Jones, 5th,	born " 5, 1871.
Mary (Whitney) Jones,	died " 9, 1788.
William Augustus Dabney,	" " 9, 1830.
Alexander Jones, 5th,	" " 9, 1872.
Mary Elizabeth Wood,	born " 14, 1811.
George Sherwood Valk,	died " 14, 1875.
Charles Christian,	born " 20, 1785.
Mary Jones Alden,	married " 20, 1840.
Henry Joseph Carver Alden Little,	born " 20, 1853.
Alice Carey Morgan,	died " 20, 1867.
Churchill Crittenden Jones,	born " 20, 1868.
Charles Henry Dabney,	" " 25, 1807.
Julia Lucinda Parker,	died " 25, 1837.
Nancy (Jones) King,	" " 25, 1845.
Emily Josephine Jones,	born " 25, 1861.
Lillian Chase,	died " 25, 1862.
William Dabney Hunter,	born " 25, 1863.
Charles Macmurdo Jones,	" " 25, 1864.
Alexander Jones Gibson,	died " 25, 1880.
Mary Farquhar Jones,	born " 26, 1826.
Eliza Ann Jones Wood,	married " 26, 1843.
Edward Alden Petit,	born " 26, 1852.
William Horatio Nelson Valk,	" " 26, 1872.
Alexander Jones, 6th,	" " 26, 1874.
Mary Elizabeth Cutler,	died Aug. 3, 1843.
Mary Farquhar Dabney,	born " 3, 1844.
Mary Crittenden,	died " 3, 1854.
Harold Cutler Whitman,	born " 3, 1883.
Alexander Jones,	" " 8, 1764.
Wiswall Jones,	died " 8, 1842.
Clara Augusta Lloyd,	" " 8, 1860.
Breckenridge Stuyvesant Gibson,	born " 8, 1873.
Jonathan Jones,	" " 11, 1746.
Frances Susan Jones,	" " 11, 1820.
Henry Monroe White,	" " 11, 1854.
Samuel Brenton Shaw, 2d,	" " 11, 1868.
Annie Maury Jones,	died " 11, 1873.
Nannie Crittenden Van Wyck,	born " 11, 1874.
Mary Elizabeth Bostwick,	married " 11, 1874.
Edward George Farquhar Green,	died " 16, 1801.
Emily Matilda Jones,	born " 16, 1814.
Ruth (Nelson) Jones,	died " 16, 1825.
Hannah (Jones) Dabney,	" " 16, 1836.
Charles Lawrence King,	" " 20, 1853.

Lewis Valk,	born	Aug.	20, 1867.
Robert Maxwell Green,	died	"	20, 1883.
Hannah Jones,	married	"	24, 1797.
Theodore Bogert Dabney,	died	"	24, 1839.
Lorania Carrington Hoy,	born	"	24, 1863.
Minnie Elizabeth Urquhart,	"	"	24, 1864.
Lorania Carrington King,	died	"	24, 1884.
Eliza Ann Jones Wood,	born	"	27, 1823.
Henry Tyler Howard,	"	"	27, 1865.
Charles Goodrich King,	died	"	27, 1881.
Edward Rawson,	"	Sept.	5, 1671.
Mary (Farquhar) Jones,	"	"	5, 1835.
Normand Knox Wood,	"	"	5, 1840.
Arthur Laidler Jones,	born	"	5, 1858.
Laura Sanchez Van Wyck,	"	"	5, 1879.
Florence Page Crittenden,	"	"	5, 1881.
George Farquhar,	died	"	20, 1779.
George William Jones,	"	"	20, 1866.
Ada Virginia Valk,	"	"	20, 1870.
Eliza Ruth Jones,	married	Oct.	4, 1810.
Nellie Farquhar Chase,	died	"	4, 1852.
Churchill Crittenden,	"	"	4, 1864.
Charles Clifton Claggett,	married	"	4, 1867.
Elizabeth Sherwood,	"	"	5, 1770.
Harriet Tyson Joliffe,	died	"	5, 1862.
Lizzie Louise Joliffe,	"	"	5, 1862.
Alfred Duval Crittenden,	born	"	5, 1882.
Lalier Elizabeth Farquhar,	died	"	6, 1776.
Josephine Howard Wood,	married	"	6, 1863.
Francis Lithgow Payson,	"	"	6, 1883.
Caroline Jones Dodge,	"	"	8, 1862.
Henry Eugene Dodge,	"	"	8, 1866.
Annie Churchill Joliffe,	died	"	8, 1862.
William Jones King, 3d,	born	"	13, 1864.
Randall Nelson Durfee,	"	"	13, 1867.
Andrew Hasel Heyward, Jr.,	died	"	13, 1872.
Rennie Lee Jones,	married	"	13, 1882.
Elizabeth Somerville Urquhart,	born	"	13, 1883.
Harriet Farquhar Chace,	died	"	14, 1823.
William Jones King, Jr.,	born	"	14, 1837.
Henry Austin Claggett,	"	"	14, 1839.
Annie Vane Jones,	"	"	14, 1866.
Arthur Bostwick DeGraw,	"	"	14, 1878.
Elizabeth Sherwood, 2d,	"	"	15, 1746.
John William King,	"	"	15, 1806.
Henry Holman Jones,	died	"	15, 1859.
Rennie Lee Jones,	born	"	15, 1860.

James Farquhar Green, 3d,	born Oct.	15, 1860.
Frank Rudolph Valk,	" "	15, 1866.
Mary Jones,	" "	16, 1740.
Samuel Brenton Shaw, Jr.,	" "	16, 1826.
Brenton Shaw Clark,	" "	16, 1857.
Clara Crittenden Jolliffe,	died "	16, 1862.
Amy Morton,	married "	16, 1866.
William Cyrus Little,	" "	16, 1878.
Caroline Clinton Durfee,	" "	16, 1879.
William Mosely Jones,	" "	16, 1881.
Abigail Lee,	born "	20, 1766.
William Jones King,	married "	20, 1832.
Francis William Jones,	died "	20, 1859.
Wiswall Jones,	born "	22, 1788.
Theodore P. Bogert, Jr.,	" "	22, 1830.
Caroline Frances Little,	married "	22, 1862.
Emily Alden Little,	" "	22, 1862.
Matthew Conrad Hoppin, Jr.,	born "	22, 1883.
Alice Bradford,	" "	30, 1587.
Abraham Jones,	married "	30, 1765.
James Francis D'Wolf, Jr.,	born "	30, 1852.
James Henry Monroe,	died "	30, 1838.
Harriet Farquhar Jones,	married Nov.	3, 1811.
Mary Price Jones,	" "	3, 1841.
Albert Valk,	died "	3, 1846.
Maria Harriet Lloyd,	" "	3, 1846.
George E. King,	born "	3, 1851.
Margaret Russell Durfee,	" "	3, 1871.
Angelletta Russell,	" "	3, 1870.
Alexander Jones, Jr.,	" "	8, 1796.
Annie Churchill Crittenden,	married " .	8, 1862.
Charlotte Morton,	" "	8, 1862.
Loraine Farquhar Jones,	born "	9, 1837.
Mary Price Jones, 2d,	" "	9, 1859.
Loraine Farquhar Jones,	married "	9, 1870.
Alexander Blodget Chace,	died "	9, 1873.
Joseph Jones,	" "	12, 1831.
Alexander George Wood,	born "	12, 1831.
Lawrence Bolton Valk,	" "	17, 1837.
Howard Crittenden,	" "	17, 1844.
Emilie Ronald Furse,	" "	17, 1875.
Margaret Wood Davis,	" "	17, 1882.
Edward Gilbert King,	" "	20, 1841.
Frances Akers Van Wyck,	" "	20, 1866.
Charles Grenville Lloyd,	" "	20, 1867.
Louisa Jones Lloyd,	died "	23, 1850.
James Reginald Foster,	born "	23, 1867.

Maggie Macmurdo Jones,	born Nov.	23, 1870.
Jane Sherwood Jones,	" "	26, 1863.
Amy Harris Bowler,	married "	26, 1810.
Mary Elizabeth Shaw,	" "	26, 1856.
Ellen Maria Shaw,	born "	28, 1830.
Emily Matilda Shaw,	" "	28, 1830.
Eugene William Claggett,	" "	28, 1848.
Clarence Duroy Claggett,	" "	28, 1848.
Charles Leverett Green,	" "	29, 1802.
John Joseph Brinsdon,	" "	29, 1871.
Wilson Rawson,	died Dec.	1, 1726.
Mary Weed Wallace,	born "	1, 1828.
William Grenville Lloyd,	" "	1, 1829.
Mary Hoppin Morton,	married "	1, 1875.
Margaret Manson Farquhar,	died "	2, 1806.
George Farquhar Green,	born "	2, 1861.
Amy Hoppin Jones,	married "	2, 1862.
Amy Elizabeth Charnley,	born "	2, 1864.
Charles Bowler Hoppin,	died "	6, 1851.
Ellen Maria Shaw,	married "	6, 1853.
Laura Crittenden,	" "	6, 1859.
Annie Lou King,	born "	6, 1860.
John Jones,	married "	9, 1762.
Charles Lee Bowler,	born "	9, 1786.
Jerry Andrew Hunter,	" "	9, 1861.
Edith Dodge Morgan,	died "	9, 1876.
John Sherwood,	" "	11, 1755.
Rebecca Churchill Jones,	born "	11, 1833.
Thomas Wallace Hoppin,	" "	11, 1858.
Noah Jones,	died "	14, 1813.
Sarah Mary Valk,	born "	14, 1835.
Edward Newton Shaw,	" "	15, 1836.
James Love Crittenden,	" "	15, 1841.
William Whittemore, Jr.,	died "	15, 1849.
Mary Hoppin Morton,	born "	15, 1849.
William Whittemore, 3d,	died "	15, 1861.
Edith Livingston Satterlee,	born "	15, 1865.
Rose Barrington Clark,	" "	15, 1871.
Charles Henry Dabney,	died "	15, 1879.
Susanna Wilson,	born "	16, 1664.
Sarah Jones,	" "	16, 1739.
William Bishop Hunter,	" "	16, 1870.
Annie Howard DeGraw,	" "	16, 1873.
George Farquhar Jones, Jr.,	" "	17, 1843.
Eugene William Valk,	died "	17, 1849.
Frances Ellen Jones,	born "	18, 1845.
Charles Arthur Payson,	" "	18, 1868.

Charlotte Alden Petit,	born Dec.	18, 1876.
Mary Farquhar Jones,	" "	21, 1835.
Mary Farquhar Jones,	married "	21, 1859.
Margaret Green Wilkinson,	" "	21, 1881.
Alexander Irving Jones,	born "	21, 1883.
Frances Placidia Wood,	" "	22, 1825.
Joseph Jones Daugherty,	" "	22, 1838.
Margaretta Brown Jones,	" "	22, 1840.
Andrew Hasel Heyward,	" "	22, 1871.
Anna Hester Bishop,	died "	23, 1859.
Alexander David Jones,	married "	23, 1862.
Clara Churchill Crittenden Jones,	born "	23, 1863.
Georgiana Hasel Heyward,	" "	23, 1869.
Mary Farquhar,	" "	24, 1773.
Joshua Crocker Wood,	" "	24, 1816.
Maria Eugenia King,	" "	24, 1847.
Caroline Jane Frances Shaw,	married "	25, 1852.
Emily Matilda Shaw,	" "	25, 1852.
Lilly Margaret Gibson,	born "	25, 1860.
Elizabeth Sherwood,	" "	26, 1714.
Mary Marchant,	" "	26, 1850.
Gertrude Clara Crittenden,	" "	26, 1869.
Annie Churchill Jones,	" "	26, 1872.
Ruth Jones,	married "	28, 1749.
Joseph Jones, Jr.,	" "	28, 1763.
Frances Eudora Durfee,	born "	28, 1841.
Ellen Louise Claggett,	" "	28, 1844.
Mary Josephine Nichols,	" "	28, 1849.
Marion Kershaw Young,	" "	28, 1864.
Julius Smith Lloyd,	married "	28, 1865.
Abigail Bradford,	" "	31, 1740.
Ada Virginia Valk,	born "	31, 1869.
Charlotte Sherwood Morgan,	" "	31, 1871.
Ellen Dabney Archer,	" "	31, 1877.

SINGULAR & UNCOMMON NAMES.

In an examination of Genealogical and Biographical registers, and particularly those in Ballou's History of Milford, my attention was arrested by some peculiar names that were given to children. Many of them are so uncommon, I gathered them, and now list them for the inspection of the curious. The large majority of those bestowed upon the boys are taken from the Bible, and in many cases the ugliest seem to have been selected by the parents. Those given to the girls, while equally curious and strange, are more euphonious and fanciful. They cover a period of nearly 200 years.

BOYS' NAMES.

Abiah.	Athlin.	Ichabod.	Nabor.	Salathiel.
Abiathar.	Aulando.	Increase.	Nahor.	Salem.
Abidah.		Issacher.	Nahum.	Salmon.
Abijah.	Baruch.	Ithiel.	Naum.	Silenus.
Adin.	Barzillai.		Noahdiah.	
Adoniram.	Benoni.	Jabez.		Theron.
Africa.	Beriah.	Jahleel.	Obed.	Thurza.
Ahaz.	Bezaleal.	Japheth.	Ora.	
Alanson.		Jared.	Oramel.	Uel.
Albertus.	Carmel.	Jason.	Origen.	Uri.
Albion.	Chiron.	Jasper.	Orimandel.	Uriah.
Almanza.	Cleophas.	Jedediah.	Orrin.	Uriel.
Almon.	Cyriel.	Jedutham.	Orson.	
Alpheus.		Jemotis.	Ozias.	Welcome.
Alvah.	Dascam.	Joazaniah.		Wisdom.
Alvin.	Dutee.	Jotham.	Pardon.	
Amariah.			Parley.	Zaccheus.
Amaziah.	Elam.	Laban.	Parmenas.	Zadoc.
America.	Eldad.	Laten.	Parseus.	Zalmon.
Amni.	Eldorado.	Leander.	Pelatiah.	Zebina.
Ammiel.	Eleazer.	Lebbeus.	Peleg.	Zebulon.
Amrilla.	Eliab.	Libbeus.	Penuel.	Zelek.
Amzi.	Elihu.	Loammi.	Perez.	Zemiah.
Angel.	Elicenai.	Loren.	Perley.	Zenas.
Ansel.	Eliphalet.	Loriel.	Pero.	Ziba.
Aquilla.	Elmon.	Luman.	Philo.	Zibeon.
Arad.	Ethan.		Phinehas.	Zimri.
Aretus.		Manoah.	Preserved.	Zubah.
Ariel.	Gershom.	Marvel.		Zuriel.
Artemus.	Grindall.	Medad.	Ralsmond.	
Arvah.		Mellen.	Revilo.	
Asaph.	Hachaliah.	Micajah.	Royal.	
Asia.	Haskey.	Myron.	Ruel.	
Athelred.	Hazen.			

GIRLS' NAMES.

Abida.
Abilene.
Abzada.
Abzina.
Achsa.
Adaliza.
Adella.
Aditta.
Adla.
Aleda.
Alena.
Alethira.
Allethira.
Alma.
Almida.
Alinda.
Alpha.
Althea.
Althira.
Angelia.
Angenette.
Anselina.
Anziana.
Arba.
Armis.
Arozine.
Arvilla.
Aurilla.
Asenath.
Axalana.
Azora.
Azubah.

Bathsheba.
Bethia.
Bettina.

Careful.
Calista.
Capitola.
Carra.
Casandana.
Cassandra.
Celinda.
Cerusa.
Charity.
Chastina.
Climena.
Clothilda.

Comfort.
Considerate.
Content.
Corazandra.
Cosie.

Dealonta.
Dealbana.
Delight.
Deliverance.
Della.
Delora.
Delphia.
Dependence.
Diadama.
Diantha.
Dilla.
Direxa.
Dorinda.
Drusey.
Dulcina.

Ede.
Edilda.
Elbertina.
Eldora.
Elinda.
Elma.
Elonia.
Emeliza.
Emolena.
Eurania.
Experience.

Faith.
Firilla.
Freelove.
Francena.

Georgietta.
Georgina.

Heaster.
Hepsie.
Hepzibah.
Hope.
Hopeful.
Hopestill.

Idalena.
Idella.
Izanna.
Izetta.

Jerusha.
Johanna.
Jula.

Keziah.
Kittah.

Laurinda.
Lavena.
Lavira.
Leonia.
Leudamia.
Lina.
Loanna.
Lodensa.
Lorena.
Lorinda.
Love.
Lovica.
Lovicy.
Lovilla.
Lovina.
Lovisa.
Lowmira.
Luella.
Lura.
Lurena.
Luna.
Laurinda.
Lutella.

Maldusa.
Malissa.
Maltina.
Mandana.
Maranda.
Marilla.
Meketabel.
Melatiah.
Mercy.
Milcha.
Mindwell.
Molita.
Mura.

Naamah.
Nabby.
Norena.
Novena.

Orilla.
Orinda.
Orissa.

Parna.
Patience.
Pedea.
Peregrina.
Persis.
Phila.
Philena.
Princis.
Prua.
Pruda.
Prudence.

Relief.
Rhana.
Rhoba.
Rittah.
Rowanca.
Rowanna.
Rowena.
Rosela.
Ruba.
Ruhannah.
Roxa.
Roxalana.
Roxalinda.
Roxana.
Rosilla.

Sabina.
Sabra.
Sabrina.
Sarinda.
Satira.
Selissa.
Semantha.
Semira.
Sena.
Serinda.
Sibbia.
Silence.

Submit.
Sylvania.
Sylvira.

Tamer.
Tamsin.
Temperance.
Thankful.
Theoda.
Thirza.
Thusa.
Trial.
Truelove.
Truth.
Tryphena.

Uella.
Ulila.
Urana.
Unity.

Valeria.
Velma.
Vera.
Versalia.
Vervilla.
Vianna.
Vida.
Vietta.
Vilora.
Virtue.

Waity.
Wealthy.

Zavina.
Zebinah.
Zelina.
Zelona.
Zervia.
Zilla.
Zilphia.
Zipporah.
Zurvilla.

POSTSCRIPT AND ADDENDA.

Owing to the great and active interest felt and shown by my sister, Mrs. E. M. Dabney, and her eager wish and generous kindness, we, together, went to Milford, Mass., to visit the place where so many of our family were born, married, lived and died. We arrived there on the 12th of August, and immediately took a carriage and rode out to the place where our ancestor, Elder John Jones, had made a clearing in the wild forest, with his own hands. The place where his large farm was, is now called "*Hopedale*," it having been purchased by a Community of that name. It had been built upon and improved by roads and streets, and hardly a trace of the old place was left.

Our first call was upon the Rev. Adin Ballou, the author of "The History of Milford," and we found the reverend gentleman at his home, not many rods from the spot where "*the old Jones House*" stood for nearly a century and three-quarters. We had a long and interesting interview, which lasted two hours, learning many little items and matters that were to us very gratifying. On being asked if there were any pictures of the old homestead, he quietly rose and took down from the wall of the room, a daguerreotype and an oil painting, both being faithful representations of the house first erected in 1703, enlarged in 1730 to 1735, and demolished in 1874. He kindly loaned us both pictures to be photographed, and the order was given the next day. They were well done by a photographer in Milford.

Expressing a strong desire to see the spot where the old house had stood for so many long years, Mr. Ballou went with us, and we soon were standing on the ground once covered by the venerable building. The space is open and uncovered by buildings, and near by are three grand old trees. The old well was there, into which a pump had been placed, and we found the large, broad and heavy "*front door stone*," which had lain at the entrance to the house, for years upon years. This, to me, was more familiar and well remembered than anything that was seen. How many feet had passed over, or stood on that doorstone! Those of the young, the middle-aged and the old—the toddling baby, the young boy or girl, the full-grown man and woman, the busy, active farmer and his wife; the aged, resting and waiting, father and mother, soon, perhaps, to lay down a wearied life for one "beyond the river;" the gay and happy had stood there, the worn, the tried, the weary, the afflicted, had stepped upon that stone. The gaieties attendant on the wedding, the solemnities of the funeral, had brought many to tread on that stone, on their way into the house of joy or of mourning, as might be the case; and now *all* had *gone and passed away.* Only three persons of all the generations who had lived in, or had visited at the venerable mansion, are now alive. "So runs the world away."

We visited the beautiful river, so clear, and pure and sparkling, as we well remembered it to be, and it is now walled up, where it passed near the old house, and is utilized for manufacturing purposes. It had been fifty-four years since my sister last visited the place, and fifty-nine or sixty years since I was there the last time. Singular sensations were ours as we stood there, and memories of the youthful and happy days passed at "the Farm," and under the old roof-tree, crowded themselves upon us. All our recollections of the scenes we saw and the events we had witnessed, came back to us vividly and with remarkable acuteness. *They were felt, but cannot be described.*

We parted from our bright, active, venerable companion (he told us that he was in his eighty-second year) with regret, but thanking him (which I repeat here, and again with much pleasure) for his courtesy and kindness to us, who till then had been entire strangers to him. His and his wife's pleasant conversation will long remain in our memory, as interesting and gratifying.

That same afternoon and evening, and during the part of the succeeding day, which we spent in Milford, we called upon or saw thirteen other persons, who, on making known our mission and the object of our visit, each and all, were kind and obliging, and gave us all the information in their power. We regretted that our visit could not have been prolonged, for we thought we could have passed several days there pleasantly, and filled with interest. When we visited Milford in our early youth, it was a small village of some four or five hundred people: now it is a busy, enterprising and handsome town, with eleven thousand inhabitants.

We could not leave without going to the cemetery, and our visit could only be a hurried one, for want of time, and because of rain. "The old burying ground," as it was called in old times, had been moved, and the remains lying there, with the grave-stones above them, were carefully carried to the new cemetery. I there found some forty graves and grave-stones of the various members of *the Jones family* (had the time been extended I should probably have found more), and of their connections by marriage. Many of the dates were 140 years old, and quite a number were 100 years back. As I stood there, my feelings and sensations were singularly interesting, for I was standing over the spot where the relics of my great-great-grandfather lay, with wife, children, and their wives and children. They live only in memory, and are fast being forgotten. So, too, must we all pass away, and in our turn, only live in the dim shadow of the years that are gone, to give place to those to come.

DEMOLITION OF "THE OLD JONES HOUSE."

After the visit to Milford, a letter came from the Rev. Mr. Ballou, in which he says: " In the multitude of matters hurriedly talked over when you and your brother were here, I strangely forgot some relics and mementos. I also entirely forgot a historic sketch of "*The Old House*," written by me and printed in the *Milford Journal*, in 1874, the year it was demolished. I wrote this before I had traced your great-great-grandfather (Elder John), to his original home in Hull, Mass. I have only two copies of the journal containing this article. I am sure you will be interested in reading it, and, therefore, enclose herein one of these copies." If those who were never related to our family can be interested in all that refers to the old mansion, it must certainly be to us a matter of great interest. They could hardly entertain any other feeling than curiosity as to matters regarding the house and its former inmates, but to us, their descendants, everything appertaining to it and to them must be highly interesting. I, therefore, give Mr. Ballou's description, or sketch, as he calls it, making one or two slight corrections and with some omissions :

THE OLD HOUSE AT HOPEDALE.

By Rev. Adin Ballou.

Messrs. Editors: In compliance with your request and recent announcement, I present your readers the following historical sketch relating to "*The Old Jones House*" in our village, which has just been demolished. That venerable mansion has been the centre of many interesting associations, transactions and occurrences. I have not been able to fix with certainty the exact dates of some important particulars in its history, but with the aid of reliable records and oral traditions, feel warranted in assuming the general correctness of my statements. It was a two-story structure facing south, 40 by 30 feet in dimensions, and until a few years ago, had a one-story kitchen appendage on the north, 26 by 20 feet, covering the ancient well, still the best in our whole village. The great stone chimney contained not less than 3,300 cubic feet, or 200 perch, or nearly 26 cords. It had, below and above, five fireplaces and the same number of ovens, the latter mostly of brick. Of the three fireplaces below, the largest had stone jambs 8 feet apart in the flue, with a huge oak mantel-beam 14 inches square, and it was capable of taking in fuel 6 feet in length. The whole stone-work was laid in clay mortar. The cellar was 6 feet in depth, and so fashioned as to leave a square body of earth under and south of the chimney, 20 by 10 feet, but strongly walled up, affording ample space east, north and south for domestic convenience. The timber frame was of solid oak, and found to be nearly all sound, with ponderous beams 12 inches square, girts 14 by 6 inches, and other pieces of corresponding strength. Some of this timber was sawed, and the western half of the house walled with solid plank, fastened to sills, plates and girts with wooden pins. Antique spikes and nails were used in other parts of the structure. The inside ceiling and ornamental work was of nice pine stuff, and has been safely stored away for preservation, as also such relics as were deemed valuable to antiquaries.

This ancient dwelling was erected at two different periods. The oldest half was built by Elder John Jones, according to my present best information, between 1700 and 1704, and the youngest half jointly by said Elder John and his son, Mr. Joseph Jones, in 1730 to 1735—the last date having been inscribed in antique figures on a wooden tablet in the western gable, and now carefully preserved. I have not found, as yet, any conclusive written evidence of the exact date at which the oldest half was built. Some 25 years ago, the Rev. David Long, the second regular Pastor of the Milford Congregational Church and Parish, a man of great accuracy, as well as information in all such matters, told me that it must be then about 150 years old. If so, it must have been built not far from the year 1700, and certainly not later than 1703 or 1704.

This accords well with an ancient deed from Seth Chapin, a near neighbor to Elder John Jones, in which a certain "drift-way" is reserved 3 rods wide, running by Jones' house on the south side towards "Magoniscock Woods," then covering the highlands northeast of Hopedale. This deed dates back to 1703 or 1704. It also accords with the well-remembered statements of the late Mrs. Roxa (Rawson) Rockwood, last wife of Deacon Peter Rockwood, and of her venerable brother, Jared Rawson. His deceased sister was a living chronicle of olden times, events and traditions, and he is scarcely less so. Their testimony is a positive tradition that the oldest section of the Jones house was *the first framed one* in the whole territory now included in the town of Milford. Thus we arrive at the conclusion that the first built portion of this edifice was at least 170 years old at the time of its demolition, and that the second built portion was 137 years old.

We now treat of persons and events in connection with this time-worn abode. Elder John Jones was a very enterprising, pious and influential man in his time. I have not learned the place of his nativity, but only that he came a young man to Mendontown, so called, some time after its resettlement in 1678–80, etc., it having been burnt in King Philip's war. Between 1690 and 1700 he took up proprietary lands on Mill River, in and about the vicinage now called Hopedale. Afterwards he extended his purchases northwardly as far as Bungy, where the first saw-mill in these parts was early erected. When he commenced clearing the wild land near the site which he selected for his dwelling-house, he lodged in old Mendon, whence he came down by an Indian path to his incipient farm with a frugal dinner in hand, consisting of plain Indian bannock and a bottle of milk, starting at early morn and plying his axe with stalwart arms until nearly night. At noon it was his invariable custom to spread his dinner on a clean stump, and before eating, invoke the Divine blessing on his knees. Bears, wolves and Indians were enemies from which he must protect himself. He therefore soon built a small, strong barrack of logs close to the little river, a few rods westerly of the site afterwards occupied by his house. Therein, with two large dogs, he took refuge from threatened danger, but seldom stayed over night until he had made a considerable clearing of the forest about him. One night, however, dark clouds overcast the skies just before sunset, and obliged him to take lodgings in his rude block house. Predatory beasts and savages came prowling around during the night, but his two brave dogs being let out, soon dispersed them, and morning dawned upon him in safety.

Whether he kept house at all with his young wife in his log barrack, is uncertain, though probably he did so, on the eve of getting up his framed house. Mr. Jared Rawson informs me that when at work for the later Joneses in 1805, he dug up the flooring and hearth-stones of the old barrack, and found the remains of firebrands, torches, etc., among the ashes overlying them.

The new settler drew his first fodder for cattle from Beaver Meadow, which is now covered by the upper section of the Hopedale larger pond—sagacious and industrious beavers having, at an earlier period, prepared the ground for nice crops of swale hay. Further up the river, one of his best cows, straggling off for pasture, got snared in the branches of a fallen tree, and partly mired, perished before being found after a tedious search. This was then, and long afterward deemed a serious misfortune, for the owner was at that time poor in cattle.

When he came to build his house, he had to get his sawing done at Bungy, over four miles off, reached by rough cart paths, mostly through heavily timbered woodlands. Having got his cellar ready for the sills and lower flooring, and covered it loosely, he is said to have lodged his wife and children in the premises, providing safe shelter for them during the night in that subterranean dormitory; while often he himself was obliged to spend the darksome hours at Bungy, going with his oxen one day and returning the next. But his prosperity was equal to his toils and privations; he grew rich in lands, cattle and goods.

In 1708, his son Abraham was born in the new house, and in 1709 his son Joseph, both of whom grew up blessings to him and his wife Sarah. They became pillars in the church and precinct. In due time he married off his daughters into good families, and his habitation was not only a house of prayer, but often of wedding festivity and innocent social merry-making. He settled his son Abraham on a goodly homestead, not far from his own, but kept his son Joseph at home with him as his partner and heir. Joseph married a wife, Mary Whitney, and began to rear a family.

In 1735 it became necessary to enlarge the domicile—so Joseph and his father united in doubling, and perhaps more than doubling, the accommodations of their residence. Moreover they rejuvenated the first built section, and garnished the whole within and without with such ceilings and ornamentations, that it became the admiration of all the surrounding inhabitants—one of the most aristocratic in this region. One Mr. Leshure was their head carpenter—a very ingenious joiner, but always poor and hunted by sheriffs and their kindred to take away his money or his body to prison. The Joneses befriended him, and secreted him as much as they could, that he might, by snatches at least, finish off their parlor and the nicer work in other parts of the house. It is said to have taken Leshure three weeks to construct the crockery cupboard, then and long afterwards called "the beaufet." It stood in the northeast corner of the parlor, and became the favorite depositary of nice china and glassware, not to mention silver and pewter, and also of choice liquors and sweetenings. On this Mr. Leshure lavished his skill—keeping meantime a sharp lookout for the officers.

Then followed social parties, festive entertainments, solemn religious meetings; for the Joneses were eminently social and hospitable, both

12

jovially and seriously. About the year 1740, a considerable portion of the mother church in old Mendon, known as *The First Church*, became aggrieved and disaffected. Most of those aggrieved members resided east of Neck Hill, in what is now Milford. The idea soon suggested itself to them of forming *a second church* and a new precinct. John Jones was the man to lead this movement. Accordingly he convened his "aggrieved" brethren in his own spacious house for consultation, April 1st, 1741. They decided to hold a day of fasting and prayer, and renewal of covenant, on the 15th of the same month in his house, to open at 9 o'clock A.M. Also to invite counsel from the churches in Hopkinton, Holliston, Uxbridge, and Upton; and further, that one of their pastors should be requested to preach a sermon on the occasion.

The appointed day and hour arrived. Pastors and elders came from Hopkinton and Holliston to their assistance—the mansion was thronged with people—and Rev. Mr. Barrett, of Hopkinton, preached an impressive sermon. A stringent covenant was subscribed to by numerous persons; the necessary church officers were elected, including, as was then customary, two ruling elders, two deacons, and a scribe, and the new church solemnly declared a properly inaugurated body. The pious, worthy and hospitable John Jones was recognized as first and chief elder of the Second Church in Mendon, which now has Rev. Dr. Richardson for its distinguished pastor. And we may reasonably infer that Elder Jones and his son Joseph, with their wives, liberally entertained their numerous guests on that 15th of April in the year 1741.

From this time onward church meetings and Sabbath preaching meetings were frequently held at the house of Elder Jones, down to 1743–44, when the first meeting-house in the then newly organized easterly precinct of Mendon was opened for public worship. On the 21st of December, 1743, a most important assembly was convened at Elder Jones' for the ordination of Rev. Amariah Frost, pastor-elect of the new church. A large council of pastors, ruling elders and messengers convened early in the day. They appear, from the record, to have been sadly discordant in opinion on certain then disputed points of church order, to have spent several hours in debate, and at length to have divided on a test question, 15 for to 7 against. Finally, after much discussion and delay, the majority arranged the programme of ordination services from sermon to charge, and went through them before night accordingly, all in this extemporized sanctuary of the Jones'; so the records of the church imply, or oblige us to infer.

In 1750 the good wife and mother, Mrs. Sarah Jones, departed this life, and funeral solemnities begloomed the home of the Joneses. In

1753 Elder John Jones himself received the most honorable burial which his revering family and friends, with the inhabitants far and near, could render. He passed away in the 84th year of his age. His son Abraham was first made a deacon, and then a ruling elder of the church, like his father before him, and he long officiated in that office with the highest esteem and confidence of his brethren. He died in 1792 in his 84th year, but his funeral was not held in the home of his childhood. His younger brother was a respected member of the same church from his youth upward; likewise Mary, his wife. They raised several children, and married them off with joyous celebrations under the historic roof. Her funeral came in 1788, and her husband, Joseph's, in 1796, when he had reached his 87th year.

His son, Joseph Jones, Jr., came from Bungy to live in the homestead, on whom the father seems to have leaned in his old age. Mr. Jared Rawson said that his wife, Ruth Nelson, was the handsomest, smartest and best woman ever raised in Milford. He and his excellent wife raised nine children, five sons and four daughters, all handsome, sprightly and enterprising, who in their youthful days drew together many a gay party, and made the stately mansion resound with music, dancing and mirth.

The eldest son, Alexander Jones, and one or two of his brothers, became adventurers in trade at the South—Charleston, S. C., if I mistake not—and grew rich, especially Alexander. He soon settled in Providence, R. I., and was long a wealthy merchant there. In the Summer season these mercantile brothers, with their families and negro servants, spent several weeks annually at the old homestead, and seldom failed to signalize this sojourn by some jovial displays and romantic festivities. One autumn a showy wedding was celebrated on the occasion of their sister Hannah's bridal union with a dashing Southern trader. But the young beaux of Milford were slighted; not one of them was invited. The guests were all from abroad, and of a higher standing in fashionable life. The wedding went off with eclat; but the young, slighted Milfordonians testified their resentment by a stealthy joke. That night they carried old Mr. Jones' nicely wrought bean arbor from his garden, transporting it to the town common, where it next day appeared as a refreshment booth, some rods in length, ready to serve a military muster then at hand. Such was the genius of those times.

At length, about the beginning of our century, the Jones house and farm passed into the possession of Alexander Jones, great-grandson of Elder John, and remained therein until 1838. He made it his summer residence, spent much money in improvements on the buildings and lands, and so rendered the estate a very attractive domain. I have not ascertained anything definite about the death of his parents, Joseph, Jr., and Ruth (Nelson) Jones, but have heard it said they ended their days with their son in Providence. Alexander placed the estate in the immediate charge of hired managers and tenants, who in succession occupied the old domicile, but for a long time he reserved one well-furnished room, which he, his children and grandchildren might resort to for a temporary stay at pleasure. This usually took place every year in the season of berries, when more or less of them came from their city home in quest of recreation, and had good times.

Mr. Jared Rawson was hired manager from 1805 to 1807, and I understand him to say that the old folks, Joseph and Ruth Jones, were then alive on the estate. Mr. John Parkhurst was managing tenant some three or four years, down to 1810 or 1811. Then Mr. Elisha Daniels, who died there in the year 1821. Then his widow and her son continued the tenancy down to 1838, when Mr. Hastings Daniels became owner. He lived to enjoy his purchase only a little while, being cut off by death early in middle age. When his estate was settled up, the real passed into the ownership of John Claflin, Esq., and our well-known neighbor, Mr. Newton Daniels, a brother of the deceased.

They rented the place in 1840 to Mr. Dominie McDavit, and the next year to my nephew, Mr. Cyrus Ballou, through whose agency I purchased it of Messrs. Claflin and Daniels, in the Autumn of 1841 for the then recently formed "Hopedale community." Two community families entered the old house as tenants that very Autumn, or perhaps one of them early in the Winter. Near the end of March, Mr. E. D. Draper, myself and others, with our families, took up our abode there. On Thursday evening, March 24th, 1842, we held our first religious meeting in the west room—the same in which the Congregational Church had been instituted a little over one hundred years before. It was a deeply interesting occasion, full of prayer, praise, thanksgiving, exhortation and fraternal congratulation—a sort of dedication to God and humanity. Oh! that the enthusiastic hopes of that hour had been better realized!

Thenceforth, for more than a year, our regular Sabbath and Thursday evening meetings were held in that ancient sanctuary. Meantime it became the temporary home of ten married pairs, who, with their children, dependents and boarding associates, numbered between forty and fifty persons in the Summer season. Its common tables were thronged, and all its available space for lodging rooms economically partitioned off in the chambers and attic, scarcely sufficed for our decent necessities. Its parlor was our reception-room for visitors (not a few), and our council-hall for discussion, legislative deliberation and official consultation. These I shall never forget. There, also, during seventeen months of residence, I solemnized thirteen marriages.

When our joint stock proprietorship was dissolved, in 1856, the old mansion passed into the ownership of Mr. E. D. Draper, who, three or four years since, sold it to the Dutcher Temple Company. Through all these years, whilst new shops and dwellings were constantly going up around it, plenty of tenants were always glad to occupy its apartments, even down to the very last. Among these was our oldest community member, Mrs. Jane Wilson, familiarly known as "Aunt Jane." She occupied the famous parlor with its *beaufet*, and the rear rooms, for some ten years, I think, and often declared it the happiest home of her lifetime. There she closed her earthly pilgrimage, in the Summer of 1872, a widow of 86 years.

I had a daguerreotype picture of the venerable domicile taken in 1852. Mr. Frank I. Dutcher recently had a stereoscopic view taken, and Miss Lizzie B. Humphrey is finishing in colors a pictorial drawing. These will be pleasant and lasting memorials. The demolition took place during the last week in October, save the great stone chimney, which stood thirty feet high, like a grim giant in sorrow, till Sunday, November 29th, when the tempestuous storm-gusts of the forenoon, prostrated it forever. Thus ends the History of "*The Old House*" at Hopedale.

Shall we indulge in a few reflections? Its oldest half, as we have seen, was 170 years of age, possibly a little more or a little less; its younger half, demonstrably 137 years old. Let us remember that in its infancy it was contemporary with Queen Anne, of England, and in its old age, with Queen Victoria; that its foundations were laid in an opening of the primeval forest, while yet its wild beasts made night hideous, and the whoop of the Indian had scarcely ceased to echo in this region; that it stood in comparative solitude *then*, as the noblest of a few crude habitations, scattered here and there, along the eastern skirts of old Mendon, but survived to see *Milford*, a town of 10,000 inhabitants, and itself closely surrounded by a bright and flourishing village, plentiful in thrifty machine shops and smiling homes. Let us not forget that it lived through "the old French war, which gave the Canadas to England;" the Revolutionary war," which made the thirteen Colonies an independent nation, now more than 40,000,000 strong;

the second war with England; the Mexican war; and the great war of the Rebellion; that it has seen the Georges and the Bonapartes of Europe, one after another, cross the stage and disappear from the rulership of nations; that it has witnessed the most astonishing revolutions, changes and progressions, in all departments of human life throughout the world; that it has welcomed the eras of steamboats, railroads and telegraphs; that it was an octogenarian when George Washington became President of the United States, and has survived to see U. S. Grant their fifteenth President. But I need not prolong the theme.

What has that old House been? The home of the Joneses, from generation to generation, whose posterity, now scattered far abroad, are forgetting the place of their ancestry. It has been the sanctuary of religion, where its pastors preached, its elders prayed, and its saints raised their best aspirations to Heaven. It has been the resort of festive parties and social assemblies, in whose chambers youth and beauty flirted, "tripped the light fantastic toe," and luxuriated in delicious entertainments. There, friendships have been formed and refreshed, and perhaps some of them broken. There, fasts and feasts, weddings and funerals, mirth and sorrow, and all the changeful experiences of domestic life, have alternated for 170 years. But the end has come. The old actors are gone, the latest, presently going. We are gathering up their memorials. Let us enshrine them in wise hearts, profit by older lessons, and be ready to join the hosts of the departed on the immortal continent. *Peace and Honor to the remains of the "The Old House," the Palace of the Dale.*

HOPEDALE, *December* 1, 1874.

NOTES.

In introducing the foregoing "historical sketch of the old Jones house," I stated that it was done with a few corrections and some omissions. Of the former, it is hardly worth while to make mention, as they were so few and slight, but with regard to the omissions, they related only to my grandfather, Joseph Jones, Jr. In this sketch, as well as in the History of Milford, the reverend author speaks somewhat desparingly of him, giving as his authority "the venerable Jared Rawson." Such authority is, without doubt, excellent, but allowance must be made with regard to "statements" of matters that were said to have occurred when he was but a lad, and remembered and made by him when "*he was then over 90 years old.*" An interval of *some 77 years* had passed by, and the recollections of what he may have heard or known in his early youth may have become exaggerated or distorted by the lapse of nearly three-quarters of a century. Again, the omission by my father to ever speak in terms of censure or regret of his father to my mother or to their older children, is something strange, for he was remarkable for his candor and freedom of speech whenever any relative or friend was concerned. He never alluded to my grandfather as having "caused trouble in the family," except the fact, which he often spoke of to us, that his father had sold lands largely, and was ruined and became poor by taking Continental money in payment, which became worthless.

Mr. Jared Rawson speaks of "his sad old age," which could not be, as he died at the age of 62 years while on a visit to his son Alexander, in Charleston, S. C. Neither was it possible that "he ended his days with his son in Providence," as he died in 1799, six years before his son removed to that place. Joseph Jones, Jr., was a genial, pleasant, social man, with a naturally bright and jovial disposition, and the unusual strictness in which Jared Rawson was brought up, may perhaps account for the disfavor with which the conduct of the older man was viewed by the Rawson family. Their lands were contiguous to "The Dale Farm," and disputes may have arisen, which produced "trouble" and resulted in bitter prejudice. The disparaging remarks can be accounted for in no other way.

Ruth Nelson Jones, his wife and my grandmother, passed the greater part of her old age, some 20 or 25 years, in Providence, living under the same roof with two married daughters, receiving daily visits from her oldest son, Alexander, who supported and cared for her with the tenderest affection, until she was called away from earth, at the age of 82 years. And here it may not be amiss to remark, that this aged and revered woman, who suffered from paralysis for twenty years, was most highly respected and honored by every one. Clergymen of every denomination called to see and converse with this aged saint and "Mother in Israel," and, as one of them said, "receiving instruction in listening to her words of wisdom."

One thing more. The author says in the sketch, in speaking of the children of Joseph and Ruth Jones, "I do not learn that they inherited very much of the religion of their ancestors." In answer to this, it is only necessary to state the fact that *all of them became church members*, and that their lives were consistent with their profession.

REVIEW AND REMARKS.

In going over the ages of many whose names and years are mentioned in this book, I find the average of longevity to be somewhat remarkable. Taking 40 of the oldest persons, fathers and mothers of families, and their lives ranging between 61 and 93 years, there is an aggregate of *three thousand and ten years*, or an average of 75¼ years to each.

With regard to the families and the number of children, I find in, say 50 families, that the aggregate is almost 400 children, or an average of 7$\frac{7}{16}$ to each. This is leaving out families where there were no children and only those of two and upwards. There are in this book three families of 15, 14 and 13 children respectively, and of 12 and 11 there are several.

Respecting names, there is certainly a large variety, some of them singular in themselves or in combination with other names. One individual rejoices *in five names*. The name of Mary occurs 33 times; Farquhar, 26; Caroline, 20; Churchill, 18; George, 15; Alexander, 13; Frances, 12; Ellen, 11; Amy, 10; Emily, 9; Sherwood, 8, and Joseph, 7. Besides the 13 named Alexander, 8 were named Alexander Jones, 5 George Farquhar and 5 Mary Farquhar.

FAREWELL.

My self-imposed task is now completed. I have endeavored to be exact and as accurate as was possible under the circumstances. If errors are found it must not be laid to my charge, but to the sometimes

GEORGE FARQUHAR JONES.
Taken in 1877.

indistinct or careless writing of those who furnished me with names and dates. The collection and ingathering of so large an amount of information involved a large amount of labor, patient waiting and much writing. Some four hundred letters were written and sent by me in the last sixteen months. But the array and classification of names, dates, etc., is now finished. The requests of various members of our family to have it all "printed in a book for private circulation" have been complied with, as is seen in the foregoing pages. On my part great satisfaction is felt that my labors (extended as they have been through such a long period), and attended with many vexatious delays and numerous disappointments, have come to an end. On the part of those whose names are here recorded, and those who may read this book, it is hoped that it will fully repay them the trouble of going through its pages.

To the children, grandchildren, great-grandchildren, the nephews, nieces, the grand and the great-grand-nephews and nieces of

Alexander and Mary (Farquhar) Jones,

the contents of this book should bring pleasure and satisfaction. If their blood and relationship does not cause a feeling of pride and gratification to rise in the heart of even the latest descendants (lineal or collateral), I confess myself to be mistaken in my estimate of them.

Their lives were just, pure and righteous in the sight of God and man, their record is on high, and their memory has been and is honored and revered by all who knew them. Surely, to claim descent or kinship with those who have lived and died esteemed and beloved, must be a source of honorable pride and heartfelt gratification.

. Going back through the five generations preceding that of Alexander Jones, those who have that blood running in their veins, have good reason to be proud of their ancestry. In a close and careful examination of all the records at my command, I could find naught against any one member of their large and prosperous families, but much that was recorded to their praise. No murder, suicide, robbery, or other crimes was ever charged against them, and

The Escutcheon is Clear and Untarnished.

The fathers and mothers, the children, the men and the women all seemed to live under a sense of their high responsibilities, and the performance of life's duties. These they endeavored to discharge in the fear of God and with devotion to Him and His service, thus bringing rich benefits to themselves and to their fellow-men. All of them have passed beyond the gates of death, and but few of *the seventh generation* of "The Jones family of Milford" now survive. There are only three.

To one and to all of our relationship (many of whom I have never seen), I send my heartfelt greetings. I trust that one and all may find much that will be of interest to them in the pages of this book. I trust also that the lives of our ancestors may incite us to live as they lived, that so living the life of the righteous our "last end may be like His."   G. F. J.

ACKNOWLEDGMENTS.

A strong feeling of obligation prompts me to record my appreciation of the interest manifested and the efforts made, to procure for me much needed information, by three of my nieces. A valued cousin also aided me greatly by her exertions. To each one of them my hearty and willing thanks are given.

And to my sister, Mrs. Ellen M. Dabney, I am greatly indebted for her warm and active interest in this book, as well as her kind efforts and generous assistance, towards its completion and publication.

                                                 G. F. J.

Philadelphia, October, 1884.

ILLUSTRATIONS.

The representation of "*The Old Jones House*," on "*The Dale Farm*," in Milford, Massachusetts, is a *photogliph*, and done by C. A. Adams, West Gardner, Mass., from a photograph by E. L. Willis, of Milford. This photograph was from a daguerreotype, taken thirty-two years ago, and is referred to by the Rev. Adin Ballou, in his interesting article, to be found on page 166 of this book.

All the others are *phototypes*, and with one exception, from photographs taken of portraits in oil, many of them painted nearly ninety years ago. It is owing to the great age of these paintings, (in addition to hard usage and subsequent restoration, *in some instances*,) that great difficulties were encountered in an endeavor to get satisfactory results. Generally, however, good likenesses have been obtained, as the few who are conversant with the portraits can testify. All are phototyped at the establishment of F. Gutekunst, on Arch Street below Ninth.

Those of Joseph and Ruth (Nelson) Jones were painted by Earl, a pupil of Benjamin West, and probably in 1798 or 1799.

Those of Alexander and Mary (Farquhar) Jones, at the ages respectively of 32 and 23 years, as also that of Mrs. Elizabeth Christian, were by the same artist, and painted in Charleston in the year 1796.

Those of William and Hannah (Jones) Dabney were also painted by Earl, and most probably in the year 1797, or perhaps in 1798.

The portraits of Alexander and Mary (Farquhar) Jones, taken later in their lives, (say at the ages of *about* 63 and 54 years,) were painted by Alexander in 1827 or 1828. He was famed for securing an excellent likeness of those whose pictures he painted, and that of my father, Alexander Jones, can justly be termed "a speaking likeness."

With regard to the remaining picture, a few words of explanation seem, to the writer of this, to be absolutely necessary. Such an idea as having his picture among such beloved and justly revered persons, was not thought of. Suggestions and wishes, however, by various relatives, with the proposition that the author of the book should be represented in its pages, overcame his scruples, and a reluctant consent was given. The phototype is from a small photograph taken in 1877.

G. F. J.

INDEX.

www.ingramcontent.com/pod-product-compliance
Lightning Source LLC
Chambersburg PA
CBHW030536040726
47497CB00008B/2478